BATTERED

Robert Banfelder

BB

~~

Broadwater Books

Riverhead, New York

This book is a work of fiction. Names, characters, places, and incidents are the product of the author's imagination, or are used fictitiously.

Broadwater Books
141 Riverside Drive
Riverhead, New York 11901

broadwaterbooksinfo@gmail.com

ISBN: 978-0-9915912-5-1

Cover Image: Federico Marsicano/123rf

Printed in the United States of America

10 9 8 7 6 5 4 3 2 1

For Donna

Books by Robert Banfelder

Fiction

The Robert Redler/Liza Downs Series:

Dick, Richard, and I
The Signing
The Triumvirate

The Justin Barnes Series:

The Author
The Teacher
Knots
The Good Samaritans

Trace Evidence

Nonfiction

The Fishing Smart Anywhere Handbook for Salt Water & Fresh Water

Coming 2016

The North American Hunting Smart Handbook
with
Bonus Feature
Hunting Africa's Five Most Dangerous Game Animals

Author's Note

This work of fiction is an amalgamation of composite sketches concerning battered women whom I have interviewed at considerable length over the course of many years. Its fusion was additionally inspired by one battered woman's jury trial and her subsequent imprisonment for the shooting death of her husband. Therefore, this narrative is based both on fact and inspiration, a *roman à clef,* [translated, a novel with a key]; that is, a thinly-guised account of many actual events. The courtroom scenes are virtually verbatim. Back-and-forth bimonthly (in this case meaning twice a month) correspondence with one female inmate over the course of several years is closely transcribed as written; that is, the inmate's misspellings, poor grammar, et cetera, albeit instances of Caitlin Fitzgerald's (pseudonym) syntax have been altered for the sake of clarity. Too, all other names and locations were changed for obvious reasons. Again, this is a factual accounting framed as fiction. Be prepared to enter a dark world of spousal violence, murder, courtroom drama, a prisoner's *life* behind bars, and Caitlin's eventual freedom. Embellishment is employed in the final chapter and epilogue solely as a tool to sensationalize and carry the story to its conclusion; otherwise, this narrative is as real as it gets.

The theme of this work is awareness: awareness of how the criminal courts work as well as how they fail; awareness of how various police departments work to build a case for the district attorney in lieu of endeavoring to ascertain truth; awareness of inept and corrupt law enforcement officers; awareness of how a criminal defense attorney misserved his client; awareness of the discretionary and unlimited powers of seated judges to rule on the admission or rejection as to what they themselves allow into evidence.

In essence, this is a story based on the frailties and failures of our criminal justice system. It is a story of supposed truths and half-truths, often concealed between the poles of outright prevarication and distortion. Firstly, it is a book about battered women and what they must do in order to free themselves from the chains of verbal, emotional and physical abuse; admittedly, easier said than done.

Lastly, it is a book about one of our so-called freedoms; namely, the perversion of the First Amendment of the United States Constitution —our Freedom of Speech—for the Son of Sam law has prevented me, as well as anonymous sources cloaked within these pages, from telling this story as nonfiction.

Keep in mind that there have been trials of battered women who have shot and killed their sleeping husbands and beaten (pun intended) the case against them in criminal court. Such a singular yet sometimes defensible action falls within the parameters of the battered-spousal syndrome and goes to the state of mind of the defendant at the time of the event. A commonplace criminal defense attorney would be far out of his or her league to argue such a case before a jury, let alone a case of self-defense as it applies to this syndrome. The intricacies are complex. A litigator would have to educate then convincingly argue that defense before a judge and jury. The task becomes altogether challenging when a consummate prosecutor attacks the credibility of that syndrome as pure junk science. One must never lose sight of the fact that a court trial, be it civil or criminal, is a contest between two lawyers—period. Win or lose at all cost is the name of the game. The truth, the whole truth, and nothing but the truth is at best a cliché that lies somewhere between the poles of guilt and innocence.

Robert Banfelder

BOOK ONE

Chapter One

Pizza Before Policy

A dispatcher transferred the 911 call to the 107th Precinct in Flushing, Queens at precisely 7:47 p.m. on Saturday August 15th, 1998. A heavyset police sergeant continued reading his magazine, finally putting down *Playboy* and picking up the phone on the fifth ring.

"107th Precinct. Sergeant Phelps."

"I need help. I'm scared to go back into my house."

"Who's there that's going to keep you from being in your home?"

"My husband, Jimmy Fitzgerald. He's threatened my life again. I'm scared to go home. I have nowhere to sleep."

"Your full name."

"Caitlin with a C, Ann Fitzgerald."

"Your address." The desk sergeant knew of the woman and that she lived close by.

"71-30½ 167th Street, Flushing."

"Where are you now?"

"I'm calling from my cell phone just outside of McDonald's on Kissena Boulevard."

"Let me have both numbers; home and cell."

Caitlin gave the police sergeant the phone numbers.

"Are you in a car or—"

"I'm in my car; a gray Honda Accord."

"License plate number."

"Give me a second . . . GKN 3209."

"I want you to wait right where you are until I call you back on your cell. Can you do that?"

"Yes, sir."

"Good. I'll call you as soon as I have two of my sergeants on their way to you. All right?"

Sobbing bitterly, the attractive 56-year-old red-haired, green-eyed woman took a deep breath. "Thank you, sir. Thank you very much."

The two hung up. Sergeant Phelps fumbled through a file in a lower desk drawer for a specific document.

"What's up, Den?" Detective Lieutenant Walter Warford questioned.

"It's that Caitlin Fitzgerald woman," Sergeant Dennis Phelps said and sighed. "Domestic dispute again. I know her husband Jimmy through the hunting and fishing club. She says she's afraid to go home. Says he'll kill her."

"What are you looking for?"

"Restraining order. Not sure if it's active or not."

"Why don't you give the husband a call and hear what he has to say?"

"I told her I'd send a car."

"Save yourself the trouble and call the guy if you know him. I got Ted and Thomas on a special detail, and manpower is an issue at the moment."

"All right." Phelps dialed the Fitzgerald residence and James Fitzgerald answered.

"Yeah?"

"Jimmy, this is Sergeant Dennis Phelps. I'm in your hunting/fishing club, buddy."

"Hey, Denny. What's up, guy?"

"Well, unfortunately this isn't a social call. It's about your wife, Caitlin. She just called us."

"Oh, yeah? The bitch drunk again?"

"Didn't seem that way. She said you threatened to kill her—again; she's afraid to come home."

"Listen, Den. We had a bit of an argument on the phone about her opening my mail when I was away in Texas on business. I just got in last night, actually this morning. I'm wiped. Jet lag. I cooled down.

Wouldn't dare touch her, Den. I just wanted to talk some sense into her about opening other people's mail. I just woke up. Where is she?"

"Waiting for me to send a car to escort her home, which is what I'm supposed to do. There's a question as to whether or not this restraining order I have in front of me is still in effect. If it is, and I send a car, you'll be removed from that house. That's mandatory, Jimmy."

"That restraining order has been rescinded, Den."

"What I have in front of me, Jimmy, is a restraining order with ambiguous written comments referencing determination as to time and date. If I send a car and have Caitlin escorted home, and she pushes the envelope, you could be arrested. Understand?"

Jimmy Fitzgerald drew a deep breath. "Please don't send a car here, Den. Please. Caitlin has nothing to worry about. Tell her to come home. Everything is going to be fine."

"All right, Jimmy. I'm going out on a limb for you. By law I have to send her home escorted. But if you tell me—"

"She has nothing to worry about, Den. I swear."

"Fine then."

"I owe you one, Den."

Sergeant Dennis Phelps smiled into the mouthpiece. "I get the starboard stern quarter on *Never Enuff I* charter out of Manhasset Bay, fellow."

"Done deal, good buddy. I'll even spring for libations and lobster salad for lunch. How's that?"

"Never better, good buddy."

The two men hung up, and Phelps immediately called Caitlin Fitzgerald.

Caitlin was sobbing. "Hello."

"This is Sergeant Phelps, Mrs. Fitzgerald."

"Yes, sir."

"I want you to listen to me carefully." Phelps thumbed through the pages of the gentlemen's monthly magazine as he spoke, opening the centerfold and studying the stately naked figure. "I just spoke with your husband, and he wants you to come home. He assures me that there will be absolutely no trouble."

"No!" Caitlin pleaded. "I beg you. If he doesn't kill me, he'll beat me. I know he will. Please have your sergeants take me home and talk to him. I don't want to be beat no more. I've been beaten for thirty years, and I just can't take it anymore. Please help me . . . please."

"Mrs. Fitzgerald, I just spoke to your husband at length, and he promises there won't be any more trouble."

"He's a liar! He'll beat me mercilessly if he doesn't kill me first."

"You're not listening to me, ma'am. If he so much as touches you, he'll be arrested. But he won't lay a hand on you. Now, you go on home, and everything is going to be fine. If there is any problem, you give me a call. Understand?"

Weeping and sobbing uncontrollably, Caitlin nodded before the mouthpiece then hung up.

Detective Lieutenant Warford sighed heavily. "You accidentally erase that last conversation you just had with her, preserve the first recording, have Ted and Thomas drive past McDonald's on their way back from picking up pizzas, making sure she's left Mickey D's, en route home, then have Ted call you and confirm."

"Yes, sir," Phelps replied, calling the two patrolmen in their sector car and giving them specific instructions.

"Now, turn off the speaker phone, and put that fucking magazine away."

"Right away, Lieutenant."

Twenty minutes later, Phelps received a call from Patrolman Ted DeVito.

"2012 gray Honda Accord, license plate number GKN 3209, has left McDonald's on Kissena Boulevard. It's sitting in the driveway at 71-30½ 167th Street, Flushing.

"Thanks, Ted."

"Yes, sir."

"Those pizzas still hot?"

"Will be unless you send us another ten blocks out of the way."

"Just get your asses back here. And if you guys see a robbery in progress, you turn your fucking heads the other way."

The two patrolmen laughed.

"Roger that," Ted acknowledged.

"Ditto," Patrolman Thomas Malanny muttered with a Dunkin' Donut in his mouth, a 7-Eleven coffee in a meaty fist.

Chapter Two

The Shooting Followed by Surrender

Caitlin Fitzgerald entered her home and quietly walked down the hallway, heading toward a separate bedroom—her bedroom. She slept and ate in that room whenever Jimmy acted out, whenever her husband was drunk, whenever he finished beating and raping her. Caitlin spent more time in that guest bedroom than in their master bedroom. The irony being that they rarely had a guest, except for when Jim's daughter by a previous marriage would visit. Caitlin's guest bedroom: complete with a 54-quart Coleman cooler, a Coleman water jug with a spout, rolls of toilet paper, and paper towels. Twice, for severe punishment by Jim, she had spent the night in a hallway closet with those items. The guest bedroom was her refuge. Two locks, one of which had been broken along with a thrice repaired doorjamb, provided a false sense of safety, for whenever Jim wanted to gain entry, kicking in the door was mere child's play and made him feel powerful. Jim loved feeling powerful. Jim loved being in absolute control. The six-foot three, two hundred thirty-five pound figure was all muscle. No one messed with Big Jimbo, a moniker given to him by his friends at the local gin mill.

The attractive 56-year-old woman entered the foyer and made it as far as the threshold of the wide-open home office doorway as Jim started to rise from his chair behind the L-shaped desk. He was furious. Sheer hatred filled his eyes.

"You fucking bitch. You called the police on me again. You goddamn cunt."

Tonight Caitlin would not run to her room, for he would surely kick the door in if not down. His wild eyes told her that he would punish her mercilessly. Tonight she would not be beaten and confined to her room until the swelling went down and all the bruises disappeared. Not this time. No, never ever again. Tonight she was ready for him.

Jim was up out of his chair. Caitlin withdrew a pistol from her handbag, leveled it at her husband and fired until she saw him fall forward. She had loved him, but she knew he had to die tonight. Not tomorrow, when once again he would say he was *so* sorry, that he would promise to stop seeing his girlfriends, that he would seek help for his uncontrollable anger, that he would never ever again hit her. Hit her? Oh, how he would always minimize everything, referring to his viciousness as simply *bad behavior.*

James Fitzgerald did not so much as twitch or move a muscle. Big Jimbo lie stone-cold dead upon the home office floor.

Caitlin made two phone calls to friends before turning herself and the handgun over to police at the 107th Precinct, ten blocks away from her home. Caitlin went up to the police sergeant on duty. Sergeant Dennis Phelps.

"My name is Caitlin Fitzgerald, and I just shot my husband."

Sergeant Dennis Phelps stared in shock as he studied the woman. He had never actually met Caitlin, nor had she met him. The two had twice spoken with one another not forty-five minutes earlier.

Caitlin set a plush cloth fishing reel bag down over the counter. "The gun is inside."

Sergeant Phelps stepped up to the counter and pulled open the bag's drawstrings, removing a .25 caliber handgun.

"Where is your husband now?" Phelps questioned.

"In his office of our home at 71-30½ 167th Street." Caitlin read the nametag on the police sergeant's shirt. "I spoke with you a little while ago. You were going to send a car to take me home and talk to Jim. But then you called me back and told me it was safe to go home." Caitlin lowered her head and began crying quietly. "Only it wasn't safe. It wasn't safe at all."

Several police officers stood frozen in the background. One of the men finally folded and discarded three large pizza boxes into a tall trash container.

Detective Lieutenant Walter Warford walked across the room and up to the counter. "Is your husband wounded or dead?" he asked firmly yet civilly, gesturing for one of his men to escort Mrs. Caitlin Fitzgerald into the precinct's inner sanctum, about to be taken into custody, about to be led into the interrogation room.

"I think he's dead."

"May I have the keys to your house, ma'am?" Warford said just as politely as he could.

"The front door is open; I mean unlocked. But you can have them if you like. I ran out—"

The escorting patrolman roughly grabbed the woman's pocketbook as he came around the partition, searching for contraband as well as her keys.

"Easy, Thomas," Warford warned, warming up for the role of good cop while Patrolman Thomas Malanny would never ever have to rehearse for the role of bad cop. Malanny was by his very nature mean to the bone. "I want you and Tim to shoot on over to 71-30½ 167th Street, immediately if not sooner. I'll call Larson to meet you over there." He turned to Caitlin. "Mrs. Fitzgerald, if you'll follow Sergeant Phelps, please. I'll be with both of you in just a moment. Sergeant Hanley, I need you to man the front desk."

"Yes, sir."

Chapter Three

Arrested Judgment

Sitting before Detective Sergeant Angelo Niverra, Caitlin wept bitterly as she was being read her Miranda rights as well as the waiver part of the form, which she foolishly agreed to and then initialed.

"May I call you Caitlin?" the detective asked.

Caitlin nodded.

"Tell me what happened, Caitlin."

"My husband went to Texas last week on business, but his business was with one of his girlfriends who he's been seeing a lot of lately. I know this because I opened up his mail when he was away. Telephone bill. American Express Card. He had booked a trip with her to Venice. I confronted him on the phone that he's been with and still seeing Theresa Manno; that's her name. That was on Friday. He was furious and told me he was going to kill me when he came home.

"Jimmy flew home very early Saturday morning, around three-thirty a.m. I had locked myself in the guestroom; that's where I sleep. I snuck out of the house around eight that morning, knowing he was fast asleep because I could hear him snoring. I drove around all day, wondering what I was going to do. If I went home, he swore he'd kill me like I told the police sergeant earlier. He almost did once. He nearly beat me to death. I just wasn't going to be beaten no more. I called him later in the day when I knew he'd be awake, to try and reason with him. He told me not to come home, that he'd kill me. You don't reason with Jimmy, but I tried."

"What happened when you went home?"

"I went inside and walked down the hallway on my way to the guest room. That's where I sleep," she repeated.

"Did you have the gun with you?"

"Yes. It was in my pocketbook."

"Where did you get it?"

"From a man at a bar in Astoria."

"Who is this man?"

"Just a stranger."

"And how did you meet him?"

"Asked around. Said I needed a gun for protection. Someone arranged for me to meet this man who I bought the gun from."

"You walk around with a loaded illegal handgun, Caitlin?"

Caitlin shook her head. "I do not walk around with a gun. I kept it under the floor mat of the front seat in my car."

"What happened as you were walking down the hallway toward the guest room?"

"Jim started to get up from the chair behind his desk. He was furious with me for having called the police. He said, 'You bitch. You called the police on me again.' He called me other curse names. His eyes were filled with hatred; he would have killed me or at the very least beaten me badly. I did not give him the chance. I withdrew the pistol from my pocketbook, pointed it at him then fired until I saw him fall forward." Caitlin took a deep breath and wiped her eyes before continuing.

"I knew I had to surrender myself to the police, so I grabbed one of Jim's fishing reel bags off the counter and put the gun inside it and ran out of the house to my car. I called a couple of friends and told them I had just shot Jimmy and was turning myself in."

Detective Niverra suddenly and purposely changed his disposition from *good cop* to assuming a rather gruff demeanor. "Mrs. Fitzgerald, I'd like to take a taped statement from you concerning what you just told me. Would you agree to that?"

A precipitous chill shot up Caitlin's back. She had been cooperative up to this point, but the detective's abrupt change of behavior frightened her and made her wary. "No, I don't think so."

Detective Niverra smiled inwardly. "I'll be back in just a moment, ma'am." Niverra gestured for Phelps to follow him.

From Caitlin, to Mrs. Fitzgerald, to ma'am. *What had I done wrong?* Caitlin wondered. *What?*

Well, for openers, you just murdered your husband, which you feel is justified, a reasonable person would have told the woman. Secondly, you waved your rights and spoke to the police without the presence of an attorney. That's what any knowledgeable soul would have told Mrs. Caitlin Ann Fitzgerald.

Just outside the interrogation room, Detective Sergeant Angelo Niverra addressed his subordinates: "You guys fucked up big time tonight. She should have been escorted home whether that restraining order was or wasn't in force. I'm not telling you anything you don't already know. The fact that she waived her rights and spoke to us, coupled to the fact that she declined to make a taped statement is what's going to save your sorry asses. Note that I did not include myself in present company. Now, we all have to be on the same page in order for this to fly. From the first moment you had contact with this woman earlier, Phelps, her attitude was cold and calculating. Besides erasing that second call you had with her, we'll have to alter the two conversations you had with Ted. Background noises, voice-overs, and other distortions will take care of that. Lousy recording system. You were under the impression that Ted and Thomas were going into the home when Ted told you that her car was parked in the driveway. Got all that?"

"Yes, sir," Sergeant Dennis Phelps said through a hard swallow.

"I can't believe you called her fucking husband. Another conversation you never had."

Phelps knew not to mention that it was Detective Lieutenant Warford who told him to make the call. "I know Jim through our hunting/fishing club, sir. I only thought—"

"I don't need for you to think, Phelps. I need for you to follow proper police procedure in the future. A smart defense attorney is going to try and crucify the 107th Precinct in open court. Understand? It will be a question of just how much latitude a judge will allow. Now, you understand exactly what has to be done?"

"Absolutely. I understand perfectly."

Chapter Four

Grand Jury Indictment

Five and a half months later, in the Queens County Courthouse in Kew Gardens, Caitlin Ann Fitzgerald testified at her grand jury hearing. Caitlin was buried alive with lies told by the police as to what she had said transpired on the night she shot her husband. The grand jury returned with an indictment. Having rejected a plea bargain offer of a maximum term of twelve years, Caitlin would be standing trial for second degree murder. If Caitlin were found guilty, she would be facing fifteen to thirty years behind bars. Caitlin was out on bail and staying with friends. Twenty-one long months followed the grand jury hearing before her murder trial began.

It was made clear from the onset that Caitlin had been verbally and mentally abused by James Fitzgerald for nearly three decades. Of this there was no doubt. However, few folks knew of the physical abuse Caitlin endured. Having lived together for practically thirty years, they were married but for one when a culmination of explosive events resulted in the deadly aftermath. Caitlin had taken out several restraining (protective) orders against Jimmy over the course of those years. Too, she had left home on more than one occasion, running to her family in Georgia, or surreptitiously staying with friends in Florida. However, Jimmy would always find her. He'd threaten folks for information of her whereabouts. And when he did find her, he'd run the gamut of menacing, admonishing, and cajoling, finally convincing Caitlin to return home with him. Why a woman would repeatedly yield to such abuse was certainly in the mind of the jurors. You could read that very question in their eyes.

There are, of course, several reasons why battered women remain in such abusive relationships. Financial dependency is but one such explanation that comes immediately to mind. However, this was not the case because Caitlin worked as a seamstress and dressmaker for several companies and shops as well as doing work on the side. She could and did support herself as well as Jimmy for significant periods of time as when he was fired from his jobs as a traveling salesman for various fishing tackle companies: fired for intimidating, drinking, arguing or physically fighting with customers.

To get a clear picture of Jim Fitzgerald's intimidation tactics, one first needs a physical description of the man. Jim stood six-foot-three inches tall and weighed in at 235 pounds. During a family dinner gathering, Jimbo had grabbed a relative inflicted with multiple sclerosis and threw the small man face-forward into a wall. The frail fellow was so frightened that he obtained a handgun permit for self-protection as Jimmy had menaced the man on more than one occasion. To call Jim Fitzgerald a bully was a sheer understatement. Jimmy Fitzgerald was a wrecking ball of a brute, having once put Caitlin's head through a plasterboard wall in their Flushing home.

Chapter Five

The Trial ~ Opening Statements

Caitlin's trial began on September 26th, 2000. The People of the State of New York versus Caitlin Ann Fitzgerald. The prosecutor, Philip Murrow, introduced himself to the jury in his opening statement before cutting to the heart of the matter. Trial was formally under way.

The tall, trim, well-dressed figure stood directly before the jury as he began.

"James Fitzgerald's body tells the only true account of how Caitlin Fitzgerald shot and killed her husband. James Fitzgerald's body, the way he suffered the bullet wounds that she caused, will prove to you beyond a shadow of any doubt that at the time she shot him, she snuck up on an unsuspecting James Fitzgerald when he was sitting in the chair at his desk, and she gunned him down."

Philip Murrow went on to explain the People's version referencing the bullets' trajectory paths. As to which interpretation was the more plausible between People versus Defendant would become the crux of the matter. Meanwhile, the prosecution had the floor, and we hear Murrow's damaging remarks as though he himself had been present at the scene:

"James Fitzgerald wasn't talking to his wife, Caitlin. He wasn't facing her. He wasn't engaging her in any manner when he suffered the bullet wounds that she caused because the bullet wounds are at a downward angle. The defendant is five-feet, seven-inches tall. James Fitzgerald was six-feet, three-inches tall. The evidence will show that the only reason she had to point that weapon downward was because he was below her. He was sitting down. The location of the bullet wounds in Jim Fitzgerald's body tell you what her intentions were that day. They tell you what her purpose was. It was to murder Jim Fitzgerald.

"The People will prove that Caitlin Fitzgerald was not motivated by fear. She was motivated by anger and jealousy." The prosecutor figuratively leads the jury to the threshold of the shooting and then tells them what Caitlin allegedly told the police.

"She told the police in her first account that she walked to the front of the house, that she looked into the window to the left of the front door and saw James Fitzgerald working at his desk. She then told the police that she walked into the house and that when she reached the doorway of his office, he stood up on his own two feet and said, "You bitch, you opened my mail. And at that time she told the police that James reached out with his two hands for her throat. She told the police that she reached in her pocketbook, drew her unlicensed handgun, shot James Fitzgerald while he was coming at her, that she saw him fall back into his chair, then saw him slump forward onto his desk; and then she left.

"James Fitzgerald's body tells the only true account of how he died. James Fitzgerald's body, the physical evidence will show, proves that Caitlin Fitzgerald's first version of the events is impossible. It's a lie!"

Again, this so-called alleged *first version* is not at all what Caitlin had told the police upon turning herself in. The police sergeant's and other officers' version of how Caitlin behaved and what she had said that evening were altered to present her in a bad light as well as to contradict the physical evidence. The desk sergeant, patrolmen, and detectives make it appear as though Caitlin had changed her story, presumably realizing at some later point that the purported physical evidence would not be in sync with her tale. To confound matters, the testimonies from ballistic experts referencing bullet trajectory with regard to where Jim and Caitlin were *precisely* positioned at the time of the shooting fall into a rather gray area. The prosecutor held tenaciously to one thesis while the defense team presented another scenario. Nothing was cut-and-dried. Nothing was black and white.

Philip Murrow rose to his tippy-toes and smiled broadly so as to emphasize his point. "Some five months later, the defendant testified before the Queens County Grand Jury and gave a different version of events relating to the shooting, a version which is also impossible based on the bullet wounds suffered by James Fitzgerald.

"She told the Queens County Grand Jury that on that Saturday afternoon, she went into the house wearing tennis shoes and that the hallway was made of marble, and she told the Grand Jury that she didn't think that Jim could hear her enter because he was hard of hearing and he was too proud to do anything about it.

"She told the Grand Jury that as she approached the doorway to his office, Jimmy was facing her while he was sitting in his chair, and she told the Grand Jury that Jim said to her, 'You bitch, you called the police on me again.'

"She claimed at that time that Jim had his two hands on the arms of his chair and that he was lifting his body out of the chair in an effort to attack her—that he was going after her.

"She told the Grand Jury that her pocketbook was on her left shoulder and that she reached into her pocketbook with her right hand, although she's left-handed, that she drew her handgun, pointed it at her husband, that she closed her eyes, that she shot Jim an unknown number of times, and that she left.

"Those are the two versions from the defendant of how she killed James Fitzgerald."

The argument that Caitlin's defense attorney will later fail to make, among several vital arguments, is to posit the fact that his client is ambidextrous, that she can sew, sketch, scribe or shoot with either hand.

Philip Murrow is about to finish his opening statement:

"And you will hear that this is not the first time that the defendant has taken a loaded handgun and pointed it at James Fitzgerald because of her anger and her jealousy. In January of 1997, she tried to kill him because of his relationship with the same girlfriend, but the gun misfired, and a bullet went into the ceiling. And you'll see evidence of that misfire into the ceiling, and you'll see the weapon itself.

"What Caitlin Fitzgerald did to her husband James Fitzgerald on August 15th of 1998 was to ambush and murder him, and ever since that moment, she's been trying to rewrite history because she's trying to get away with murder."

Mr. William Baxter, attorney for the defense, standing a good distance from the jury, begins his opening statement:

"For almost three decades, Caitlin Fitzgerald suffered emotional, verbal, and physical abuse by James Fitzgerald. On August 15th, 1998, Caitlin Fitzgerald was in fear for her life. Yes, a life has been lost. We try to understand. We try to make some sense of this human tragedy, and in trying to make some sense of this human tragedy, we think about the woman who had the gun. She's now fifty-eight years old. She has no criminal record."

A minute of monologue continues as Baxter pretentiously leads the jury to the separate guest bedroom in which Caitlin slept; a room with a door that James Fitzgerald had broken down on more than one occasion; a doorjamb that had to be repaired repeatedly because of James' violent behavior; a door with locks that had been installed by a neighbor so that Caitlin could barricade herself within that room.

Baxter dramatically drives home points with body language that speaks of overacting; his wording becomes disjointed; he speaks too quickly; he appears and *is* obviously unprepared. One will learn just how unprepared as the attorney continues. Evidenced in this regard is the court transcript set forth by the official court reporter (courtroom stenographer). Testimony is not nor could not be taken verbatim. The defense attorney's jumbled words and phrases are omitted from the text.

Charles Winfield, a freelance writer and part-time reporter for *The North Shore Towers News*, sitting toward the front of the courtroom along with other news correspondents and television commentators, listens intently—listens in disappointment and disbelief.

William Baxter continued.

"And on this night, the night that she was going to intentionally murder her husband, she was barricaded in that room; well, what she had in there, you see, she spread a white towel right next to the bed on the floor, a white towel, and right next . . . you ever see a Coleman's water jug? Blue around the top, white at the bottom with a little spout; you know, you usually see them at soccer games. She had that Coleman's bottle of water, and right next to it was a roll of toilet paper, and next to that was a Tupperware bucket because that was her bathroom. That's where she planned to spend the night, you see."

Judge, jury, court reporter, and spectators looked on with a mix of mild amusement to outright incredulity. Did Baxter actually say, "And on this night, the night that she was going to *intentionally* murder her husband . . . ."? Was it the defense attorney's attempt to be ironic and facetious? It definitely did not come across that way. Not remotely.

Having the benefit of live *Court TV* audio-videotaping, pundits had a field day with William Baxter's opening statements, virtually all agreeing that the man's performance fell far short of expectations. Does a defense attorney have to be an eloquent speaker in order to properly defend his or her client? No. What the defense attorney must be is prepared, not only in terms of delivery, but on points of law. By comparison, prosecutor Philip Murrow literally and figuratively stood head and shoulders above William Baxter. The prosecutor was well-prepared. The defense attorney was not. The contest between the two lawyers proved to be no contest at all. Not that William Baxter didn't have a moment or two where he shined; however, those moments were few and far between.

Those courtroom episodes continuously and lucidly displayed the incompetence of Caitlin Fitzgerald's defense attorney. The presiding judge, Judge Hershfield, on more than one occasion had instructed William Baxter at sidebar—and out of earshot of the jury—to visit the law library in lieu of the attorney taking his lunch hour. Caitlin learned quickly, but too late, that you get what you pay for. Caitlin had initially retained a competent attorney that she quickly dismissed after a girlfriend of hers said that Caitlin was paying way too much for representation. Caitlin's friend advised her to go with an acquaintance of hers who had said he would take her case for far less money, and so Caitlin wound up with William Baxter, Esquire. You do not make trouble for or aggravate the presiding judge, which Baxter did quite often throughout the proceedings.

Chapter Six

Caitlin's Childhood to Adulthood

The trial continues with William Baxter presenting a slice of Caitlin Ann Fitzgerald's early childhood, taking the jury from that juncture to the threshold of adulthood. It is a wise move on the defense attorney's behalf, and lucky for the defense that the judge had agreed to allow it. Caitlin's story certainly doesn't begin on the night she shot her husband. It doesn't even begin practically thirty years earlier when Caitlin Ann Reeves and James Fitzgerald first met. The relevant part of the story unfolds when Caitlin was a mere child, a child who was the product of a dysfunctional family, a child who grew up in an abusive environment. Still it is interesting to note that Judge Hershfield had allowed Baxter to address Caitlin's early history because a good many judges simply would not have permitted it. Few folks realize how discretionary a judge's allowance of what will and will not be allowed into evidence can be. Autonomy may be the perfect word referencing a judge's power. However, Judge Hershfield apparently noted the relevance as to how the case connected to Caitlin's state of mind at the time of the shooting, for a pattern of abuse has certainly followed her through the years.

Baxter gives the jury a snapshot of Caitlin's childhood, a snippet here and there of what the young girl's life was like growing up in Macon, Georgia, circa 1955, when Caitlin was about thirteen years old. Her father was a day laborer and a strict disciplinarian.

The defense attorney lucidly explains that a young Caitlin is under the porch of a next-door neighbor's house. She has her report card in hand. She has all A's and B's, except for a single grade of C. Caitlin has attempted to change it, but it is obvious that the grade has been altered. As a matter of fact, the paper has a tiny tear in it from rubbing while trying to erase the grade. She knows what will happen when she gets home and her father sees the report card. Her father places the report card, along with her brother's, upon the kitchen table. If either child has a C, they are going to receive a beating. The father sees his son's grade of C and Caitlin's obvious changing of a grade. He becomes furious and climbs over his wife to get to the two children— first Caitlin, and then her older 15-year-old brother, Shawn.

As this situation worsened, Baxter goes on to explain that because of the father's increasing rage, Caitlin's mother arranges for her fourteen-and-a-half-year-old daughter to marry a seventeen-year-old boy who is the son of Caitlin's mother's close friend. Caitlin's mother puts her daughter on a bus, sending Caitlin off to South Carolina to marry the boy for fear that her husband would seriously injure Caitlin out of sheer anger. The marriage lasted a couple of months.

"Across the span of years," Baxter continues, "Caitlin's relationships and unions fail. And why wouldn't they? With no parents at hand to nurture and guide the child." *Might as well address it now*, Baxter figures, for he knows that Caitlin's other marriages are going to be brought up by the prosecution and placed in a quite negative light.

"By the age of twenty-seven, Caitlin has her high school diploma and her trade as a seamstress and dressmaker," Baxter goes on. "She is living alone and about to turn twenty-eight in 1970, working as a dressmaker and designer in Raleigh, North Carolina. Her girlfriend has planned a surprise birthday party for her. It is there that she first meets Jimmy Fitzgerald. After six months, Caitlin moves to Jim's town of Fayetteville, North Carolina. She has her own apartment. She didn't know that Jim Fitzgerald was still married. The violence has not yet begun. Eventually, Caitlin and Jim move in together."

Baxter informs the jury that the first act of violence occurs one day when Caitlin is in the shower.

"Jim Fitzgerald bangs open the bathroom door, rips open the shower curtain and punches Caitlin in the face. Later he tells her that he did that to her because she had done something that was her fault."

Charles Winfield noted that the attorney fails to tell the jury what precipitated that horrific event, only to add that Caitlin believed that she *was* at fault. The impact is seemingly lost on the jury. More importantly, William Baxter fails to explain the elements of Battered Woman Syndrome and how the recipient of such abuse comes to rationalize that she *is* somehow at fault. A person suffering in such a situation will make extraordinary efforts to have things work. The first

25

mistake is to remain in that position. Yes, so easy to say but hard for many outsiders looking in to understand, Winfield knew. For the need to please becomes powerful and overwhelming, especially when you're involved with someone you love, the writer mused. *It must be me*, the abused party decides. But when the abuse repeats itself and then repeats itself anew, why doesn't that person pick themselves up and leave? Winfield realizes that most members of the jury are asking themselves why Caitlin didn't leave Jimmy. William Baxter explains that Caitlin *did* leave, and on more than one occasion. But James Fitzgerald always found her and manipulated Caitlin into coming home.

Many folks think of a battered woman as being trapped in a situation where she is completely dependent on her spouse or domestic partner, no friends to turn to, no money of her own, no place to go. Caitlin does not fit the criteria. She was self-sufficient; she had her own circle of long-time friends and customers, some who became her confidants; she earned decent money as a seamstress and dressmaker; she did have a place to go, even to temporarily hide when the going got tough. But Jimmy Fitzgerald was relentless in his pursuit of Caitlin. He had threatened those who tried to help and/or hide her. When Jimmy finally found her, he would attempt to charm Caitlin. When those tactics no longer worked, he would beg, and cry, and promise to change for the better—forever and always.

Yes, maybe things will work out, Caitlin hoped against all hope . . . and so she takes Jimmy back.

Charles Winfield had done his homework, having spoken to more than a dozen family members, friends, and acquaintances of Caitlin and James Fitzgerald.

"The years fly by," William Baxter proceeds. "They buy a home together, but the house is in his name. Unstable, Jim Fitzgerald is dependent on Caitlin, for he was fired from job after job and eventually went well into debt. Jim wanted to have his cake and eat it, too. He was a bully and a player. He had scores of girlfriends, the equivalent of the proverbial sailor with a girl in every port. As a down-and-out traveling salesman, he ran up exorbitant charges on Caitlin's credit cards. Caitlin stops the card, and Jim threatens to kill her. He owes Caitlin a lot of money. Jim is desperate and says he'll put the house in her name, promising, too, to marry her."

As Caitlin's defense attorney points out, this is James Fitzgerald's trump card. Caitlin Reeves loves this man and desperately believes that marrying James will change the man. He'll give up his girlfriends. He'll settle down. He won't beat her any more. They'll be happy. Yes, a real marriage; not like the mock marriage ceremony they had some years ago at the Playboy Club in Manhattan, having friends and relatives believing that Caitlin and James had tied the knot. Caitlin was unaware of the sham at the time. Off to Vegas they go to get married, for real this time. Three days later, James is on a plane to Rome with one of his girlfriends, Theresa Manno.

"We're into May of 1998," Baxter tells the jury. "A month later, Jim tells Caitlin that he and Theresa Manno want the house for the weekend and that Caitlin has to get out. But Caitlin answers back this time, reminding Jim, who has been drinking heavily, that he had signed the house over to her and that she's not leaving." Baxter informs the jury that they will see how badly Jim beat her with her own shoe, photographs in evidence taken by the 107th Precinct in Flushing, showing Caitlin's legs beaten black and blue. "Caitlin has learned over the course of years not to fight back, for the beatings will only be worse. So she lies there, still as stone. Next, Jim takes Caitlin by the neck and puts her head through a sheetrock wall. She cleverly distracts Jim, who has as I said been drinking, by asking him to make her a drink. While he does, she bolts out the door and runs to her car. Jim goes after her. Now there are neighbors who are witness to this violent domestic scene.

"This abuse is one vicious cycle. Caitlin is out of the house, but where will she go? She knows that wherever she runs, Jim will find her as he always does. She actually returns and begs for him to take her in. He obliges Caitlin by taking her back inside the house, dragging her down the hall into *his* bedroom and raping her . . . later holding her in his arms while weeping and begging for forgiveness.

"When Jim is in Texas on so-called business, Caitlin has opened Jim's mail and finds two airline tickets. She sees the phone bill with many calls made to Theresa Manno, suspecting that he is still seeing her and is probably with her at that moment. Caitlin calls Jim to confirm her suspicions. He is furious that she has opened his mail, threatening to kill her when he returns home. Caitlin believes that she is in store for more than just a beating. She is in fear for her life. That's

27

when Caitlin walks the streets of Astoria to buy a gun as a last resort for self-protection. We are now a day away from when James Fitzgerald is due home. Caitlin can either get another restraining order as she had in the past, or she can ask the police for help when Jim returns home from Texas. As the latter is more expedient, Caitlin is hoping that the police will defuse a volatile situation that is looming on the horizon."

The jury will have two versions of what transpired on the evening of August 15th, 1998. They have the People's version as explained by the prosecutor, Mr. Murrow, referencing both the grand jury and this impaneled jury. Shortly, they will have the defense's version set forth by Mr. Baxter.

In the prosecutors opening statements, Philip Murrow has accused Caitlin Fitzgerald of having two versions as to what happened on the night of the shooting; one version that she supposedly gave to the police, and a second that she told to the grand jury. It will become obvious that either the police or Caitlin Fitzgerald is flat-out lying. Is it the police who initially dropped the ball? Or is it Caitlin Fitzgerald who wanted to paint a more dramatic story in order to further justify her actions as well as have her story fit the physical evidence?

The jury will have their work cut out for them. They will have to reach a decision by weighing in on not only the dilemma of dual versions as it applies to the police versus Caitlin's statements, but also by versions of what they will hear from other witness testimony. Who will prove the more credible? Witnesses for the People, mainly comprised of James Fitzgerald's relatives? Or witnesses for the defense, comprised of Caitlin's family and friends?

During Philip Murrow's opening statement, the prosecutor had covered details involving other police officers who were present on the evening Caitlin turned herself in, having handed over the firearm shortly after fatally shooting her husband. Following a brief recess, the prosecutor calls his first witness to the stand, Sergeant Dennis Phelps of the 107th Precinct, the police officer to whom Caitlin first spoke, asking for help. Philip Murrow begins with direct examination of his first witness for the People concerning Caitlin's earlier call to police.

Chapter Seven

First Witness ~ The Fix is In

A Question and Answer Transcript of the Trial Proceedings is being recorded by the Official Court Reporter (stenographer).

DIRECT EXAMINATION

Prosecutor Philip Murrow: Sergeant, did you realize during the course of that evening that you had spoken with Mrs. Caitlin Fitzgerald earlier that same night?

Sergeant Dennis Phelps: As soon as I came back into the dispatch room, I realized I had spoken to Mrs. Fitzgerald; yes, sir.

Murrow: What were the circumstances of your speaking to her earlier that night?

Phelps: Mrs. Fitzgerald had called headquarters and had spoken to the dispatcher, and he put Mrs. Fitzgerald through to me, and I spoke to Mrs. Fitzgerald.

She stated something to the effect that her husband had come home from Texas, and she had stayed in her room that night because she said he had threatened her on the phone when he was in Texas.

She said that she wanted to go back to her house. I said okay, and I said, Where are you calling from? And she said, McDonald's. And I asked her if it was the McDonald's on Kissena Boulevard. She said, yes.

I told her, okay. I told her to wait there and that I would send two police officers over to her and escort her back to the house and find out what was going on.

Murrow: Did any police officers actually bring the defendant home?

Phelps: No, sir, they didn't.

Murrow: Why not?

Phelps: I don't know why.

Murrow: Do you acknowledge, Sergeant, that police officers should have brought her home that night?

Phelps: Absolutely.

The prosecutor then addresses a distorted audiotaped cassette conversation between Sergeant Phelps and patrolman Theodore DeVito. The defense attorney had asked for further clarification regarding distorted voices and background noises of that tape as well as other recordings relating to Caitlin's phone conversations with the police on the evening of August 15th, 1998. The police maintain that there was no other phone conversation between Sergeant Phelps and Caitlin Fitzgerald other than the initial call made by her at 7:47 p.m. that Saturday. The judge gives the jury specific instructions along with copies of that transcript to be compared to what they will hear referencing the cassette recording. No pleading or sobbing by Caitlin can be discerned on that tape or is indicated in the transcript copy of that tape. William Baxter begins his cross-examination of Sergeant Phelps.

CROSS-EXAMINATION

William Baxter: Sergeant, you testified on direct that you didn't know why the police didn't take Caitlin back home. Yes?

Sergeant Phelps: Yes, sir.

Baxter: You do know why they didn't take Caitlin back home, don't you? You found next to your desk—

Murrow: Objection, Your Honor.

Baxter: I'm withdrawing it. At some point during your first phone conversation with Caitlin Fitzgerald, you checked the drawer next to your desk and found a restraining order, didn't you?

Phelps: I only had one phone conversation with Mrs. Fitzgerald; that being when she called the precinct. And, no, I didn't find any restraining order. Sergeant Hanley did, sir.

Baxter: You didn't call Caitlin Fitzgerald back after you spoke to her and tell her that you spoke to her husband and that it was safe for her to go home?

Phelps: No, I did not.

Baxter: Let me show you what's been marked D-11 for identification and ask if you can identify this. Just answer me if you can identify it.

Phelps: Looks like some part of a restraining order.

Baxter: Does it look to you as though that might have been the cover sheet of a restraining order, the type you have at the 107th Precinct?

Phelps: It looks like it; yes, sir.

Baxter: Let me show it to you again. Do you see your own handwriting on this document?

Phelps: Yes. Right there. That's my writing.

Baxter: And what does your writing say on this document?

Phelps: *Plaintiff states order dropped 10/97. Please contact Judge Fallow. Why not pulled?*

Murrow: That's your question written on the cover sheet, which you signed by abbreviating your title and name: Sgt. D.P.; Sergeant Dennis

Phelps. Is that correct?

Phelps: Yes, that's me.

Murrow: And that's because this was an active restraining order as far as you knew on August 15th, 1998. Isn't that correct, Sergeant?

Phelps: No, sir.

Baxter: Then what does it tell you?

Phelps: I wanted to know why it wasn't pulled.

Baxter: That's what this says?

Phelps: Yes, sir.

Baxter: But you say you later spoke with Caitlin Fitzgerald at the precinct after she turned herself in and asked her if she had an active restraining order; didn't you?

Phelps: Yes, sir.

Baxter: And didn't you tell her that you had had a restraining order at that time?

Phelps: Eventually, I did; yes, sir.

Baxter: So you knew you had an active restraining order; isn't that correct?

Phelps: No, sir.

Baxter: You didn't have an active restraining order?

Phelps: No. I was satisfied that that order was not active.

Baxter: All right. Let's talk about—she called you initially?

Phelps: Yes.

Baxter: Do you know the purpose of her call?

Phelps: Yes, sir.

Baxter: What was the purpose of her call?

Phelps: To go back into her residence.

Baxter: And did you send somebody back with her into her residence?

Phelps: I told the dispatcher to send a car. Yes, sir.

Baxter: And didn't you have a conversation with Jim Fitzgerald that same evening after Mrs. Fitzgerald called you for assistance?

Phelps: No, sir. I did not.

Baxter: You wanted to check with him to make sure that everything was okay at the house; isn't that correct?

Phelps: No, sir.

Baxter: But you wanted to get Caitlin Fitzgerald back in the house that night; yes?

Phelps: Yes, sir.

Baxter: Isn't it a fact, Sergeant, that if you have an active restraining order, your job as a police officer is to act on that active restraining order?

Phelps: Absolutely.

Baxter: And you had an active restraining order in your hands, did you not?

Phelps: Okay. I'm telling you I was—stated that as far as I was concerned, that restraining order had been dropped, sir. Had there been an active restraining order Jim Fitzgerald would have been arrested and removed from 71-30½ 167th Street, Flushing, Queens. Period.

Baxter: So you later took information from the complainant, Caitlin Ann Fitzgerald, confirming your belief that the restraining order had been dropped, that it was no longer active. Is that correct?

Phelps: Sir, if I thought for one second that that restraining order was still in effect, sir, Mr. Fitzgerald would have been arrested by my men. That's mandatory.

Baxter: Well, what convinced you that it wasn't in effect?

Phelps: My conversations with Mrs. Fitzgerald.

Baxter: But you couldn't confirm that initially?

Phelps: No, sir, I couldn't.

Baxter: You tried.

Phelps: Yes, sir.

Baxter: Even after she told you that it wasn't active?

Phelps: Repeat that, sir.

Baxter: Even after she told you that it wasn't active, you weren't convinced, because you then called Kew Gardens. Yes?

Phelps: No, sir. I was convinced, but, you know, in my position with domestic violence, I'll go ten, twelve steps past that because—

Baxter: And you're confident—you're confident that you did that on this case for Caitlin Fitzgerald.

Phelps: Yes, sir, I am, because if I wasn't, sir, Mr. Fitzgerald would have been arrested.

Baxter: Well, then, let me ask you this. After—why after you're finished with the restraining order, why after Mrs. Fitzgerald told you that her life had been threatened, why didn't you tell her what the law requires you to tell her?

Phelps: My intention was that the dispatcher was to send two officers over to that residence, and they would make a determination as to what's going on. They would instruct Mrs. Fitzgerald as to what her options were.

Baxter: But didn't you tell Mrs. Fitzgerald that it was safe to go home, that you had spoken to her husband, Jimmy?

Phelps: No, sir. I did not. I never told her that. I thought she was being escorted home.

Baxter: You indicated that at approximately 8:30 p.m. Caitlin Fitzgerald walked into police headquarters and handed you the gun?

Phelps: Yes, sir.

Baxter: And your heart dropped through your shoes, or words to that effect?

Phelps: I didn't say that, but I was—I was—the elevation was up there. Yes, sir.

Baxter: Isn't it a fact, Sergeant Phelps, that the reason why you were so upset is because the same person who came in and told you she was Caitlin Fitzgerald is the person you had just spoken with forty-five minutes earlier?

Phelps: No. I was concerned because of the fact the woman had just come in and dropped a handgun in front of me.

Baxter continues to press Sergeant Phelps with regard to the restraining order and whether or not it was still in effect in Phelps' mind. "Asked and answered," were the grounds for the objections put forth by Philip Murrow. "Sustained," were Judge Hershfield's rulings. On redirect examination by the prosecutor, Murrow makes it clear to the jury, via Sergeant Phelps' answers that Caitlin Fitzgerald did not ask for a *new* restraining order when she called the police that evening. The prosecutor posits that Caitlin knew the process but did not pursue that procedure.

Charles Winfield was familiar with police procedure, knowing that a police officer would go to the scene, and if the complaint was so deemed domestic violence, the officer would phone a judge in front of the complainant and state the facts. The judge would then talk to the complainant in person before making a ruling. Again, Philip Murrow hammers home the point that Caitlin Fitzgerald *did not* ask for a restraining order that evening.

However, the fact remains that Caitlin Fitzgerald had asked for help that evening; help that never came. Had she been assisted, had a police officer heard her plight, a judge might have been called and a new restraining order may have been issued.

On recross examination of Sergeant Phelps, William Baxter wanted to play another tape that the judge would not allow at that juncture because of procedure, which Baxter has a great deal of trouble following. Baxter was about to fold, failing to further question Phelps. Baxter said he would put the tape in via another witness. Pundits felt that William Baxter could have strengthened his argument by firmly pressing and positing the fine points of law concerning police responsibility, making it crystal clear to the jury that the 107th Police Precinct failed miserably in its duty to protect citizen Caitlin Fitzgerald that evening.

Baxter: One further question, Sergeant Phelps. The two police offers who were supposed to escort my client home were patrolmen, not ranked as sergeants but rather P.P.O's; that is, Probationary Police Officers; is that not correct, Sergeant Phelps?

Murrow: Objection.

Baxter: I withdraw it. [there is a long pause]

Charles Winfield sadly shook his head as William Baxter hung his own head, staring fixedly at the floor.

Judge Hershfield: You have no further questions, counselor?

Baxter: No further questions, Your Honor.

Chapter Eight

Police Prevarication Continues to Support the Physical Evidence

Other witnesses for the prosecution were police officers from the 107th Precinct, testifying to the location of the spent cartridges recovered in the home office (study) where James Fitzgerald's body had lain. Detective Lieutenant Walter Warford gave testimony referencing police photographs taken at the crime scene.

During cross-examination, William Baxter is called to sidebar for a rather lengthy reprimand by Judge Hershfield.

Judge Hershfield: Now, Mr. Baxter, this is the third or fourth time you made reference that you have a tape, and you wish to play it. We have rules of evidence; we have foundation rules of evidence. If you have some evidence and you want to ask a question that's relevant, competent, probative, and appropriate through an appropriate witness, you may lay a foundation, mark the evidence, and move it. Don't keep saying in front of this jury, "I have a tape that I want to play," and make it look like I'm not letting you play some evidence.

You know the rules of evidence, or you're supposed to. You want to lay the foundation, put something into evidence, this is cross-examination; ask the questions, lay the foundation, and if it's proper, probative, relevant, and material, and not outside the scope of direct examination, and not subject to an objection that's sustainable, I will permit it. But if you do it one more time, there's going to be a problem. I repeat. Don't keep saying that, "I have a tape I want to play," unless you properly lay a foundation, properly authenticate it, and properly move it into evidence.

Proceedings resume in the jury's presence.

Through Detective Lieutenant Warford's testimony, we hear of Caitlin Fitzgerald's "matter-of-fact behavior," that Caitlin was properly

Mirandized (read her rights) at 9:15 p.m. that evening by Detective Sergeant Angelo Niverra, and that she waived her rights. In the interrogation room, Caitlin had told her story of the events leading up to the shooting of her husband. During direct examination, Warford reiterates those injurious comments, the most damaging being the penultimate moment when Caitlin enters the house.

Philip Murrow: Detective Warford, Mrs. Fitzgerald had said that she went in the house, located Jim in his office, and that Jim started a verbal fight with her about her opening his mail, and at some point she said he came at her with his hands in this position (indicating), going for her throat. Did the defendant show you this motion?

Warford: Yes, she did.

Murrow: She demonstrated this for you?

Warford: Yes.

Murrow: And did she stand up when she did that?

Warford: Partially. She was more or less up like this.

(Witness indicating)

Murrow: And she indicated to you that her husband stood up and was coming at her with his hands outstretched?

Warford: That's correct.

Baxter: Objection, Judge. He's testifying as far as what he saw—

Judge Hershfield: Overruled.

Murrow: What did she tell you next?

Warford: That she reached into her pocketbook and pulled out a gun and shot an unknown amount of times.

Murrow: And did she tell you that she saw what happened to Jim after she shot him?

Warford: That he fell back into the chair then slumped forward.

Charles Winfield duly noted that there was no audio or videotaping of Caitlin's story as to what actually transpired, that the interview was conducted orally and only the Mirandized segment had been audiotaped. Again and again, Caitlin is emphatic that she never said or indicated what Detective Lieutenant Warford testified to, sticking to her story that Jim Fitzgerald placed his hands on the arms of his chair and started to get up, saying, "You bitch, you called the police on me again," other profanities notwithstanding.

Mr. Murrow finishes up on direct examination of Detective Lieutenant Warford. The judge asks Mr. Baxter, "Cross-examination, counselor?"

Baxter: No questions, Judge. Thank you.

The fact that William Baxter had no questions to ask of Detective Lieutenant Warford is amazing, Charles Winfield entertained. Was Baxter intimidated by the judge having reprimanded and overruled him continuously? Baxter certainly could have questioned Warford's use of the word *partially* and his phrase *more or less up* when Murrow asked the detective, "And did she stand up when she did that?"

Warford: <u>Partially</u>. She was <u>more or less up</u> like this.

(Witness indicating)

The same held true after Murrow finishes up with his next witness, Roy Smith, a neighbor who lives a few houses away from the Fitzgerald residence. On the morning of the shooting, Mr. Smith testifies that he saw Caitlin sitting on the front porch drinking a cup of coffee at approximately 9 a.m., then cutting and watering the grass and that they waved to each other. Caitlin tells her co-counsel (a mousy-looking young woman who sits by and says scarcely a word) that none of this is true. "I never saw Roy Smith in my life until he walked in the courtroom."

Charles Winfield overheard the defendant, as did others in the courtroom who sat in proximity, make that statement. Caitlin was warned by co-counselor to lower her voice.

Winfield pondered what Murrow was trying to establish in calling this witness to the stand, except perhaps to indicate that nothing seemed amiss as Caitlin went about her chores, normally that morning. To dispel any lingering doubts or suspicions in the jury's mind, one might suppose that Mr. Baxter would have had question of this witness on cross-examination. Once again, the judge asks:

Judge Hershfield: Cross-examination, Mr. Baxter?

Baxter: No questions, sir.

The prosecutor's next witness is Detective Myers of the Queens County Sheriff's Department, assigned to the Criminalistics Unit, charged with preserving evidence and examining crime scenes. A videotape had been made and measurements had been taken so as to prepare a floor plan and diagram of the Fitzgerald residence at 71-30½ 167th Street, Flushing, on the evening of the murder. The video is played for the jury, a walk-through depicting the front exterior of the house, leading to the entrance foyer, down along the hallway, showing the connecting rooms and eventually the crime scene; that is, Jim Fitzgerald's office. Little red cups cover the spent shell casings placed earlier by responding police officers. Jim Fitzgerald's body is shown exactly how he was found, lying upon the floor of his office. When asked by Murrow, Detective Myers indicates where those casings are in relationship to the body, giving the impression that Jim Fitzgerald was ambushed up close and personal.

The detective explains a hole in the closet wall where a bullet had ricocheted off a pad atop the desk. The camera zooms in on other projectiles that found their mark: an entrance wound to the victim's left temple, upper shoulder, et cetera.

Following the video, the detective shows the jury a diagram indicating relevant measurements referencing James Fitzgerald's body in relationship to areas of the house. For example, the distance from the front door of the home to the home office crime scene; the spent casings in relationship to James Fitzgerald's desk.

Murrow then asks the detective questions concerning the chair in which Jim Fitzgerald sat at the time of the shooting.

Philip Murrow: Did you conduct what's known as a presumptive test for blood on this chair at that time?

Detective Meyers: Yes, sir. I took two samples of what they call a Hemident McPhails Reagent test.

Murrow: What does that mean?

Meyers: What a McPhails test is, is a presumptive test for blood. That would give us an indication of whether or not a specific area is or is not blood.

Murrow: And what were the results of those tests?

Meyers: One of them was negative, and one of them was positive.

Murrow: Okay. And where—from where on the chair did you get a positive result?

Meyers: Number one [indicating] is in the front of the chair where it's negative; however, to the right, right underneath the right arm, was area number two where we did get a positive test.

Murrow then leads the detective to the prior handgun incident where a bullet was discharged into the ceiling in the master bedroom years earlier. This will certainly leave a lasting negative impression in the minds of jurors.

First addressing the spent shell casings referencing the husband's home office during cross-examination, Mr. Baxter *hopefully* dispels the notion that Caitlin ambushed her husband—up close and personal:

CROSS-EXAMINATION

William Baxter: It's Detective Myers, yes?

Detective Myers: Yes, sir.

Baxter: In any of the casings found in the study, can you identify precisely the velocity or the direction that the casings move when they are ejected from a gun?

Meyers: I couldn't, sir, no.

Baxter: Can anyone?

Meyers: That would depend highly on the amount of powder in the casing that would cause the action to work inside the weapon—looks like a finger, and when the slide comes back from the explosion of the bullet going off, it just pops it and sort of springs—just ejects it out, and so the next one—

Baxter: And, of course, the empty cartridge would bounce around the room and hit say any furniture, yes?

Meyers: Yes. That's pretty much going off to the right, but they can go all over. Yes, sir.

Baxter has *hopefully* dispelled the impression that Caitlin rushed into the room and gunned down her husband . . . though the rather inarticulate wording by the detective referencing cartridge ejection leaves a lot to be desired in terms of clarity.

Regarding the hole in the master bedroom ceiling, a convoluted Q & A continues between Baxter and the detective. After a back-and-forth concerning triangulation to determine from where the gun was fired, it all boiled down to the detective stating that the bed was not directly under the hole in the ceiling. What Baxter fails to address, after an objection by Murrow and the judge asking Baxter to rephrase, is that the bed *was* directly under the hole in the ceiling at the time of the shooting but was subsequently moved against a wall during ceiling repair then left in that position. Jim Fitzgerald was on top of Caitlin on that bed, choking her, when the gun went off. Baxter fails to adequately explore this area of questioning.

Charles Winfield had made it his business to visit the Fitzgerald home when it was up for sale a year after the fatal shooting, having located and spoken with their housekeeper who confirmed the fact that the bed had been directly beneath the hole in the ceiling, moved against a wall during repair, and remained in that position until the very day the house was sold. The housekeeper had told Charles that both she and Caitlin had moved the bed while Jim shot orders as to where it should be placed precisely.

Baxter: Did it appear to you, Detective, from your examination that the bullet that went through the master bedroom ceiling was shot from a position in the center of the room?

Meyers: The measurement is 22 inches, sir.

Baxter: Thank you. I have nothing further.

Of course, the prosecutor chose to ask nothing on redirect. The damage had been nicely accomplished in that the jury is now privy to the initial handgun incident, some of its members certainly considering that Caitlin had tried to kill her husband earlier in time, which is exactly what Philip Murrow wants the jury to believe.

Detective Dean Fowler with the Queens County Sheriff's Department, Criminalistics Investigation Unit is the prosecution's next witness. Like Detective Meyers, Fowler's responsibilities include collecting, preserving, and sorting evidence. Detective Fowler collected the five spent shell casings recovered from the floor of Jim Fitzgerald's office as well as the bullets recovered from the victim's body during autopsy. Two bullets were recovered from the right lower chest and body cavity, one bullet from the right arm, one bullet from the left arm, and one from the back of the head, which had entered the victim's left temple. Next, the detective addresses the blood-stained clothing: hat, shirt, and shorts.

On cross-examination, Baxter finally hammers home an important point with respect to bullet holes in the victim's shirt.

William Baxter: Detective, could you just get the bag out that has the shirt in it again?

Detective Fowler: Could I possibly get another set of gloves? I'm sorry. I took these off.

Baxter: I'll get you another pair.

Judge Hershfield: That's exhibit S-39, Detective?

Fowler: Yes, sir.

Baxter: Can you take it out and take a look at the *front* of the shirt?

Fowler: Yes, sir.

Baxter: Do you see any bullet holes in the *front* of the shirt?

Fowler: Yes, there are holes that I can see.

Baxter: Do you recognize them to be bullet holes?

Fowler: They're—yes—well, yes. They were matched up with the victim's body, yes.

Baxter: Are they in the *front* of the shirt in the chest area?

Fowler: Yes.

Baxter: Thank you.

Baxter addressing the court: Nothing further, Judge.

Judge Hershfield: Redirect?

Murrow: No, your honor.

Judge Hershfield: You can step down. Thank you, Detective.

Fowler: Thank you, Judge.

(Witness excused)

Score that round in favor of Baxter, Charles Winfield entertained, for Detective Fowler's testimony hopefully showed how inconclusive the prosecution's assertion is that Caitlin *ambushed* her unsuspecting husband from the sidelines. As a matter of fact, the word ambush is not at all accurate in the sense that Caitlin Fitzgerald did not issue forth a surprise attack from a place of hiding. She was at the threshold of the office, and Jim was definitely at his desk. Was he firmly seated in his chair? Was he rising from his seat? Was he up and out of his chair? Was he up and out of his chair and coming toward Caitlin in a threatening fashion? Winfield considered the possibilities.

What Charles knew for certain of Jim Fitzgerald's past behavior is that he was unlikely to sit calmly by after his wife had called the police on him—again. Jim most probably did rise from his chair and start to come after her with the intention of hitting or beating Caitlin. "You bitch. You called the police on me again," short of other expletives, are the final words that Jim Fitzgerald did most presumptively utter before Caitlin shot and killed her husband.

Several other law enforcement officers were called to the witness stand by the People, giving their sworn testimony as to the .25 caliber Smith and Wesson handgun used in the shooting, elaborating on enlargements of photographs taken at the crime scene, the containment bag and items within of Jim Fitzgerald's personal effects: keys, cell phone, clothing. Next, photos of the office desk were presented. Finally, the office chair had been marked into evidence and rolled out on display.

An investigator with the Queens County Prosecutor's Office, assigned to the Major Crimes Unit, testified to the reclamation of a ricocheted bullet, shell casings, and projectiles recovered from Jim Fitzgerald's body during the autopsy.

The next witness for the prosecution is the medical examiner who performed the autopsy on James Fitzgerald.

Chapter Nine

The Good Doctor on Direct Examination

Judge Hershfield: Good afternoon, Doctor.

Doctor Daniel T. Kurtz: Good afternoon.

Judge Hershfield: Your witness, Mr. Murrow.

Philip Murrow: Thank you, Your Honor.

DIRECT EXAMINATION

Murrow: Dr. Kurtz, do you perform autopsies for Queens County?

Dr. Kurtz: Yes, I do.

Murrow: And are you licensed in the state of New York?

Dr. Kurtz: Yes.

Murrow: Would you tell us what type of licenses you hold?

Dr. Kurtz: I have a license to practice medicine.

Murrow: You're a medical doctor?

Dr. Kurtz: Yes.

Murrow: And you're a pathologist, correct?

Dr. Kurtz: Yes, that's correct.

Murrow: Can you give the jury the benefit of your educational background, Doctor?

Dr. Kurtz: Yes. I graduated Johns Hopkins University, School of Medicine, Baltimore, Maryland—1965.

Murrow: Can you give us the benefit of your professional experience, Doctor.

Dr. Kurtz: Yes, I worked as a staff pathologist at different hospitals. During the past twelve years, I spent most of my time doing autopsies; that is, forensic pathology.

Murrow: Can you explain forensic pathology for us?

Dr. Kurtz: Forensic pathology is the application of knowledge in pathology as it relates to legal issues; primarily performing autopsies to determine cause and origin of death.

Murrow: How many autopsies have you performed, Doctor?

Dr. Kurtz: At least two thousand.

Murrow: How many autopsies have you performed where the cause of death is multiple gunshot wounds?

Dr. Kurtz: Many hundreds of such cases.

Murrow: Have you previously qualified in Superior Court of New York as an expert in forensic pathology?

Dr. Kurtz: Yes.

Murrow: On approximately how many occasions?

Dr. Kurtz: Approximately half a dozen times a year.

Murrow: Half a dozen times a year.

Dr. Kurtz: Yes.

Murrow: And have you offered testimony on those occasions?

Dr. Kurtz: Yes.

Murrow: Your Honor, at this time the People are asking the Court to recognize Doctor Kurtz as an expert in forensic pathology.

Judge Hershfield: Mr. Baxter?

William Baxter: I'll stipulate, Your Honor.

Judge Hershfield: All right.

(The judge then addresses the jury)

Judge Hershfield: Ladies and gentlemen of the jury. Doctor Kurtz has been offered as an expert in forensic pathology and is so recognized by the Court as an expert. I'll have some instructions for you with regard to this at the end of the case, but the qualifications allow Doctor Kurtz to offer his opinion as an expert.
    Mr. Murrow, you may proceed.

Murrow: Doctor Kurtz, did you perform an autopsy on James Fitzgerald?

Dr. Kurtz: Yes, I did.

Murrow: And when was that autopsy performed?

Dr. Kurtz: May I look at my report?

Judge Hershfield: If it's necessary to refresh your recollection, Doctor, just indicate that you're doing so for the record.

Dr. Kurtz: Yes. I performed an autopsy on James Fitzgerald on August the 16th, 1998.

Murrow: And where was that autopsy performed, Doctor?

Dr. Kurtz: At Queens General Hospital in Jamaica.

Murrow: And how long did it take you to perform the autopsy?

Dr. Kurtz: Approximately two hours.

Murrow: Was the body received in a sealed bag?

Dr. Kurtz: Yes.

Murrow: What clothing was received on the body, Doctor?

Dr. Kurtz: I'm referring to my report (indicating). A long sleeve beige pullover shirt and a pair of dark brown pants.

Murrow: In the pockets of clothing, were there any items?

Dr. Kurtz: Yes, a cellular phone and a set of keys.

Murrow: What was the condition of the beige shirt?

Dr. Kurtz: The shirt had large blood stains on the right side and small blood stains and three holes with typical bullet wipes on the left upper front of the shirt.

Murrow: What do you mean when you say typical bullet wipes, Doctor?

Dr. Kurtz: Bullet wipes are gray stains along the edge of the hole indicating that the bullet usually has some lubricant or stain that usually leaves a mark on the edge of the bullet, consequently the edge of the hole on the shirt.

Murrow: What other observations of the shirt did you make, Doctor?

Dr. Kurtz: There was a bullet hole in the left sleeve of that shirt.

Murrow: And did you compare the shirt to the body?

Dr. Kurtz: Yes.

Murrow: And what further observations did you make?

Dr. Kurtz: There were three holes on the upper left front of the shirt and one hole on the sleeve that corresponds to the entrance gunshot wounds on the body.

Murrow: What was the condition of the dark brown pants that James Fitzgerald wore?

Dr. Kurtz: The pants had small blood stains on the front.

Murrow: What was the size of Mr. Fitzgerald?

Dr. Kurtz: The body measured approximately 75 inches in length.

Murrow: Was he weighed, Doctor?

Dr. Kurtz: Yes. The body weighed approximately 235 pounds.

Murrow: And did he look to be consistent with his stated age?

Dr. Kurtz: Yes.

Murrow: And what was that?

Dr. Kurtz: The stated age was 55 years old.

Murrow: What initial observations did you make, Doctor?

Dr. Kurtz: Initial?

Murrow: Did you look at his face, Doctor?

Dr. Kurtz: Yes.

Murrow: And what observation did you make of his face?

Dr. Kurtz: The face was covered with blood, blood trailing from the left temple area.

Murrow: And what observations—what initial observations did you make of Mr. Fitzgerald's head?

Dr. Kurtz: There was a gunshot entrance wound to the left temple.

Murrow: And did you locate precisely where on Mr. Fitzgerald's temple the entrance gunshot wound was?

Dr. Kurtz: The entrance wound is exactly two-and-a-half inches from the top of the head and four inches to the left of the anterior midline.

Murrow: Doctor, I show you a photograph that's marked S-75 for identification. Do you recognize this?

Dr. Kurtz: Yes.

Murrow: That photograph has previously been identified as having been taken at Mr. Fitzgerald's autopsy. Does it refresh your recollection of the bullet wound to the left temple?

Dr. Kurtz: Yes, it does.

Murrow: With the court's permission, Your Honor, I'd ask that it be published so that the doctor can show it to the jury.

Judge Hershfield: What's the marking again?

Murrow: S-75, Your Honor.

Judge Hershfield: In evidence?

Murrow: In evidence.

Judge Hershfield: It may be shown.

Murrow: Would you show it to the jury, Doctor Kurtz?

Dr. Kurtz: Yes.

Murrow: And indicate where the gunshot wound is.

(Witness indicating)

Murrow: Thanks, Doctor. Now, what type of hole into the skin did that bullet make?

Dr. Kurtz: The bullet made a typical entrance wound. In other words, it's a hole on the skin with what I describe as a circular marginal abrasion.

Murrow: Does the shape of the hole into the skin tell you anything, Doctor?

Dr. Kurtz: Yes. The shape of the hole was a relatively round circle, indicating that the bullet went into the skin more or less perpendicular. In other words, straight through the skin.

Murrow: What evidence did your internal examination of Mr. Fitzgerald's head wound reveal relating to the injuries that the bullet caused?

Dr. Kurtz: The internal examination shows that the bullet had coursed rightwards. In other words, from left to right, slightly backward and downward, striking the cranial cavity before entering and exiting the brain. The bullet was recovered on the right rear side of the head, beneath the skin, just outside of the skull.

Murrow: You said that the bullet traveled backwards. What do you mean by that?

Dr. Kurtz: Toward the back of the decedent and slightly downward, assuming that the head was straight up.

Murrow: Doctor, do you know what the medical result on a human being would be having suffered this type of head wound?

Dr. Kurtz: The person would likely become unconscious when a bullet goes through the brain.

Murrow: Are you able to determine whether this wound in and of itself could have been fatal to James Fitzgerald?

Dr. Kurtz: Yes, this wound could have been fatal.

Murrow: Which was the next gunshot wound that you examined?

Dr. Kurtz: The next gunshot wound is one of three entrance wounds on the left side of the torso. This one was on the left upper chest, three inches below the top of the shoulder and two-and-a-half inches to the left of the midline on the front.

Murrow: Doctor, let me show you a photograph that's been marked S-80 in evidence.

Dr. Kurtz: Yes.

Murrow: Do you see a second bullet wound that you describe in your report in that photograph?

Dr. Kurtz: Yes.

Murrow: And would you hold up the photograph and show the jury by pointing to the bullet wound that you're talking about now; that is, the second one?

Dr. Kurtz: Yes, this one, which is one of the three.

Murrow: Doctor, is there anything about the shape of that wound into Mr. Fitzgerald's upper left chest that is significant to you?

55

Dr. Kurtz: The shape is more or less a typical entrance gunshot wound.

Murrow: Were you able to tell the direction that the bullet came from by the shape of the wound for that bullet?

Dr. Kurtz: Not from the shape of the wound alone. Of course, there is a better way of ascertaining a bullet wound's path.

Murrow: And what way would that be? Could you explain?

Dr. Kurtz: Certainly. The way one could establish the direction of a bullet's path is by examining the inside of the body to see which way the bullet went through.

Murrow: And what did your examination of this second bullet wound in the chest tell you, Doctor?

Dr. Kurtz: That the bullet had entered the left chest cavity, coursed rightwards, slightly downwards, and slightly backwards.

Murrow: Can you explain what you mean by that—rightwards, backwards, downwards?

Dr. Kurtz: Rightwards is the bullet traveling from the left side of the decedent to the right side of the decedent, slightly downwards and slightly towards the back of the decedent's body.

Murrow: And what precisely was the path that this bullet took through James Fitzgerald's body?

Dr. Kurtz: The bullet went into the decedent's left lung and crossed the midline of the torso, entering the right chest cavity.

Murrow: Which was the next gunshot wound that you examined, Doctor?

Dr. Kurtz: Right here. (Witness displaying a photograph to the jury)

Murrow: That's utilizing S-75, showing the middle of the three in the left upper chest?

Dr. Kurtz: Yes.

Murrow: This is the second gunshot wound to the chest that you examined?

Dr. Kurtz: Yes.

Murrow: And what did your examination of this gunshot wound tell you, Doctor? Where was it located?

Dr. Kurtz: This was located on the left upper chest, approximately four inches below the top of the shoulder, and one inch to the left of the midline.

Murrow: And what do you mean when you say midline?

Dr. Kurtz: The midline is the vertical line on the front of the chest, and the bullet was one inch to the left of that line. In other words, slightly on the left side of the chest.

Murrow: What did your examination of that bullet tell you?

Dr. Kurtz: The bullet entered the chest from the left side of the midline, again coursing rightwards. In other words, from left to right and then slightly downwards and slightly backwards, passing through the right lung and into the right chest cavity. It went through and exited the torso, entering the right arm, where the bullet was recovered.

Murrow: Doctor, let me show you a photograph that's been marked S-77 in evidence and ask if you recognize what's in that photo.

Dr. Kurtz: Yes. This photograph shows the exit wound from the right side of the chest then entering the inner aspect of the right arm.

Murrow: And what do those wounds tell you about the position of the right arm at the time that bullet wound was suffered?

Dr. Kurtz: The entrance, exit, then reentrance wound, approximately two inches below the armpit, indicate that the arm was in the usual position; that is, lowered, not raised, when he was shot.

Murrow: The arm was down by his side?

Dr. Kurtz: Yes, that's correct.

Murrow: And could you show that photo to the jury, indicating where those wounds are?

(Witness indicating to the jury)

Murrow: Was there a third gunshot wound to the chest that you examined, Doctor?

Dr. Kurtz: Yes.

Murrow: And where was that?

Dr. Kurtz: The entrance of this third gunshot wound on the torso was approximately five inches below the top of the shoulder and three inches anterior to the left armpit. In other words, three inches from the left armpit.

Murrow: What type of hole did that bullet make?

Dr. Kurtz: That also had a fairly typical entrance wound; however, the shape of the wound—do you have the photograph that I may look at?

Murrow: S-78 in evidence.

Dr. Kurtz: The marginal abrasion that I described earlier, most of the entrance wounds have an abrasion along the edge of the hole in the skin. But in this case, the marginal abrasion is not perfectly circular. It is more or less elliptical or elongated.

Murrow: And what does that tell you, Doctor?

Dr. Kurtz: It indicates that the direction of the bullet is not perpendicular to the body.

Murrow: What was the path that this bullet traveled within Mr. Fitzgerald's body?

Dr. Kurtz: Again, the bullet coursed from the left side of the torso to the right side of the torso and slightly downward as it went into the heart. There's a sack, if you will, that surrounds the heart, and the bullet went through the heart, penetrating the diaphragm, which is the muscle between the chest and the abdomen. The bullet continued to travel through the liver, struck and exited a bone on the right side of the ribcage between the seventh and eighth rib. The slightly deformed bullet was recovered from the right side of the lower chest wall just beneath the skin.

Murrow: Doctor, was this bullet wound to the heart in and of itself capable of causing death?

Dr. Kurtz: Yes.

Murrow: And did you examine a fifth gunshot wound?

Dr. Kurtz: Yes.

Murrow: And where on Mr. Fitzgerald's body was that wound?

Dr. Kurtz: The fifth gunshot wound of entrance was on the left side of the left arm, five and a half inches below the top of the shoulder. The bullet was recovered from the deep muscles of the left arm; the bone was broken.

Murrow: Doctor, let me show you what's been marked S-79, which is in evidence. Do you see a gunshot wound to the arm in that photograph?

Dr. Kurtz: Yes.

Murrow: Would you show the jury, please?

Dr. Kurtz: Certainly.

(Witness complies)

Murrow: Thank you, Doctor. Would that bullet wound in the left arm have prevented Mr. Fitzgerald from using that arm?

Dr. Kurtz: That is difficult to say.

Murrow: Now, Doctor. Is the angle of entry of the three wounds in the left chest of James Fitzgerald basically the same for each bullet?

Dr. Kurtz: Yes.

Murrow: And the path traveled by those bullets gives you an indication of where the shooter was at the time those bullets were fired into Mr. James Fitzgerald, doesn't it?

Dr. Kurtz: Yes.

Murrow: And do you have an opinion based upon your medical and professional experience as to where the shooter was when Mr. Fitzgerald suffered the three rounds into his chest?

Dr. Kurtz: Yes. The shooter was on the left side of the decedent.

Murrow: Do you have an opinion within a reasonable degree of medical certainty where the shooter was at the time Mr. Fitzgerald suffered the wound to his left arm and the wound to the left side of his head?

Dr. Kurtz: Yes.

Murrow: And what is that opinion, Doctor?

Dr. Kurtz: That the shooter was standing to the left side, aiming down and shooting at the person seated at his desk.

Murrow: Is it your opinion that the shooter was on the same side of Mr. Fitzgerald for all five bullet wounds that he suffered?

Dr. Kurtz: Yes.

Murrow: Doctor, you're aware that the State has hired an expert to reconstruct the circumstances of the shooting of Mr. Fitzgerald?

Dr. Kurtz: Yes.

Murrow: Which is based on your autopsy report, correct?

Dr. Kurtz: Yes, that's correct.

Murrow: And do you agree with that reconstruction report?

Baxter: Objection.

Judge Hershfield: Basis for your objection?

Baxter: Dr. Kurtz is not a ballistics expert. He's an expert in the field of his study. I don't believe he can render an opinion about the ballistic expert's opinion.

Judge Hershfield: Well, the doctor's been qualified as an expert in forensic pathology. As to the limited degree of expertise and the question the prosecutor has asked, I'll allow the question within that area of limitation.
Restate the question, Mr. Murrow.

Murrow: Doctor Kurtz. Have you reviewed the report of the State's ballistics expert who has reconstructed the circumstances of Mr. Fitzgerald's shooting?

Dr. Kurtz: Yes.

Murrow: And you understand that his report is based on your autopsy report, yes?

Dr. Kurtz: Yes.

Murrow: And do you agree with the findings that he has set forth in his report?

Dr. Kurtz: Yes, I agree.

Murrow: Doctor, I show you a photograph that's been marked S-86 for identification. Have you seen that photograph before?

Dr. Kurtz: Yes.

Murrow: And is that photograph a photo of a reconstruction based on the State's expert report?

Dr. Kurtz: Yes, the direction of the bullet is in agreement with the autopsy findings.

Murrow: I show you what's been marked S-87 for identification. Have you seen that photograph before today, Doctor?

Dr. Kurtz: Yes.

Murrow: And does that photograph depict a valid reconstruction of the shooting of James Fitzgerald based on your autopsy report?

Dr. Kurtz: Yes, it does.

Murrow: Thank you. Doctor, have you reached an opinion within a reasonable degree of medical certainty as to the cause of death of James Fitzgerald?

Dr. Kurtz: Yes.

Murrow: And what was the cause of his death?

Dr. Kurtz: The cause of death was multiple gunshot wounds.

Murrow: And have you reached an opinion within a reasonable degree of medical certainty as to the manner of the death of James Fitzgerald?

Dr. Kurtz: Yes.

Murrow: And what was the manner of his death?

Dr. Kurtz: The manner of death is homicide, meaning that he was killed by another person.

Murrow: I don't have any other questions, Your Honor.

Judge Hershfield: Cross-examination?

Baxter: Thank you, Judge.

CROSS-EXAMINATION BY MR. BAXTER

William Baxter: Doctor Kurtz, can we agree that the angle of flight of the bullets—of all five bullets—that hit the decedent was the same angle?

Dr. Kurtz: More or less the same angle, assuming that the victim was sitting straight up.

Baxter: So we can agree that the angles were basically the same, yet the bullets went into different parts of the body. Isn't that correct?

Dr. Kurtz: Yes.

Baxter: And we know that the bullets were fired serially; that is, one after another. Isn't that correct?

Dr. Kurtz: That's correct.

Baxter: And you've already testified that a bullet that would enter the brain of this individual would have caused unconsciousness and death. Isn't that correct?

Dr. Kurtz: Not death necessarily, but—

Baxter: Unconscious was the word?

Dr. Kurtz: Yes, unconscious.

Baxter: And therefore there would be no motor activity; isn't that correct?

Dr. Kurtz: Motor activity?

Baxter: Well, for example, let's take the wounds to the body. Did you find a great amount of blood emanating from the wounds of the torso of the decedent?

Dr. Kurtz: Yes.

Baxter: Did you find blood on the inside of the hands of the decedent?

Dr. Kurtz: Inside of the hands? You mean the palms?

Baxter: Yes.

Dr. Kurtz: I have to look at my report.

Baxter: Let me show you what's been marked S-70 in evidence. Can you see Mr. Fitzgerald's hands in that picture?

Dr. Kurtz: Yes.

Baxter: Does there appear to be blood residue on those hands?

Dr. Kurtz: The left hand looks fairly clean.

Baxter: Judge, if I may, I think there are other pictures of the hands.

(The Court complies)

Baxter: Now, Doctor, let me show you what's been marked S-12 in evidence and have you take a look at this photograph. Do you see blood on Mr. Fitzgerald's left hand in that picture?

Dr. Kurtz: Yes. I see a little bit of blood on the left thumb. But may I ask what the significance of—

Baxter: Do you see any bullet wounds on the hands of Mr. Fitzgerald in the area of the blood on his hands?

Dr. Kurtz: The bullet wound is in the left upper arm, and I see the blood stain on the shirt. The left arm is fairly clean except for blood stains on the thumb and the index finger.

Baxter: So there's blood on his hand, isn't there?

Dr. Kurtz: Yes.

Baxter: But there's no bullet wounds on his hands, are there?

Dr. Kurtz: No.

Baxter: But there's blood on that hand. Is that correct?

Dr. Kurtz: Yes, that's correct.

Baxter: Now, do we see any hand marks on the head of Mr. Fitzgerald, indicating that a hand might have touched his head after he was shot?

Dr. Kurtz: Hand marks? What do you mean, hand marks?

Baxter: Well, there's blood on the left hand, is there not?

Dr. Kurtz: Yes.

Baxter: Are there any blood marks on the skull of Mr. Fitzgerald that would indicate that his hand touched his head?

Dr. Kurtz: I see some blood coming from the left temple area, down to the front of the head.

Baxter: You referred to that as trailing, did you not, on direct examination?

Dr. Kurtz: Yes.

Baxter: Does it appear to be smudged in any way?

Dr. Kurtz: No, I don't see any smudging in this picture.

Baxter: So it's a clean trail of blood that ran directly from the temple wound hole, down to his face. Isn't that correct?

Dr. Kurtz: Yes, that's correct.

Baxter: But there's more blood on his torso, isn't that correct?

Dr. Kurtz: You mean—this is just a picture? We're just looking at the surface.

Baxter: Yes, but it tells us things, doesn't it?

Dr. Kurtz: Yes, but— I described this relatively free of blood. The left arm is relatively free of blood except for some blood stains on the hand.

Baxter: Okay. If an individual had been shot in the torso, could he take his hands and place them on his torso as I am doing now, having been shot there?

Murrow: I object, Your Honor. Shot where in the torso? I don't think there's any foundation for this question.

Baxter: There's blood on the torso, Judge, and he's the expert.

Judge Hershfield: Well, I'm going to ask you to restate the question because I'm not sure that I understand it.

If you understand the question, Doctor, you may answer it. But I'm not sure that I understand it.

Otherwise, I'm going to ask you, Mr. Baxter, to rephrase it.

Baxter: I'll rephrase it, Your Honor.

Doctor, let's assume for a moment that the first bullet hit Mr. Fitzgerald in the torso. You've seen the bullet wounds. Could he have, with the bullet wounds in his body, taken his hand and touched his torso with the kind of wounds that you observed?

Murrow: I object. First we're talking about the first bullet wound, and then we're talking about other bullet wounds.

Baxter: Any bullet wounds to the torso.

Judge Hershfield: One question at a time. Is your question, Mr. Baxter, "Could an individual have reacted to a gunshot wound by moving his hands to his body?"

Baxter: With specific reference to James Fitzgerald in this photograph.

Judge Hershfield: Or are you asking Doctor Kurtz, "Is there any evidence in this photo that that's what this victim did in response to any gunshot wounds?"

Baxter: Ultimately, that's the question.

Judge Hershfield: Because they're two different questions.

Baxter: And that's ultimately the question, Your Honor.

Judge Hershfield: Well, then let's state the question that you're asking. And that is, if I may, Mr. Baxter, "Is there any evidence in this photograph, Doctor Kurtz, for you to draw a conclusion or the opinion that this victim touched his hands to his body after he was shot in response to any gunshot wounds that you testified to?"

Dr. Kurtz: No, I do not see any evidence indicating that the victim touched his torso.

Baxter: Yet he could have, but you see no evidence of it?

Dr. Kurtz: Yes, he could have touched his torso without leaving marks as he was wearing a shirt. But, again, I see no evidence of that.

Baxter: Okay. Now, you testified that the third bullet wound that went into the torso went into the front of his chest, exited, then went into the right arm. Correct?

Dr. Kurtz: The third one is the second wound that I described of the torso.

Baxter: Entering the torso, exiting the chest then entering the right arm two inches from the armpit. Is that what you testified to?

Dr. Kurtz: That's correct.

Baxter: So that means that his arm was close to his body. Isn't that correct?

Dr. Kurtz: Yes. The right arm was down.

Baxter: So that would be consistent with somebody who could have been sitting in his chair. Isn't that correct?

Dr. Kurtz: Yes, sitting.

Baxter: Sitting with his right arm lowered like this?

(Baxter indicating)

Dr. Kurtz: Yes.

Baxter: Is it consistent with somebody who could have been doing this?

(Baxter indicating)

Do you see what I'm doing? I moved my position.

Dr. Kurtz: I see your arm going backward. The victim's arm was more or less in contact with the chest, ascertained by the location of the entrance, exit, then reentrance wound. But I see your arm moving backward, which is not consistent.

Baxter: All right. How about if I move up to where my arm is now, almost straight, about a foot off the chair?

(Baxter indicating)

Dr. Kurtz: Only as long as your arm is in contact with the chest, yes, it's possible.

Baxter: Okay. Thank you, Doctor. Nothing further, Your Honor.

Charles Winfield could not believe his eyes or ears. Reading the faces of other media personnel present, Charles saw that they, too, could not believe what had just happened. Baxter had dropped the ball. Baxter had just handed the prosecution a slam dunk; a sure thing.

William Baxter could and should have pursued a thorough line of questioning on cross-examination concerning the People's star witness, Dr. Daniel T. Kurtz, Queens County Medical Examiner. However, Baxter's cross-examination was short, hollow, and confusing. As no one truly knows the sequence of the five shots that were fired, the defense needed to make that perfectly clear while hammering home the point that the first shot need not have been the fatal shot. James Fitzgerald could have reacted to a nonlethal wound, thereby supporting a theory that Fitzgerald turned to the side after he started to get up to assault his wife, not that Caitlin snuck up on his blind side and shot him unaware. There lies the probable doubt for the jury to process and digest. Hopefully, jurors so noted Baxter's convoluted attempt to establish this reasonable doubt.

Baxter is failing his client in more than one way, for he did not satisfactorily address battered woman syndrome when he had the chance—not even remotely.

Judge Hershfield: Redirect?

REDIRECT EXAMINATION BY MR. MURROW

Murrow: Dr. Kurtz, the bullet that traveled across the chest and into the right arm indicates that the right arm could not have been in this position, correct?

(Murrow indicating)

Dr. Kurtz: That's correct.

Murrow. That's all I have, Your Honor.

Judge Hershfield: Recross?

Baxter: No, thank you, Judge.

Once again, Charles Winfield and other knowledgeable folks present in the courtroom knew the disservice William Baxter did to his client. Caitlin Fitzgerald got what she paid for: an incompetent criminal attorney. *Criminal*, was the word that ran repeatedly through Winfield's brain.

Judge Hershfield: Thank you, Doctor Kurtz. You may step down.

(Witness excused)

Murrow: May we approach, Your Honor?

Judge Hershfield: Yes, you may.

(Sidebar held off the record)

Judge Hershfield: All right, ladies and gentlemen. It's seven minutes to four. We're going to recess now for the evening. I'll remind you not to discuss the case amongst yourselves or with anybody else. I'll remind you to avoid any media coverage of this trial whether it be in print, on television, on radio, or in any form whatsoever. I'll ask you to return tomorrow morning at nine o'clock. Go directly to the jury assembly area. Please be there by nine o'clock, and my staff will come and get you shortly thereafter, and we'll start once again with testimony. Thank you for your attention, ladies and gentlemen. Good evening.

(Jury excused)

Judge Hershfield: Mr. Murrow, I'm going to expect you to stay with our Court Reporter until she marks all of those items that we moved into evidence, and then keep them in your chart as we have in the past.

Murrow: Yes, sir.

Judge Hershfield: With regard to the chair—oh, the videotape; did we ever get the videotape out of the TV, Brendon?

Sheriff's Court Officer: Yes, we did.

Judge Hershfield: We did?

Sheriff's Officer: Yes, sir.

Judge Hershfield: Are you going to take that back to your office?

Murrow: I have the videotape, Your Honor.

Judge Hershfield: You want to leave the chair here rather than drag it back to your office?

Murrow: I would like to leave it here.

Judge Hershfield: All right. You may leave it here. The courtroom's obviously secured while I'm off the bench. Anything else, gentlemen?

Murrow: No, Your Honor.

Baxter: No, Judge.

(Matter concluded for the day)

Chapter Ten

James Fitzgerald's Girlfriend for the Prosecution

The following morning, a colloquy among Judge Hershfield, Philip Murrow, and William Baxter was conducted. A witness for the defense, Marco D'Angelo, a civil rights lawyer, sitting in the courtroom as a spectator and concerned neighbor, was questioned on the record by Judge Hershfield because Baxter had, once again, fouled up, failing to notify the gentleman that he was on the witness list. Baxter was severely reprimanded; D'Angelo was removed as a witness.

Of the several witnesses for the People called that day, Theresa Manno, Jim Fitzgerald's girlfriend, was the woman of the hour. The jury hung on her every word.

Philip Murrow: People call Theresa Manno, Your Honor.

(Theresa Manno, witness for the People is sworn)

Judge Hershfield: Mr. Murrow, please proceed.

Murrow: Thank you, Your Honor.

DIRECT EXAMINATION BY MR. MURROW

Murrow: Ms. Manno, you knew James Fitzgerald; is that correct?

Manno: Yes, I knew Jimmy.

Murrow: When did you first meet Jim?

Manno: I met him in December of '96 at a Christmas party.

Murrow: And where was that?

Manno: At a restaurant in Manhattan. Felidia, midtown east. Fab.

Murrow: Excuse me?

Manno: Fabulous.

Murrow: Oh, I see. Can you give us the history of your relationship with Jim Fitzgerald?

Manno: Uh-huh. After I met him, you know, we ended up exchanging phone numbers, and he called me. And we dated. And, you know, he appeared to me very, very nice. I really enjoyed myself with him, and he enjoyed himself with me. And that was our relationship. We were really very good friends and had a good time together.

Murrow: And you also had an intimate relationship with Jim Fitzgerald, didn't you?

Manno: Uh-huh.

Murrow: Would you please answer yes or no.

Manno: Sorry. Yes, I did.

Murrow: So you had a relationship with Jim Fitzgerald from December of 1996 to August of 1998?

Manno: Yes.

Murrow: During that period of time, did you travel with Mr. Fitzgerald?

Manno: Yes, I did.

Murrow: And how did that come about?

Manno: Well, he had a lot of business travel. And if I was available to travel, he wanted someone to go with him, and I would accompany him. And we also did some pleasure trips as well.

Murrow: What was Jim Fitzgerald like when he was with you?

Manno: Oh, he was a real gentleman. He was beyond nice. Respectful. Kind. A really good friend.

Murrow: Was he ever physically abusive to you in any way?

Manno: Oh, no. Never.

Murrow: Did there come a point in time when you had contact with Caitlin Fitzgerald?

Manno: Yes.

Murrow: Do you remember when that was?

Manno: Yes. It was in December, shortly after the Christmas Party at Felidia Restaurant.

Murrow: How was it that you first had contact with Caitlin Fitzgerald?

Manno: Well, I was talking to Jim on the phone when all of a sudden we got disconnected. And probably within thirty seconds, the phone rang, and it was this woman on the other end. And she said to me, "Were you talking to Jim Fitzgerald of River Bend Tackle?" And I said that I was. Then she said, "Who is this?" And, naively, I said my name. And she said, "Well, was this business or personal?" I said it was personal. And from then on, you know, she continually harassed me.

Murrow: From the first time that you had telephone contact with Caitlin Fitzgerald, until mid-August of 1998, did you receive telephone calls from her?

Manno: Yes, numerous times.

Murrow: Had you ever met Caitlin Fitzgerald in person?

Manno: I was never introduced to her in person, no.

Murrow: Were you ever physically in her presence?

Manno: I was in her presence once when we were all on a fishing boat trip.

Murrow: Do you recognize her in court today?

Manno: Yes, I do.

Murrow: Is that the same person?

(Prosecutor indicating)

Manno: Yes.

Murrow: Your Honor, I'd ask the record to reflect that the witness has identified the defendant.

Judge Hershfield: Record is so reflected.

Murrow: Ms. Manno, what was the nature of these phone calls that you received from the defendant?

Manno: They were abusive, harassing, vulgar; occurring at all hours of the night. She would call me continuously, sometimes four or five times a night. It went on for practically the whole time I was with Jim.

Murrow: For more than a year and a half this continued?

Manno: Well, for a period she would lay off when I wasn't seeing Jim. Sometimes she would call and just assume I was with him and leave these terrible messages.

Murrow: During the course of this period of time, did she ever make any threats to you about your relationship with Jim?

Manno: Yes. She said, "If you don't stop seeing each other, I'm going to blow you away."

Caitlin, sitting at a table between her counselor and co-counselor, says in a low voice, "I never threatened anyone."

Murrow: She said that to you?

Manno: Yes, she did.

"Liar!" Caitlin shakes her head and exclaims in a voice well above a whisper.

She is immediately cautioned by counsel to remain silent.

Murrow: And did she make any threats to you about what she would do to Jim if you continued your relationship with him?

Manno: I don't remember anything like that.

Murrow: Do you know if Jim Fitzgerald knew that the defendant was calling you and harassing and threatening you?

Manno: Yes, he did.

Murrow: He was aware of that?

Manno: Yes.

Murrow: Let me show you what's been marked S-103, which has been previously identified as a 1998 daily planner. Now, let me show you a page from that planner. Do you see your name there?

Manno: Yes.

Murrow: And is there an address in New York listed there?

Manno: Yes, there is.

Murrow: And at one time did you live at that address?

Manno: Yes, I did.

Murrow: Is there a phone number below that address?

Manno: Yes, there is.

Murrow: Area code 212 652-5787?

Manno: Yes.

Murrow: Was that your phone number at one time?

Manno: Yes, it was.

Murrow: Is this still your phone number?

Manno: No.

Murrow: You changed your phone number?

Manno: Definitely.

Murrow: There's a phone number below that number. Do you recognize that number?

Manno: That's the place where I work.

Murrow: Did the defendant ever call you at work?

Manno: Yes, she did.

Murrow: To harass you?

Manno: Yes.

Murrow: And to threaten you.

Baxter: Objection, Judge.

Judge Hershfield: Don't lead the witness. I will sustain the objection.

Murrow: I will rephrase, Your Honor.

Ms. Manno. What was the reason why the defendant called you at work?

Manno: To harass me.

Murrow: There's a name below the second phone number. Do you recognize that name?

Manno: Yes, I do.

Murrow: Whose name is that?

Manno: My daughter's name.

Murrow: What is her name?

Manno: Maria.

Murrow: And there's an address reflected below her name. At one point in time, was that ever a correct address?

Manno: Yes, it was.

Murrow: There's also a phone number there: 718-789-3770. Are you familiar with that phone number?

Manno: Yes.

Murrow: And how are you familiar with that phone number?

Manno: That was Maria's number.

Murrow: Let me show you an item that's been marked S-127. Do you recognize what kind of item that is?

Manno: Well, like—it's like an address book.

Murrow: On the page for the M's, do you see your first and last name?

Manno: Yes.

Murrow: And does that page have a phone number recorded?

Manno: Yes.

Murrow: And was that your phone number?

Manno: Yes.

Murrow: Did you spend Christmas Eve of 1997 with Jim Fitzgerald?

Manno: Yes, I did.

Murrow: Where did you spend that evening?

Manno: We went to a restaurant, Café Boulud in Manhattan, with some friends. A beige-on-beige bistro; also, fabulous.

Murrow: And did you travel with Jim Fitzgerald during the week of August the 8th 1998 to August the 14th of 1998?

Manno: Yes.

Murrow: Where did you go?

Manno: We went to Texas.

Murrow: At any point during your trip to Texas, did Jim Fitzgerald appear to be angry with the defendant, if you know?

Manno: From what I know, no.

Murrow: On August the 15th of 1998, did you receive a number of calls from the defendant?

Manno: Oh, yes.

Murrow: Did you have any conversation with the defendant on that day?

Manno: No.

Murrow: What was the nature of the calls, if you know?

Manno: To be honest with you, she called so many times that I never really listened to the messages. I would erase them as soon as I heard them. She would call and say, "Hello, Theresa." As soon as I heard her voice, I would get chills—I was so upset. Then she would keep calling back, and I would pick up, hang up the phone then erase them.

Murrow: Did you speak to Jim Fitzgerald over the phone on Saturday, August the 15th, 1998?

Manno: Yes, I did.

Murrow: And during what part of the day did you talk to him?

Manno: It was late afternoon. Maybe four or five o'clock.

Murrow: Do you recall his demeanor, how he was acting?

Manno: He was very tired and upset. I had told him on the phone that Caitlin had been calling me. And he said that she had been harassing him also. And while I was on the phone with him, he got another phone call from her. So I said to him, "Just hang up the phone on her, and eventually she won't bother you because that's what I did, and she finally stopped calling me." And that's what he did. And that was the last I heard from him.

Murrow: When you say he was upset, what do you mean by that?

Manno: Well, he was upset because she kept calling him, just like, you know, like she had been calling me.

Murrow: Did he appear to be angry?

Manno: Oh, no. He wasn't angry at all. Just tired and upset that she kept calling both of us.

Murrow: When did you find out about Jim Fitzgerald's death?

Manno: Well, it was very early in the morning the following day . . . like around three a.m. I really don't remember exactly.

Murrow: Did someone go to your house later that day to interview you?

Manno: Yes.

Murrow: That's all I have, Your Honor.

Judge Hershfield: Cross-examine?

William Baxter: Your Honor, may we approach sidebar?

Judge Hershfield: Yes.

Baxter: At this stage, I request that I be given some time to prepare a cross-examination for this witness and to organize my witnesses for this afternoon.

Judge Hershfield: You told me earlier that you needed time to organize your witnesses. You didn't tell me you needed time to prepare for cross-examination.

Baxter: At sidebar I had said that there's one more witness, and that I'd like to take a break after direct examination.

Judge Hershfield: You were talking about taking a break between the People's case and your case to prepare your witnesses. You didn't tell me you needed a break between direct and cross-examination. You're telling me now that you're not prepared to cross-examine this witness at this time?

Baxter: Judge, I'm asking for a chance to prepare. I had a different witness that I thought was going to be on, and things got fouled up. I'm doing this in good faith. I will be prepared at 1:30.

Judge Hershfield: Prosecutor?

Murrow: It's a matter for the Court's discretion, Your Honor.

Judge Hershfield: Well, quite frankly I don't understand why things always get *fouled up* with you. It's an hour that we'll be wasting; however, I will grant your request.

Baxter: Thank you.

(Sidebar concluded)

Judge Hershfield: Ms. Manno, would you step down, please.

(Witness steps down)

Judge Hershfield: Ladies and gentlemen, we're going to take a recess now for lunch. I will ask the officer to escort you back to the jury assembly area. I will ask you to return to the jury assembly area at 1:30 sharp. Do not discuss the case, and avoid any media coverage of this trial event during the recess. Thank you, ladies and gentlemen.

(Jury excused for lunch)

Judge Hershfield: All right, we are going to stand in recess. I won't expect this kind of inconsistency in the future. I will expect everybody to be prepared to proceed and not waste valuable time. Are we clear?

Mr. Baxter: Yes, Your Honor.

Mr. Murrow: Of course, Your Honor.

(Luncheon recess taken)

AFTERNOON SESSION

Judge Hershfield: All right. Let's get Ms. Manno back on the stand, please.

Ms. Manno, please resume the stand. I will remind you that you are still under oath, having previously been sworn in these proceedings.

THERESA MANNO, Witness for the People, previously sworn, resumes the stand.

Judge Hershfield: Let's have the jury out.

(Jury in the box)

Judge Hershfield: Ladies and gentlemen, before we commence testimony, I will ask if any of you discussed the case, otherwise viewed, heard, or saw any media coverage about the case during the luncheon recess.

Jurors: No.

Judge Hershfield: Not so involved. We may continue. Cross-examine, Mr. Baxter.

William Baxter: Thank you, Your Honor.

CROSS-EXAMINATION BY MR. BAXTER

William Baxter: Ms. Manno. What is your educational background?

Theresa Manno: I have two degrees.

Baxter: Which are?

Manno: A Bachelors and a Masters from the University of Houston.

Baxter: In what field or fields?

Manno: Social Services.

Baxter: And are you presently employed?

Manno: Yes.

Baxter: And were you employed when you started your relationship with Mr. Fitzgerald?

Manno: Yes.

Baxter: And where were you employed?

Manno: Office of Administrative Services, Houston.

Baxter: You worked in Texas?

Manno: Yes.

Baxter: And do you work in the same job today?

Manno: I'm with the Human Resources Department, Department of Social Services, Manhattan; downtown. I do a lot of traveling between Houston and New York.

Baxter: Now, you indicated on direct examination that you first spoke with Caitlin Fitzgerald quite by accident in a phone call; is that correct?

Manno: By accident? Probably. Sure. She called me on the phone I guess by accident.

Baxter: That must have had a devastating effect on you, didn't it, to find out that you were talking to a woman who's living with your boyfriend of so many months.

Manno: No, because I didn't know that then.

Baxter: Well, did you eventually talk to him about it? Did you confront him?

Manno: No, not really.

Baxter: You didn't find it at all unusual that a woman would be living at the house where your boyfriend lived?

Manno: I thought it was his place of business. And when she called me back, I casually mentioned it to him, and he said that it was an old girlfriend who had come by to get some papers and later hit redial because she was being nosy.

Baxter: So when did you find out that he had been with this woman for practically thirty years?

Manno: Well, to be honest with you, I never really knew he was really with her. He always said that she was an old girlfriend that was jealous and just wouldn't let go. Later he told me that he was having financial difficulties, that he had lost his job, and that Caitlin was having money problems, too, and that as part of a strictly financial arrangement, she was moving in with him. Separate rooms and all.

Baxter: I see. But—

Manno: At that point, it was a kind of an on-and-off thing between us.

Baxter: Did there ever come a point in time at which Jim told you that he had gotten married to this woman while he was dating you?
Manno: No.

Baxter: He never told you that?

Manno: No, he never told me.

Baxter: Now, you said there was a time that you first saw Caitlin Fitzgerald.

Manno: Right. On a fishing trip.

Baxter: On a boat, yes?

Manno: Yes.

Baxter: Were you on the boat *with* Jim?

Manno: No, I came by myself. He was with Caitlin.

Baxter: But how did you know it was Caitlin?

Manno: Because she was with Jim. I mean, she didn't fish or anything. She just came along for the boat ride.

Baxter: Were you supposed to be with Jim, or was this fishing trip just a coincidence?

Manno: Caitlin had insisted she come along. Jim and I spoke briefly and said we'd meet later after the fishing trip. He told me to keep a low profile, said he didn't want to do anything to upset their financial arrangement.

Baxter: And you had no idea that he and Caitlin were married.

Manno: No.

Baxter: You didn't see a wedding band on his or her finger?

Manno: I'm sorry, could you repeat the question?

Baxter: You didn't see a wedding band on his or her finger?

Manno: Jim did not wear any rings. And I did not notice any ring on her finger, no.

Baxter: Did you meet Jim later that evening?

Manno: Yes.

Baxter: Where?

Manno: At a yacht club.

Baxter: And you had no idea that he and Caitlin were married.

Murrow: Objection. Asked and answered.

Judge Hershfield: Sustained.

Baxter: Now, Ms. Manno. Did you know that Jim Fitzgerald went through bankruptcy in 1995? Did he ever tell you that?

Manno: No, I did not know that, and he never told me that.

Baxter: Were you ever in the Bahamas with Jim?

Manno: Was I ever in the Bahamas with Jimmy? I was in the Bahamas with Jimmy probably three times, yes.

Baxter: Now, on August 16th you testified that you gave a statement to the police; is that correct?

Manno: Yes, that's correct.

Baxter: The day after Jim died, the police are in your apartment in New York; is that correct?

Manno: Correct.

Baxter: You were willing to talk to the police about this tragic event that had just taken place in your life; is that correct?

Manno: Yes.

Baxter: And you gave a taped statement; is that correct?

Manno: Yes.

Baxter: Let me show you this taped statement that's been marked D-92.

Manno: Okay.

Baxter: Take a good look at it.

(Witness complies)

Baxter: Is that your statement?

Manno: I didn't finish reading it. Can I finish it?

Baxter: Certainly.

(Witness finished reading document)

Baxter: Is that accurate?

Manno: Well, there are a lot of things missing, but what I saw of it seems to be accurate.

Baxter: Do you recall the police asking you whether Jim was afraid of Caitlin?

Manno: Yes.

Baxter: And what did you tell them?

Manno: I told them, yes.

Baxter: That he was afraid of Caitlin?

Manno: At times he said that he was afraid of her.

Baxter: And were you afraid of her, too?

Manno: Yes, I was.

Baxter: Okay. Were you afraid of her when she would call the house and leave messages?

Manno: Yes, her voice would scare me to death. The vulgarity, the drunkenness, the inappropriateness. Was I scared? Sure I was scared. And after she killed him, I was very frightened.

Baxter: Did you ever make a threatening phone call to Caitlin, a message that was left for her on Jim's answering machine at the house?

Manno: I don't believe I did, no.

Baxter: Judge, with the Court's permission, I have a tape which I'd like to play for the witness to see if it refreshes her recollection.

Judge Hershfield: Come to a sidebar, counsel.

(The following discussion takes place at sidebar)

Judge Hershfield: How many times do I have to tell you, Mr. Baxter? I told you a few times earlier. In this case, the People's case, that's not the way to lay a foundation to play a tape. The way you lay a foundation to play a tape is that you have the tape authenticated through a witness.

Baxter: But she's the witness.

Judge Hershfield: Excuse me?

Baxter: Sorry.

Judge Hershfield: Once again, you do not stand up in front of this jury and say, "I have a tape that I want to play." That's not how you do it. This is *his* witness. This is cross-examination. If you have a tape, it's going to be authenticated. You have to lay the foundation. And then if you want to play it, you can. Got it, counselor? You just don't get to play it whenever you feel like playing it. I told you before, don't be making statements, "I have a tape, and I want to play it," or "I have a transcript that I want to read, which in this case is in evidence and you may read." We have rules of evidence and procedure. I expect you to learn them and follow them. I have an evidence book if you'd like to borrow it.

(Sidebar concluded)

Judge Hershfield: Mr. Baxter, you may continue.

Baxter: Thank you, Judge.

(Continued Cross-Examination)

Baxter: Now, Ms. Manno, just one more area. You indicated that you received abusive, harassing and vulgar phone calls from Caitlin. Correct?

Manno: That is correct, yes.

Baxter: Identifying herself as Caitlin Fitzgerald?

Manno. Yes.

Baxter: But you didn't know that she was the wife of Jim Fitzgerald; is that what you're saying?

Manno. I thought Caitlin was his girlfriend and that she was just making that up.

Baxter: Did you ever make such phone calls to Caitlin: abusive, harassing and vulgar phone calls?

Manno: No, not to the degree that she had.

Baxter: Tell us about your phone calls to Caitlin Fitzgerald, please.

Manno: Caitlin had called my daughter a second time, and I was really, really upset. The first time I called her was to tell her that I was truly upset that she had brought my child into it. The second time she called her, Caitlin accused me of being with Jim, and I wasn't at that time. It was an on-and-off thing with Jim as I had said earlier.

Baxter: Let me show you what's been marked D-97 for identification and ask you to review it.

Manno: Ah, hum.

Baxter: You're nodding your head.

Manno: Seems like they're my statements.

Baxter: "Hi. I'm to tell you not to call me or my daughter ever again." Is that your statement, Theresa Manno?

Manno: Yes.

Baxter: "I'm going to tell you something, *Cunt*lin. You're a sick motherfucker, and I don't ever want you to call here again. Is that your statement?

Manno: Yeah.

Baxter: "You have no fucking pride, no respect for yourself." Is that your statement?

Manno: Yes, that's my statement.

Baxter: "I have not seen Jimmy in weeks, but let me tell you something. You ever call my daughter or me again, and I swear to God I'll get back with him just to hurt you, bitch." Is that your statement?

Manno. Yes.

Baxter: You're speaking with Caitlin Fitzgerald, referring to Jim Fitzgerald, are you not?

Manno: Yes.

Baxter: "I'm sick of your fucking shit. You're a fucking loser." Is that your statement to Caitlin Fitzgerald?

Manno. Yes.

Baxter. "You're fit to live in the gutter. Better uplift yourself and get some religion because that's all you really are; a fucking loser. Go and seek God so you can find some fucking respect for yourself and other people." Is that your statement?

Manno: Yes, it was.

Baxter: I have nothing further, Judge.

Judge Hershfield: Redirect?

Murrow: Yes, Your Honor.

REDIRECT EXAMINATION BY MR. MURROW

Philip Murrow: Ms. Manno, for how long a period of time had the defendant been calling you directly with the type of phone calls that you described on direct examination before you left that message for her.

Theresa Manno: Probably since early '97 to when that message was given.

Murrow: Do you know when you left that message?

Manno: I don't recall exactly, but it was a pretty long time after she started calling me.

Murrow: After you learned that the defendant shot and killed Jim Fitzgerald, what did you do?

Manno: I left the state and went to New England. I hired an investigator to find out what was going on because she was out on bail and I was frightened for my life. I wanted to know her mental state because I felt maybe she was going to stalk me and kill me.

Murrow: That's all I have, Your Honor.

Judge Hershfield: Recross?

Baxter: Yes, Your Honor.

RECROSS EXAMINATION BY MR. BAXTER

William Baxter: Ms. Manno, were you frightened for your life when you left that message for Caitlin Fitzgerald that I just read to you?

Theresa Manno: No, I was very frustrated and very angry when I called her and left that message. I was at my wit's end when I used that kind of language because she had used that kind of language with both me and my daughter. I felt maybe she would understand that language.

Baxter: So you had to get down to her level?

Manno: Yes, and I'm sorry that I did sink to her level because that's not really me.

Baxter: Oh, I understand. Thank you very much.

Judge Hershfield: Redirect?

Murrow: No, Your Honor.

Judge Hershfield: Thank you, Ms. Manno. You may step down.

(Witness excused)

Mr. Murrow: Your Honor, subject to moving certain items into evidence, the People would rest at this time.

Judge Hershfield: Thank you, Prosecutor.
　　Ladies and gentleman, we're going to take a recess at this time. We have some administrative matters to attend to at this point. I will remind you that during the recess you are not to discuss the case. Please step into the jury room.

(Jury retires)

　　After taking care of administrative issues concerning items marked into evidence, Baxter makes a motion.

Judge Hershfield: Go ahead, Mr. Baxter.

Baxter: Judge, at this time the Defense would make a motion for a judgment of acquittal based upon the statute and the rule.

Judge Hershfield: Prosecutor?

Murrow: Your Honor, the People submit, based on the testimony under People vs. Reyes, the People submit that it has brought forward sufficient evidence on each material element of all offenses charged in the indictment sufficient for the jury to find the defendant guilty.

Judge Hershfield: Clearly, at this stage of the proceedings, under the law, the prosecution is entitled to all presumptions in its favor. Even without those presumptions, their prima facie case has been made as to the elements charged in the indictment. Your motion is denied, Mr. Baxter.

Baxter: Yes, Judge.

Judge Hershfield: Let's have the jury out.

(Jury in the box)

Chapter Eleven

Caitlin Fitzgerald's Brother for the Defense

Judge Hershfield: Ladies and gentleman, the People have rested, and now we're ready to begin the defense's side of the case.

Mr. Baxter, do you have a witness?

Baxter: I do, Judge. Shawn Reeves.

SHAWN REEVES, Witness for the People, sworn.

Judge Hershfield: Mr. Baxter.

Baxter: Thank you, Judge.

DIRECT EXAMINATION BY MR. BAXTER

William Baxter: Mr. Reeves, where do you live?

Shawn Reeves: I currently live at 103 Buckhorn Road, in Buckhannon, West Virginia.

Baxter: And what do you do for a living, sir?

Reeves: I manage real estate properties.

Baxter: Are you related to Caitlin Fitzgerald?

Reeves: She's my sister, and I'm her brother.

Baxter: And what is your age difference?

Reeves: Two years.

Baxter: Who is older?

Reeves: I'm the oldest.

Baxter: And did you grow up with Caitlin?

Reeves: I did.

Baxter: In the same house?

Reeves: Same house.

Baxter: And where was that?

Reeves: That was in Macon, Georgia.

Baxter: And who else lived there with you?

Reeves: Just my father, mother, and my sister.

Baxter: Could you describe the neighborhood in which you lived and grew up?

Reeves: We lived on the outskirts of the city, but kind of rural for what you would call a city. Mom and Dad rented a small three-room house; later they bought it from the owner and added on another room and a bathroom.

Baxter: What did your folks do?

Reeves: My father worked as a handyman until he had a heart attack; my mom was a housewife up until that time, and then she took a part-time job as a secretary at my school.

Baxter: How would you describe the family atmosphere in the Reeves household?

Reeves: Well, there were good times and there were bad times. We were not wealthy. I had a paper route that I worked before school. My father was a strict disciplinarian. He didn't punish us often, but when he did, it was quite severe.

Baxter: Did you feel his wrath?

Reeves: I did. I remember when I was six years old. I didn't come home from school right away. I was about an hour late. He took me into the garage, and he made me strip off all my clothes. Then he pulled off his belt and beat me with the buckle end of the belt, not the leather part. I had blood running down my legs; later there were many bruises.

Baxter: Were you the only person in the house to feel his wrath?

Reeves: No. In fact, my sister felt it much worse than I did. Not when she was very young, but when she was about ten. That's when it started. It was terrible.

Baxter: Can you tell us about that, please.

Reeves: When she was in school, I remember we were at the kitchen table . . . it's hard for me to tell this. Caitlin changed a grade from a C to a B on her report card, but she didn't do a very good job of it. She was an excellent student in all but one subject, and that was English. Our father put a lot of pressure on us for good grades. Actually, great grades. He wanted to see all As and Bs. When he saw, obviously, what Caitlin had done, he knocked her to the floor.

Baxter: Did she do anything to get away?

Reeves. You didn't escape punishment from our father. Caitlin tried a couple of times, but it only made things worse. One evening she spent the night in the bathroom of a service station because she knew that he would beat her mercilessly for coming home late like I did once. Another time, she stayed under a neighbor's house. That home was built up, and there was room for her to hide. When she finally did

99

come home, she paid a dear price. I can't . . . won't . . . even tell you what he did to her even if you put me in jail—but it was horrible.

Baxter: I see. Would you call Caitlin an unruly or an obedient child?

Reeves: My sister was definitely not an unruly child. She was 99.9 percent of the time a very obedient and disciplined child. In fact, she was rather meek, if you know what I mean. I have never known her to be anything but caring of people, loving, and an extremely hard worker. She was that way from early childhood and on through the years. I never saw her talk back to our parents, even when she was being verbally abused or beaten by our father. Caitlin was a very good child.

Baxter: What was the point in time, Shawn, where Caitlin first left home?

Reeves: She was about thirteen going on fourteen years old. Mom had arranged with a girlfriend's seventeen-year-old son, Bobby Lee Reynolds, for Caitlin to marry this boy and move to South Carolina. Mom gave Caitlin the bus fare to leave town. When Dad came home, he went absolutely crazy and beat Mom badly. Anyway, that marriage was later annulled.

There was another time when Mom and Dad got into an argument in the kitchen. He hit her hard across the face. I stepped between them to stop him from hitting her again. He pulled out his switchblade and threatened to cut my throat.

Baxter: Did you keep in touch with Caitlin after she left home?

Reeves: Yes, I did. Not as often as I would have liked to, but I did.

Baxter: Did Caitlin's marriage to that seventeen-year-old boy last very long?

Reeves: Oh, no. They were married so young, and they were both immature. No, it did not last very long at all.

Baxter: Did Caitlin have another marital relationship soon after that, do you know?

Reeves. Yes, she was married again at a very early age.

Baxter: Do you know who arranged that marriage, if in fact it was arranged?

Reeves: No, I don't. But it didn't last long, either.

Baxter: Did there come a point in time that Caitlin remarried and had a child?

Reeves: Yes, a boy. She was married to an older man, Billy Hendrickson, and she did have a child with him.

Baxter: Did that marriage last?

Reeves: It lasted until Billy was killed in a tragic car accident. It had been a happy marriage. Both she and Billy were very, very happy together. It was a terrible misfortune he was killed.

Baxter: How old was the child when Billy Hendrickson was killed?

Reeves: I really can't say for sure. A week old I think. All I can say is that the boy's alive and well and that he's hopefully coming to this trial to testify and support his mother.

Baxter: Did there come a point in time that Caitlin had a profession?

Reeves: Yes. She became a seamstress and dressmaker, and a very good one. She worked for companies then later went into business for herself. She did very well.

Baxter: Do you recall the time when you first met James Fitzgerald?

Reeves: Oh, yes, indeed. And I'm going to be very honest. Honest to a fault. I couldn't believe Caitlin had married a guy like that. I mean the guy was overbearing, a person who had to have complete control all the time.

He was in the fishing tackle industry; sales, promotion and such. When we first met, well, it was a kind of heated discussion because I took issue with what he had to say about people. He said he never met a person he could trust.

Murrow: Objection, Your Honor. I'm going to object about the specific instances, prior acts.

Judge Hershfield: Well, I haven't heard anything that's objectionable yet, Prosecutor. But if we can ask specific questions, Mr. Baxter, rather than ask for a narrative response, we can avoid potentially objectionable testimony coming before the jury before the prosecutor has an opportunity to impose an objection.

Baxter: All right, Judge.

Mr. Reeves. Did you have occasion to socialize with Caitlin and Jim Fitzgerald?

Reeves: I did.

Baxter: In what ways did you socialize with them?

Reeves: Well, I visited their home two times in Flushing, New York, and would have visited more except that Jim prevented it. He prevented Caitlin from seeing her family. She only got to spend one Christmas Eve since the day she met him.

He prevented Caitlin to come home to see her family and friends. This was very disappointing to our mother who was so looking forward to seeing Caitlin.

Baxter: Did your sister ever talk to you about any abuse she suffered at Jim Fitzgerald's hands?

Murrow: I am going to object, Your Honor.

Judge Hershfield: Sustained.

Baxter: Did there come a time in which you found out that Caitlin had been arrested?

Reeves: I did. I received a phone call from a Queen's County jail, but I didn't know at first what they were calling about. I initially thought that Jim had killed my sister. But then they told me that Caitlin was in jail because *she* had shot *him*.

Baxter: Thank you. I have nothing further, Judge.

Judge Hershfield: Cross-examine?

Murrow: Thank you, Your Honor.

CROSS-EXAMINATION BY MR. MURROW

Philip Murrow: Mr. Baxter brought up on direct examination two of your sister's marriages. Are you aware Mr. Reeves that your sister was married five times?

William Baxter: Objection. As to relevance—

Murrow: I'll withdraw it.
    Mr. Reeves, did you ever hit your sister when you were young?

Shawn Reeves: Yes. I did, as a sibling, hit my sister on the shoulder. We'd argue over who would wash the dishes and who would dry. It was no big deal.

Murrow: I see. No big deal. Was it no big deal when you were fourteen and Caitlin was twelve that you choked your sister until she passed out in the street, Mr. Reeves?

Reeves: No, not in the street. And I don't know how you even know anything about anything like that.

Murrow: My question to you, Mr. Reeves, was did you choke your sister until she passed out in the street when you were fourteen and

Caitlin was twelve?

Reeves: (No response)

Murrow: Did you? Yes or no?

Reeves: We weren't in the street. And yes, I did choke my sister. It was an accidental mistake. She passed out, but she woke right back up, thank goodness.

Murrow: Was it an accident, or was it a beating?

Reeves: No, I didn't beat her. I know I shouldn't have done what I did.

Murrow: You said that your father was a disciplinarian. Did he impose discipline when he thought discipline was necessary to correct bad behavior or judgment?

Reeves: He was a violent disciplinarian. I told the Court how he beat me. On two different occasions, he punched me out with his fists. And he used his fists on Caitlin, too.

Murrow: So as a result of that, the two of you grew up tough, didn't you?

Reeves: I think we grew up two different ways. I think I grew up tough. And I think Caitlin grew up not knowing how to get out of bad situations, always trying to please, always believing that it was she who created these bad situations when it wasn't Caitlin's fault whatsoever.

Murrow: Now, you said that Jimmy Fitzgerald prevented your sister from spending Christmas with your family. Correct?

Reeves: That's correct.

Murrow: And that's based on what your sister told you. Right?

Reeves: Certainly. She'd say that she was coming for Christmas Eve or Christmas. And then one or two days before the holiday, she'd call and say that she was unable to come because Jimmy wouldn't let her come.

Murrow: But that's what she told you, yes?

Reeves: Yes, but it was firsthand, and it happened right then, and it happened time and time again, sir.

Murrow: Mr. Reeves, isn't it true that your sister is the type of person who doesn't take grief from anybody?

Reeves: No, that's not at all true.

Murrow: It's not?

Reeves: It's definitely not true. Everyone in the family knows that the few times we did see Caitlin and Jim together, he'd abuse her and push her around, and she took it without saying a word.

Murrow: Pushing her around physically?

Reeves: No, not physically. Not that any of us saw.

Murrow: That's all I have, Your Honor.

Judge Hershfield: Redirect?

Baxter: No, Judge, nothing.

Judge Hershfield: Thank you, Mr. Reeves. You may step down.

(The witness is excused)

Judge Hershfield: Mr. Baxter, your next witness:

Baxter: Judge, may we approach sidebar, please?

Judge Hershfield: You may.

(The following discussion takes place at sidebar)

Baxter: Judge, that's the best I can do with the witnesses I could prepare for today. I don't have any others. I ask the Court's consideration of a recess at this time, most respectfully.

Judge Hershfield: Mr. Baxter, we've been through all of this before.

Baxter: I know, Judge.

Judge Hershfield: For the balance of this trial, I will expect you to have your witnesses lined up so that we don't waste valuable time as we have wasted earlier this afternoon.

Baxter: I understand, Judge.

Judge Hershfield: I'm not so sure that you do, Mr. Baxter. However, I'm going to grant your request. I want both sides—defense, rebuttal, surrebuttal, whatever—to have witnesses ready. We have already wasted a full hour of bench time this afternoon. You, Mr. Baxter, have to be flexible enough to adjust to however fast or slow this trial moves so that we do not inconvenience the jury.

This is a long trial to begin with. Let's not make it any longer than need be just because we allocated three-and-a-half to four weeks of these good jurors' time to sit in this matter. Let's not let this happen again.

(Sidebar concluded)

Judge Hershfield: Ladies and gentlemen, we're going to stand in recess this afternoon. Apparently, we got a little further along than was anticipated by Mr. Baxter. He doesn't have another witness available for us right now. I will remind you that you are not to discuss the case, read, review, or be involved in any media coverage. I'm going to ask you to come back tomorrow morning at nine o'clock to the jury assembly area. We'll send for you shortly thereafter when we return to the testimony part of the case.

Thank you, ladies and gentlemen. Go with Officer Hanwick; he will take you back to the jury assembly area where you can be released.

(Jury dismissed for the afternoon)

Chapter Twelve

James Fitzgerald's Sister for the Defense

William Baxter's next witness was Elizabeth Saunders, James Fitzgerald's sister.

ELIZABETH SAUNDERS, Witness for the defense, sworn.

DIRECT EXAMINATION BY MR. BAXTER

William Baxter: Good morning, Mrs. Saunders.

Elizabeth Saunders: Good morning.

Baxter: Will you tell us where you live and with whom?

Saunders: I live in South Carolina with my husband, Christopher Saunders.

Baxter: Are you employed?

Saunders: Yes.

Baxter: And what is your occupation?

Saunders: I'm an engineer; I design aircraft for the federal government.

Baxter: Are you related to Caitlin and the decedent, James Fitzgerald?

Saunders: Caitlin Fitzgerald is my sister-in-law. Jimmy was my brother.

Baxter: Did you grow up with your brother Jim Fitzgerald in the same household?

Saunders: Yes.

Baxter: With your parents, Jim and yourself?

Saunders: Yes, until I was nine and my father died in a boating accident. Then it was just my mom, Jimmy and me.

Baxter: Did that accident change the relationship that you had with your mom and Jim?

Saunders: Drastically and dramatically.

Baxter: How so?

Saunders: My brother was thirteen at the time, and he became progressively out of control, very violent. He had to have everything his way.

Baxter: Did he exhibit this behavior before the accident, to your knowledge?

Saunders: No.

Baxter: Did he act out in your presence, to your knowledge, in any instances?

Saunders: Oh, yes.

Baxter: Please tell us what those instances were.

Saunders: When he didn't get his way, he used to beat my mother, badly, in front of me.

Baxter: Did there come a point in time in which he left home?

Saunders: He left home as soon as he was seventeen.

Baxter: To do what?

Saunders: He went into the military.

Baxter: Do you recall whether he got married at some point after that?

Saunders: Yes. He got married right after he got out of the service.

Baxter: Was that marriage to Caitlin?

Saunders: No, it was to his first wife.

Baxter: Did their come a point in time in which you first met Caitlin?

Saunders: Yes, it was around 1970 or '71.

Baxter: What were the circumstances of that meeting, if you would, please?

Saunders: Jimmy and Caitlin were visiting the area.

Baxter: Did you socialize with Jim and Caitlin?

Saunders: Yes. They came for dinner.

Baxter: Okay. Did you have a chance to observe the relationship between Jim and Caitlin?

Saunders: Yes.

Baxter: And what did you see, generally or specifically, if you can recall?

Saunders: Jimmy had not changed. He was in his abusive mode.

Baxter: How so?

Saunders: Being verbally abusive, yelling and screaming at her.

Baxter: At Caitlin?

Saunders: Yes.

Baxter: Do you recall any specific words that he used?

Saunders: He'd call her a bitch and much worse. Very foul language that I'd be ashamed and embarrassed to repeat.

Baxter: Did this happen on more than one occasion?

Saunders: It happened virtually every time they visited.

Baxter: Did you ever talk to Caitlin about Jim's behavior?

Saunders: Yes, a couple of times.

Baxter: And what was the result of that conversation?

Murrow: Objection, Your Honor.

Judge Hershfield: Well, the result of the conversation is different than eliciting the conversation. I will allow it.
     But, Mrs. Saunders, you have to tell us the result of that conversation as opposed to anything that Mrs. Fitzgerald may have said to you.

Saunders: Okay. The result of the conversation. Well, I would say, "How can you stand this?"

Baxter: Did Caitlin continue to live with Jim after that?

Saunders: Yes. She loved him. Those were her words: I love him.

Murrow: Objection, Your Honor.

Judge Hershfield: Sustained.

Mrs. Saunders, please refrain from stating what the defendant may have said to you.

Saunders: Sorry.

Baxter: Did you ever see any physical indications of injury to Caitlin?

Saunders: Yes, a black eye. He would push her around and hit her.

Baxter: You saw him push and hit her?

Saunders: Yes.

Baxter: Can you tell us about that specifically?

Saunders: It was during a Thanksgiving dinner at their home; he knocked her across the room.

Baxter: Do you know why?

Saunders: Yes. Dinner was not up to his spec. Something was cold.

Baxter: What happened as a result of that?

Saunders: Caitlin was totally subservient to him. She cringed in the corner.

Baxter: Were there any other specific instances which you are aware of that were violent or aggressive as you just testified to?

Saunders: Yes, it was a repeat of the same behavior every time we visited them: Jim yelling, screaming, pushing and punching her across the entire kitchen. It was very uncomfortable being with them. Very uncomfortable.

Baxter: Did you ever talk to Jim about his behavior?

Saunders: Yes. I would say to him, "Leave her alone, Jimmy. Just leave her be."

Baxter: You were married by 1995, yes?

Saunders: Yes.

Baxter: Taking you back in time to 1995, did you have occasion to witness an incident between your husband and James Fitzgerald?

Saunders: Yes.

Baxter: Would you tell us about that occasion, please?

Saunders: My mother was very ill and was in Carolinas Medical Center University Hospital in Charlotte, North Carolina. My brother was not happy about that.

Baxter: Why was that?

Saunders: He felt that my mother was a millionaire and was going to leave him a lot of money.

Baxter: Did Jim communicate with you regarding the money?

Saunders: Oh, definitely.

Baxter: Did he have an opinion about what you were doing with your mother's money?

Saunders: Oh, definitely, definitely.

Baxter: And what was that opinion?

Saunders: His opinion was that I was stealing her money.

Baxter: And who was taking care of your mother at this time?

Saunders: I was.

Baxter: Was Jim in any way helping you take care of her?

Saunders: No, not at all.

Baxter: Drawing your attention to approximately November, 1995, was there an event that took place with respect to Jim and your husband at that time?

Saunders: Yes, I was visiting my mother at the hospital as I did every day when Jim came into the room and—

Baxter: Who did he come there with?

Saunders: Jim came with his son by his first marriage and Caitlin.

Baxter: They were there in that hospital room?

Saunders: Yes.

Baxter: Did you know Jim was coming, or did he just show up?

Saunders: He just showed up. I was surprised because he never visited her in the hospital. At home, he saw my mother maybe once a year.

Baxter: What, if anything, occurred in that hospital room?

Saunders: Jim accused the hospital, my husband, and me of not taking good care of Mother. He grabbed my husband and literally threw him into a wall.

Baxter: How big was your brother Jim at the time?

Saunders: My brother is six foot three and weighed approximately 230 pounds at the time.

Baxter: And your husband?

Saunders: My husband is five ten, weighs 140 pounds, and has multiple sclerosis.

Baxter: As a result of that confrontation, were the police called?

Saunders: Yes.

Baxter: Did Jim speak to you at this time?

Saunders: Obscenities, saying that my mother wasn't getting good care in this hospital. I told him that Carolinas Medical Center University Hospital was the best hospital in the area.

Baxter: Was anything else said between you?

Saunders: Yes. Jim wanted to see a copy of her latest will and said that he'd better be in it for half or he'd put all of our heads through a wall.

Baxter: What happened next?

Saunders: The police came and calmed him down.

Baxter: Did you have any contact with Jim after that incident?

Saunders: There were threatening messages left on our answering machine, letters filled with more threats and obscenities.

Baxter: You have these messages and letters recorded?

Saunders: Oh, yes.

Baxter: When was the last time you saw your brother, Jim Fitzgerald?

Saunders: That day in the hospital.

Baxter: When and how did you find out that your brother had died?

Saunders: I was at work when my husband received the call at home.

When I returned from work, my husband told me. We both believed that, if anything, Jim would be the one to shoot Caitlin.

Baxter: Thank you. I have nothing further.

Judge Hershfield: Cross-examine?

Murrow: Thank you, Your Honor.

CROSS-EXAMINATION BY MR. MURROW

Philip Murrow: Mrs. Saunders, you never had a very close relationship with your brother Jim, did you?

Elizabeth Saunders: Yes, I did.

Murrow: You did?

Saunders: Yes, sir.

Murrow: When you were children, you had a close relationship with Jim?

Saunders: Yes, we were three years apart, and we were very close.

Murrow: Okay. This incident referencing the care of your mother; that created some strong and very, very bitter feelings between you and Jim, didn't it?

Saunders: Yes, it did.

Murrow: Jim was very upset about the way that he believed you and your husband were treating your mother; correct?

Saunders: No.

Murrow: Well, wasn't the dispute actually about sending your mother to a nursing home after being released from the hospital and what was going to happen to her assets? Isn't that what it was all about?

Saunders: It was only about what would happen to her assets that Jim was concerned with. My brother was very upset because my mother made me executrix, and therefore I had legal control over her care and her assets to pay for her care.

Murrow: But didn't Jim accuse you and your husband of killing your mother when she passed away?

Saunders: She died at our home and under the care of hospice; no one killed her.

Murrow: Would you please answer the question? Didn't Jim accuse you and your husband of killing your mother when she passed on?

Saunders: Yes.

Murrow: And Jim was very upset about that, wasn't he?

Saunders: My brother was very upset that he was left out of the will.

Murrow: So as a result of that, the relationship between you and Jim became very, very bitter; didn't it?

Saunders: He became bitter far earlier. When my mother was very sick she told him that he was no son and that he would regret how he treated her. She called him a control freak.

Murrow: From the 1970s until 1998, you didn't see your brother very often, did you?

Saunders: I saw him maybe every other month. He saw our mother maybe once a year.

Murrow: Let's go back to the 70s. Did you believe that your brother was married to Caitlin at the time?

Saunders: Yes, I did.

Murrow: But you later found out that they were only married in 1997; correct?

Saunders: Yes.

Murrow: Did you attend the wedding?

Saunders: No. They were officially married in Las Vegas.

Murrow: So over the years, you really didn't spend much time with Jim and Caitlin; either before or after their actual marriage. Isn't that correct?

Saunders: As I had said, maybe half a dozen times a year at family get-togethers. Or he'd drop by if he was alone. We'd go out to dinner, or I'd make dinner at home.

Murrow: You said on Thanksgiving, on one occasion, you saw your brother push and punch Caitlin. Yes?

Saunders: Yes.

Murrow: And that was the only physical contact that you ever saw between Jim and Caitlin; isn't that correct?

Saunders: No, it happened almost every time we visited.

Murrow: One time you saw her with a black eye, you said; correct?

Saunders: Yes.

Murrow: But you didn't actually see how she got that black eye, did you?

Saunders: (No response)

Murrow: I asked you a question, Mrs. Saunders.

Saunders: I assume that it was from all the pushing and punching around.

Murrow: Around the entire kitchen area you testified to, yes?

Saunders. Yes.

Murrow: And when you say punching, were these forceful blows to Caitlin's—body?

Saunders: Well, they weren't love taps.

Murrow: And when you say pushing, could this movement be construed as more of a shove than a push?

Saunders: I guess it could.

Murrow: So then he didn't actually push Caitlin across the entire kitchen, did he? It was more of a limited shove, was it not?

Saunders: You're twisting my words.

Murrow: And with all of Jim's yelling and screaming, as you testified to, it could have magnified the moment in your mind as to what was actually a single limited shove exclusive of continued punching a person across the entire kitchen area, could it not, Mrs. Saunders? Is that not possible?

Saunders: Anything is possible, but that is not what happened. I am not prone to hyperbole, Mr. Murrow. I state things clearly so that there is no confusion.

Murrow: Just as you would have the Court construe on direct examination that Caitlin Fitzgerald received a black eye from being punched in the eye by your brother when in fact you didn't see how she got that black eye; yes?

Baxter: Objection, Judge. Argumentative.

Judge Hershfield: Sustained. Refrain from badgering the witness, counselor. Continue.

Murrow: Mrs. Saunders, I ask you if you knew that your brother was coming to the hospital when he had the incident with your husband, Geoffrey, in 1995?

Saunders: No, I didn't know.

Murrow: Isn't it true that Geoffrey was wearing a tape recorder that day?

Saunders: Yes.

Murrow: Have you ever listened to the tape recording of that event?

Saunders: No.

Murrow: You never have?

Saunders: No, I haven't.

Murrow: Wasn't your husband wearing a tape recorder because your brother Jim called two days prior and said that he was coming to the hospital to see his mother?

Saunders: No.

Murrow: You weren't aware of that?

Saunders: First of all—

Murrow: Excuse me!

Saunders: First of all, my brother—

Murrow: Judge, please instruct the witness to answer my question.

Judge Hershfield: Mrs. Saunders, you have to answer questions that are asked by the prosecutor, ma'am.

Saunders: Okay.

Judge Hershfield: You can't just volunteer information. All right?

Saunders: All right.

Murrow: You weren't aware that your husband was wearing a tape recorder?

Saunders: No, not initially.

Murrow: But you later knew that a tape recording was made of the incident between your husband and your brother, yes?

Saunders: Yes.

Murrow: Okay. Now, isn't it a fact that the reason your husband was wearing a tape recorder was because Jim had called your home and said: "I'm coming on November 18th to visit Mother in the hospital"?

Saunders: No.

Murrow: Isn't it a fact that it wasn't a surprise to you at all because Jim called in advance and that's why Geoffrey put the tape recorder in his pocket?

Saunders: No.

Murrow: Do you know that on that tape recording your husband alleges that Jim hit you in the hospital on that day.

Saunders: No, he did not, no. What I mean—

Murrow: Your brother Jim did not hit you on that day; did he?

Saunders: No.

Murrow: That's all I have, Your Honor.

Judge Hershfield: Redirect?

REDIRECT EXAMINATION BY MR. BAXTER

William Baxter: Mrs. Saunders, on cross-examination, you indicated that your brother was quite upset about the financial issues surrounding your mother; yes?

Elizabeth Saunders: Yes.

Baxter: Did Jim ever suggest or offer that all of you meet together to try and resolve matters peacefully?

Saunders: No. I suggested it on more than one occasion. He would not meet.

Baxter: Thank you. I have nothing further.

Judge Hershfield: Recross?

Murrow: No, Your Honor.

Judge Hershfield: Thank you. You may step down.

(Witness excused)

Judge Hershfield: Your next witness, Mr. Baxter.

Chapter Thirteen

The Verdict

William Baxter called several additional witnesses, none of whom had the impact as when weighed against the testimony of the People's previous witnesses; namely, law enforcement officers that presented Caitlin Fitzgerald as a callous individual from the moment she surrendered herself and handed over the illegal handgun at police headquarters. The officers' lies and half-truths notwithstanding, Doctor Kurtz's forensic testimony carried a great deal of weight in favor of the prosecution.

The jury would have to wrestle with and weigh the elements of Second Degree Murder: one (1), that the defendant *caused* the death of James Fitzgerald; and two (2), that the defendant did so with the *intent* to cause the death. Judge Hershfield's explanation of the charges took up a good part of the morning, with notes sent to the judge from the jury forewoman in the form of questions and requests: requests for a tape recorder and a tape in evidence, a smoking break, further elaboration and clarification on the precise legal definition of the elements.

In the afternoon, the jury further inquired about the legal definition of "intent," "premeditation," "reasonable doubt," as well as the lesser included offenses. It was abundantly clear that they were working hard. Had the jury ruled out Murder in the Second Degree (an A-1 Felony–Intentional Homicide)? Were they now considering First Degree Manslaughter Charges (a B Felony–Intentional Homicide Under Influence of Extreme Emotional Disturbance)? Or Manslaughter Second Degree (a C Felony–Reckless Homicide)? Rule number one: never second-guess a jury, for anything can happen.

Deliberation went into a second day. Read-back requests of testimony referencing five witnesses for the prosecution preceded a request for adjournment for the weekend, which was granted.

On the afternoon of October 10th, 2000, following a break for lunch, Judge Hershfield received a note from the jury forewoman saying that the jury had reached a verdict.

Judge Hershfield: Now, we have a lot of spectators here this afternoon. Let me first say, before I bring the jury out, that we do not know what the verdict is. And when the verdict is announced, I will expect everybody who is in this courtroom to control themselves whether you are in favor of the verdict or against the verdict.

I won't expect any outbursts one way or the other. If you don't think that you can sit through the verdict without some type of outburst, then I would ask that you get up and leave now, 'cause I will not tolerate any outbursts in my courtroom. That said, let's have the jury out.

(Jury present 1:07 P.M.)

Judge Hershfield: Madam Forelady, I have your note. I'm advised that the jury has reached a verdict.

Foreperson: Yes, we have, Your Honor.

Judge Hershfield: Would you please stand up and announce the verdict to the Court?

Foreperson: All right.

Count Number One: Count One of the Indictment charges the defendant, Caitlin Fitzgerald, with Murder Second Degree. As to the count of Murder Second Degree, (Intentional Homicide), we, the jury, find the defendant not guilty.

The foreperson paraphrases formally from statute law:

Foreperson: If we find the defendant, Caitlin Fitzgerald, not guilty of Murder Second Degree, (Intentional Homicide), we, the jury, must consider the lesser-indicted offense of Manslaughter First Degree (Intentional Homicide Under Influence of Extreme Emotional Disturbance).

The foreperson resumes the jury's findings and subsequent charges:

Foreperson: Therefore, as to the charge of Manslaughter First Degree (Intentional Homicide Under Influence of Extreme Emotional Disturbance), we, the jury, find the defendant guilty.

Count Two of the Indictment charges the defendant, Caitlin Fitzgerald, with possession of a weapon for unlawful purposes.

As to the count of possession of a weapon for unlawful purposes, we, the jury, find the defendant guilty.

Count Three of the Indictment charges the defendant, Caitlin Fitzgerald, with unlawful possession of a weapon.

As to the count of unlawful possession of a weapon, we, the jury, find the defendant guilty.

Judge Hershfield: Thank you, Madam Forelady.

Ladies and gentlemen of the jury, my clerk is now going to announce, not by your name, but rather by number, whether or not you agree or disagree with the verdict. This is called polling the jury.

(Jury polled: verdict unanimous)

After both the jury and alternates were instructed, advised, thanked for their services, and escorted out of the courtroom, Philip Murrow stepped forward.

Judge Hershfield: Prosecutor.

Philip Murrow: Your Honor. The People ask that the defendant's bail be revoked and that she be held without bail pending sentencing.

Judge Hershfield: Mr. Baxter.

William Baxter: Judge, my client has made every court appearance over the past two years. She's been here on time or earlier than that. She's been found not guilty of the main charge, Judge. Sentence will be rendered within the next several weeks. I ask that bail be continued until she can get her affairs in order.

Judge Hershfield: Well, the circumstances are quite different now, counselor. Prior to the jury returning a verdict, each defendant enjoys the presumption of innocence. Mrs. Fitzgerald has now been found guilty of First Degree Manslaughter in this homicide.

The circumstances are that she faces between 15 and 30 years of incarceration, to serve 85%. No Early Release Act applies. Again, the circumstances are substantially different now. I will discharge her bail and remand her to the County Jail, pending sentence.

When is the sentencing, please?

Court Clerk: January 12th, Judge.

Judge Hershfield: Sentencing in this matter will be January 12th, 2001, at 9:00 A.M.

Clear the Court.

(Matter concluded)

Chapter Fourteen

Caitlin Ann Fitzgerald's Sentencing

While awaiting sentencing, Caitlin Ann Fitzgerald spent the next three months sitting in a cell at the Rose M. Singer Center (RMSC) for females, one of ten jails on Rikers Island. On January 12th, 2001, the defendant told Judge Hershfield that someone was going to die on the night of August 15th, 1998.

"Your Honor, I knowingly state and believe that it would have been me on that office floor instead of Jim if I had not shot him that evening. He abused me for practically thirty years. I know in my heart of hearts that we would not have made it to thirty years. Because the police failed to escort me home that evening, it was the night that one of us was going to die. Had they taken me home and spoke to Jim, that might have calmed him down for the moment, the evening, perhaps the following morning. But Jim was a time bomb, waiting to go off. Each beating was worse than the one before it. Each rape was more violent than the earlier one. I want the Court to know that I did truly love Jimmy better than anything else in the world. I would go so far as to say I worshipped him. I did not shoot him out of jealously like Mr. Murrow would have the jury believe. I left him in 1976, 1977, and again in 1989. I left him three times in 1997. But he always found me. I believe he was very mentally disturbed, and for me to keep going back to him, I must have been mentally disturbed, too. I also want the Court to know that the police officers at the 107th Precinct viciously lied to protect themselves. I never said or behaved the way they said I behaved. That's all I have to say, Your Honor."

"All right." Judge Hershfield addresses all present in the courtroom.

"First off, I wish to express my sincere sympathy to all family members affected by this trial, to both the Reeves and Fitzgerald families and friends of the deceased, the defendant, as well as all others with an emotional investment in this case. This trial and trials of such nature are but a frame, a snapshot of a far broader epidemic panoramic of what I view now and again in this courtroom; specifically, domestic violence involving the illegal possession of handguns. That said, my sentencing duties are not painted with a broad brush that covers a single canvas or a collection of prejudiced declarations. My obligation is to offer up a fair and just decision in the instance of the defendant, Caitlin Ann Fitzgerald, shooting and killing James Fitzgerald on August 15th, 1998.

We have listened to a voluminous amount of testimony covering a span well-beyond a twenty-seven year domestic partnership followed by one year of marriage, a period fraught with domestic violence. What the jury found, beyond a reasonable doubt, was that Caitlin Fitzgerald knowingly possessed an illegally obtained .25 caliber semi-automatic handgun with the intention of using it unlawfully, discharging five bullets into the body of James Fitzgerald."

After several more minutes of rhetoric, Judge Hershfield imposed judgment, sentencing Caitlin Ann Fitzgerald to the maximum term of thirty years behind bars, ten more years than the assumed time period of incarceration.

A court officer escorted Caitlin out of the courtroom, first making sure that her handcuffs were not only secure but very tight. Once outside the courtroom, the officer leaned forward and whispered in her ear. "Hey, Caitlin, you're finally being escorted *home*, just like you wanted. Only your home will be three walls and a cell door for the next thirty years. Oh, by the way. My uncle, Sergeant Dennis Phelps from your murdered husband's hunting/fishing club said to say bon voyage. You're just gonna love Bedford Hills's maximum security Correctional Facility State Prison for cunts, Caitlin. Rapes there are on the roster regularly. Trust me on that. I already made arrangements to make sure that happens soon after you arrive. You see, I know people. One c/o there in particular is just going to love your old but lovely butt."

Caitlin's head and heart pounded as she was taken to a holding cell, awaiting transportation to one of three correctional facilities for woman. Albion Correctional Facility and Taconic Correctional Facility were both medium security prisons, one of which her attorney, William Baxter, had said she would be sent. However, as the court officer had told her, she was to be sent to Bedford Hills Correctional Facility, New York State's largest maximum security state prison.

Caitlin believed her life was over. In a very real sense, a good part of it was and would be. She was cold, frightened and fearful. Frightened at the moment. Fearful of what tomorrow would bring.

Chapter Fifteen

Caitlin's Incarceration

Immediately following a break in wintry weather, Caitlin was transported to the Bedford Hills maximum security state prison in Westchester County, New York. A set of sheets, one blanket, a pillow, a toothbrush and toothpaste were lying on the bed. Suddenly, a series of steel doors started slamming closed with a clang of finality that immediately chilled Caitlin to the bone. She started crying loudly and could not stop for the better part of an hour. *Thirty years*, she kept thinking. *I'll surely die in prison*, she truly believed. *Surely*.

Several weeks had gone by before Caitlin was allowed visitation rights. During a visit to the Bedford Hills Correctional Facility by Caitlin's best friend, Mary Jennings, who had testified at trial on Caitlin's behalf, Caitlin had asked Mary if she knew of anyone who might want to write her story of almost thirty years of emotional and physical abuse at the hands of her husband, Jimmy; a story about the lies that the police had told at both the grand jury and jury trial—lies that Caitlin believed buried her alive and put her in a cage, a cage that would hold her like an animal for eighty-five percent of thirty years. Caitlin cried the entire time, explaining lie after lie that the police had told. She spoke of the incompetence of her defense attorney, William Baxter. Caitlin told of how she had wished she had taken the plea offer.

Mary told Caitlin that she was not sure that she knew of anyone who would write her friend's story but said that she would look into it for her. Mary had seen Charles Winfield in the courtroom on many occasions, but the two had never met. She believed she heard that the man was a freelance writer.

That evening, Mary found Charles Winfield's phone number and home address in the directory. She called and asked if he would be interested in writing Caitlin Ann Fitzgerald's story. Charles sadly explained that the timing was out of joint, that he had just signed a contract for a trilogy on which he was working, a project that would keep him busy for several years. "Perhaps when I'm finished," was the author's offer.

Mary had contacted a good many agents as well as publishers who she believed might be interested in Caitlin's story, all to no avail. She had tried to write an impressive cover letter and synopsis but knew she was no writer. Neither was Caitlin, English being her worst subject in school. Mary certainly knew the facts of the story as she attended Caitlin's trial every day after testifying on her behalf. Also, Mary had followed news reports and made copies of the coverage, inclusive of *Court TV* and *20/20*. Too, through William Baxter's office, Mary retained copies of all court transcripts as well as copies of letters written to Judge Hershfield from supporters and dissenters alike.

Seven years later, Mary Jennings reconnected with Charles Winfield when she saw that his trilogy, three lengthy novels, was published. She called him at home once again. Charles was reluctant to take on the project, having already started another novel.

"May I ask you why you sat in that Queens County courtroom every day? You're not a relative or friend. You must have had some interest in the case."

"I did, but then I got busy. As I told you seven years ago, the time was out of joint. I was made an offer that I couldn't refuse."

"And now?"

"And now I'm busy with another book."

"Your books are fiction, Mr. Winfield, are they not?

"They are."

"Then why not write the true account of a woman who was emotionally and physically battered by her deranged husband for almost three decades. Write the true account about the lies that the police had told at both her grand jury hearing and jury trial. Lies that buried Caitlin alive and put her in a maximum security prison for thirty years. Write a true account about her incompetent attorney. About how William Baxter coaxed her to 'hang in there' rather than accept a plea offer, which would have gotten her twelve years instead of thirty. About how he dissuaded her from taking the stand and testifying before a jury of her peers."

"From what I gleaned referencing the grand jury proceeding, I'm not so sure Caitlin would have fared well by taking the stand."

"Maybe yes, and maybe no. But at her trial, Caitlin would have been credible in telling the jury that Police Officer Dennis Phelps and other officers had lied through their teeth. I believe Caitlin when she said that Officer Phelps said that he called her husband then told her that it was safe to return home—unaccompanied by police. I'm sure that there exists a phone record which shows that a call was made from the 107th Precinct to Caitlin's residence that evening. Why Baxter didn't press those issues including distorted tapes along with a missing tape is positively amazing."

"In part he tried, I'm sure you recall."

"In part," she echoed and frowned into the mouthpiece.

"You'll recall the judge saying that he is not going to allow Baxter to try the officers of the 107th Precinct, that Caitlin Fitzgerald is on trial, not the police."

"There are so many things that smack of impropriety. Like Baxter nowhere to be found outside the grand jury room during proceedings while she is in there being hammered by the prosecutor, Philip Murrow. Baxter was supposed to be right outside that door in case she had a question or twenty."

"The man's an incompetent, Mary Jennings."

"Tell me something I don't know," she said sourly.

"How about the fact that William Baxter has been disbarred," Winfield put forth matter-of-factly.

"What?"

"Embezzlement."

"You're kidding?"

"Would I kid a kid?" Charles Winfield teased.

"You don't know how old I am, mister."

"You'll be seventy next month, Ms. Mary Jane Jennings."

"How in the world—?"

"I've kept a file on every witness concerning Caitlin's case."

Mary Jennings paused for a long moment. "But why?"

"Because I've made it my business to investigate this case from the beginning."

"But you said—"

"I said that I was busy at the moment with another book."

Mary Jennings beamed brightly. "You mean you're going to write her story?"

"Caitlin's story is going to be my swan song, Ms. Jennings."

"And when do you plan on writing this story, Mr. Charles Winfield?" she asked rather impatiently.

"Let me ask you a question, Mary."

"Ask."

"I don't mean to sound insensitive, but is your friend going anywhere anytime soon?"

Mary Jennings smiled sadly and shook her gray head of curls from side to side.

BOOK TWO

Chapter Sixteen

Charles Winfield's and Caitlin Fitzgerald's Initial Correspondence

Two years later, after receiving a phone call from Charles Winfield, Mary Jennings paved the way for the author to send a letter of introduction to her good friend, Caitlin Ann Fitzgerald, providing Charles with Caitlin's address and inmate I.D. number at the Bedford Hills Correctional Facility in Westchester County, which, of course, the writer already had.

Charles Winfield
72-61 113 St.
Forest Hills, NY 11375

October 8, 2010

Caitlin Fitzgerald
#00G1442
Bedford Hills Correctional Facility
247 Harris Road
Bedford, New York 10507-2400

Dear Caitlin,

Mary Jennings had sent you a letter and paid you a recent visit with regard to the two of us putting together a manuscript then hopefully securing a literary agent to represent the work and find an interested publisher.

If you are interested in working together, we can go about this a couple of ways: I could ask you a series of questions—some of them *tough* questions—to which you'll respond directly and succinctly. At a later point, I'll ask you to elaborate on your answers. This might be a good way to begin.

Or you could start by telling me your story from the beginning, initiating the emotional and physical abuse you endured through the years—commencing with your father and continuing on to the final abuse charge you filed against your husband, James Fitzgerald, on May 16, 1997; the events with the police both before and after the shooting on August 15th, 1998; your grand jury experience and impressions, pre-jury trial and trial impressions, your incarceration—right up to the present.

With either approach, this will have to be handled via written back-and-forth correspondence between us. Would you be able to handle that, or are there any restrictions regarding written communication from Bedford?

Think about these two approaches; feel free to come up with your own suggestion(s). It will be a lot of time and work on our behalf. At the very least, your attempt may prove cathartic. If we succeed, you will be helping women who find themselves in abusive relationships.

Sincerely,
Charles Winfield

cc: Mary Jennings

****

Nov. 3, 2010

Dear Charles,

I received your letter and wrote to Mary Jennings. I gave her my permission to send you all court transcripts, TV tapes, DVDs, photos, correspondence, etc. Mary has a good feeling about you and your partner Madeline. Mary spoke to Madeline at length. I trust you both. Am sure this book will be a best seller. I know your concern is the Son of Sam Law. It is my concern also. If there is no easy loophole to write my story as nonfiction, I would like for you to write my story as fiction.

Sincerely,
Caitlin

****

November 7, 2010

Caitlin Fitzgerald
#00G1442
Bedford Hills Correctional Facility
247 Harris Road
Bedford, New York 10507-2400

Dear Caitlin,

Just to let you know, I received all materials from Mary Jennings. Madeline and I are extremely busy and in the middle of a project, so this letter is going to be short.
Take care.

Best,
Charles Winfield

****

Nov. 11, 2010

Dear Charles,

Glad that you received all the materials from Mary. This will be a great help to you I'm sure.
Billy Jr. was in the Marine Corps for 20 years. He now lives in Virginia with his wife. He would have been a great witness if my attorney had asked him the right questions. Billy got out of the Corps in 2002. He had a very hard time finding a job. I don't hear from him or his wife anymore the last three years. And don't know why. I only send Birthday and Christmas cards to him and her because I got tired of writing letters that were never answered. I'll be 73 years old when I get out of here with nothing, which is better than 89, less 15%, which it could have been. But I had someone here appeal my conviction

because Judge Hershfield made a mistake by not allowing my trial attorney, William Baxter, to present a passion-provocation defense instead of self-defense, arguing battered women's syndrome. That means manslaughter but without premeditation. I did not plan on shooting Jimmy but was terrorized at that moment, afraid that he would kill me. And I believed it at that moment when he started to come after me, and I believe it today. Still, if I had taken the plea offering that I considered taking, I would be getting out in 2013 instead of 2015. If I didn't win on appeal, it could have been 2031. Actually 2027 with 15% off that sentence. So I thank both God and my appeals attorney.

You and your family have a wonderful Thanksgiving.

Sincerely,
Caitlin

****

November 26, 2010

Caitlin Fitzgerald
#00G1442
Bedford Hills Correctional Facility
247 Harris Road
Bedford, New York 10507-2400

Dear Caitlin,

I have now finished reading each and every letter from your friends and relatives have written to Governor Christopher Emanuel Drew, Judge Hershfield, and Prosecutor Philip Murrow (copies of which were initially sent to your attorney, William Baxter, and later retained by your friend Mary Jennings) asking for leniency, clemency, a pardon, or simply attesting to your fine character. I am presently going through the transcripts of the trial proceedings as well as tapes and DVDs.

Mary suggested, after visiting you recently, that you start unfolding your story to me from the beginning, recollecting as far back as that sharp mind of yours allows. Do not take a chapter of your life and try to honey-coat it so as to paint yourself in a better light. Readers see through that. This does not mean that you can't relate how you truly felt or feel about an incident. Be direct, blunt and above all, truthful . . . truthful to a fault. Start chipping away with this (I know) very painful process. Apart from having read Eldridge Cleaver's *Soul On Ice*, I know very little about prison life. If I have questions along the way, I'll ask you to answer them. Mary suggested, too, that you should continue your story right on through to the present, illuminating prison life at a women's correctional facility for the past decade. Take it nice and slow. You are going to educate many of us.

Thanks for wishing Madeline and me a happy Thanksgiving.

Very best regards,

Enclosure: $20 postal money order for stamps.

****

Dec. 11, 2010

Dear Charles,

Received your letter and a receipt saying you had sent $20, and that was put into my account. Thank you.

Well, I'll start telling my story. Please excuse my spelling, punctuation and grammar. English was my worst subject in school. Here we go.

I was born Dec. 7, 1942, Caitlin Ann Reeves. I did not know I was an accident until my brother Shawn told me. At that time I was about 9 years old. Shawn is 2 years older than me. I went to ask my Mom if I was an accident. Mom told me they had waited 7 years before Shawn was born and that my Dad didn't want any more children, but that she loved me alot and was very happy to have a little girl.

My Mom and Dad did not get along very well. Dad was a day

138

laborer who left the house very early every morning. My Mom found work wherever she could. Anything from cleaning homes to working part-time as a secretary at my school.

My Dad had made a stool for me to stand on so that I could see what was cooking on the stovetop. I always made breakfast for the 3 of us. My brother and I were home alone 5 days a week before school started up. Each morning, Shawn made me do all his chores, and of course, I had to do mine to, while he went back to bed before getting dressed for school.

Shawn had a paper route on Saturdays, and I helped him collect money. One time I had lost a dime. We were at the end of the street. No cars were coming. Shawn choked me until I passed out. You can see my brother's statement in the court transcript. He started crying on the stand at my trial. Mary said you were there everyday so you probably remember. He also told how our Dad beat me alot. He even kicked me in the ribs.

Shawn has come to see me twice in the last ten years. But it is o.k. because that's a long trip. We were never close growing up. We did not like each other. As adults we lived in different states. Sometimes we didn't see each other for as long as 5 years at a time.

When I was in 8th grade, my brother was in the same school. He saw me in the hallway at my locker. I had on light pink lipstick. That evening he told Dad. I received a bad beating with a black leather razor strap that he used for sharpening his straight razor. My Dad beat me so many times I can not remember the first time or how old I was. Shawn beat me when we were home alone. But not often.

I know you know about the report card story from the trial so I won't go into that. My brother did not have to study hard for his grades so he didn't get beat often for that. But he did get a few beatings for other things. One time 3 boys had beat my brother. When he come home, Dad wouldn't let him into the house. He told him to go back and beat up one boy at a time before he could come back in the house.

I run away many times after my Dad beat me. My Mom took the hits while I got up and run out of the house. Sometimes I run and hide under peoples houses. Sometimes I stayed and slept at gas station bathrooms. Sometimes I slept at my Aunt and Uncles house, two houses away from our own house. One time I run to my girlfriends house about 2 miles away. I waited outside sitting behind big shrubs until her Mom left for work so I could go inside, shower, put on some of my friends clean clothes, and get something to eat. I wouldn't go to school those days. I would call home when I knew no one would be there but my Mom. The school would call the house and Mom would tell them I was home sick. I would tell my Mom I was o.k. but wouldn't come home until she could get my Dad to promise not to beat me anymore. I would call back at 5P.M. and see if he would tell me that on the phone himself. Then I would go home.

Many times at school I refused to put on my gym suit because my legs had belt marks all over them. I would tell my gym teacher that I couldn't play basket ball because I had my menstrual period.

Twice, my Mom put my brother and I in a cab with her while my Dad was somewhere with another woman. We went to my Grandfathers house. My Mom begged him to let the 3 of us live with him and his new wife. My Grandmother died when I was 4 years old. He told my Mom, you made your bed, now you lay in it. For many years I didn't know what that means. My Mom didn't think that she could raise my brother and I by herself. Mom always gave Dad her pay check. She made her own clothes. That's how I learned to sew.

On Fridays Dad would fill his car with gas, get his suits out of the dry cleaners, go to the liquor store and buy a fifth of whiskey, then hide the rest of his money. He did not believe in banks or credit or later on charge cards. He never charged a thing in his life. He bought a new car with cash in 1949. Dad had Mom, Shawn and me live very modestly. Dad however deprived himself nothing. We were the first ones on our street to have a T.V. Also, we were the only ones in the neighborhood to have a boat for water skiing. He bought that boat in 1952. I remember that year because my brother and I learned how to water ski. Shawn was 12 and I was 10 years old. In Dec. of 1952, I wanted to make sure I didn't forget how to ski because before summer came again. I asked Dad if we could go water skiing. He thought it was a great idea and told Shawn and I to put our bathing suits on under our clothes. He told Mom we were going to the river and put the boat in just to go for a boat ride. Mom never liked the boat because she couldn't swim. She was always afraid that Shawn and I were going to drown. That whole summer Mom had sit in a chair on the weekends on the shore, watching us learn to ski and prayed nothing would *happen to us.*

Years before my Dad bought the boat, he threw me in the deep end of a large swimming pool and said swim or drown. I don't remember when Shawn learned to swim, maybe the same way. I do know my brother and I became excellent swimmers and outstanding water skiers.

That Saturday in Dec. while we were skiing, a newspaper reporter saw us from the highway, come down and made many pictures of us. Next day we were in the Sunday paper. Headline read, Reeves Family, Up-Up and Away. My Mom found out that we went water skiing that cold Saturday. My Dad got pictures from the reporter, had four 8 x 10 pictures made in color. Those pictures were in our living room for years.

Lots of weekends my dad would have car keys in hand and about to leave the house. Mom would ask him where he was going. He would say I'm going to see a man about a mule. Which was an old as dirt southern saying that pretty much meant that he had business to take care of and was not about to share it with any of us. But my Mom and I knew he was going to have sex with one of his women. We only had two bedrooms in our house. I slept with my Mom. Shawn slept with Dad. On weekends Dad would come in Moms bedroom to wake her up to have sex in the garage. I would pretend to be asleep. My Mom never wanted to go, but she did because he kept saying lets go. I know she only went so his voice wouldn't wake me up, so she thought.

We had what was called a party line phone at that time. Whenever my Dad picked up the phone and the lady that lived across the street was on the line, he would hang up, look at his watch, gave her five minutes to get off, and picked up the phone again. If she was still on it, he would cuss her out, then open the front door and cuss her out again. Then she would hang up. A few times when this lady would hear my Dad screaming and cursing, she knew he was beating one of us. Mrs. McGowen would call the police. But each time the police did come, Dad talked his way out of it. Plus they never got into the house or ask to see my Mom, my brother or me. He would say, Oh, guess my T.V. was to loud.

My Dad only drank on weekends. One time my Mom poured his whiskey down the sink. But believe me she only did that one time. Whatever he did to her I don't remember. I've blocked that out of my mind. I guess you would say my Dad was a weekend drunk.

The last time I was beaten by my Dad, I had gotten on the bus from taking piano lessons to buy a piece of sheet music with my lunch money I had saved. Some boogie-woogie blues. I hated taking piano lessons and had begged to take dancing lessons. But Dad said I was going to be a schoolteacher and piano teacher. I hated both. I was thirty minutes late getting home. He accused me of having sex, saying that's why I was late. He called me a little whore. This time while he was beating me and I'm on the floor, I looked up at him and said I am still a virgin. My Dad said I know you were out screwing some boy. He kept right on beating me. My Mom kept screaming at him to stop-stop, you are going to kill her! She hasn't did anything wrong. He pushed Mom away and she fell backwards crying. He stopped beating me when he was out of breath.

I started developing alot at 12 years old. My Mom bought me some bras around 11 years old. My Dad had a fit then to. I had seen that the bigger my boobs got the more beatings I got. At 14 years old I looked like 18.

My Mom came up with a plan to get me out of the house and marry Bobby Lee Reynolds. I know you also know about it from the trial and transcripts, so I won't go into that part of the story. My attorney Mr. Baxter told what was going on in the house without telling the whole story. Which I don't like talking about anyway. I lived with Bobby Lee and his grandparents and went to school there. I did most of the cooking and cleaning because Bobby Lee's grandparents both had health problems. Bobby Lee's stepbrother Frankie also lived in the house. He was ten years older than Bobby Lee and very big and strong. When the grandparents were on a weekend holiday and Bobby Lee was working nights part time at the gas station, Frankie comes into the bed room at about 11 o'clock and rapes me. I was 15 years old. After that, our marriage didn't last very long.

I'm telling you parts of my life that my attorney and the prosecutor Mr. Murrow did not cover in detail in the courtroom. My second husband was killed in an auto accident. He was a good man and we had a child together.

When he was killed, I tried to raise the child on my own. I was very young and immature. I had 2 other marriages. I don't like to talk about that part of the story either. Many years later when I was 27 years old, I met Jimmy . . . 27 years of hell followed. But I was determined to make things work. I truly loved Jimmy. But Jimmy could not love just one woman. I knew that. Somehow I became Jimmy's mother. When Jimmy beat me, I truly believe he was beating his mother. I shot the man I loved because I didn't want to be beat no more. I had to many years of beatings between Jimmy and my Dad. Maybe when I shot Jimmy, I was shooting my own Dad.

That's part of the story of my life up until the time I was sent to this prison. For almost ten years I've been a model prisoner. I'm determined to find myself and make things work. In here I can't run and hide from myself. In here I face three walls and a cell door.

Again, please excuse my spelling, punctuation and grammar. I try and get help from one of the other inmates when I can.

Sincerely,
Caitlin

****

December 20, 2010

Caitlin Fitzgerald
#00G1442
Bedford Hills Correctional Facility
247 Harris Road
Bedford, New York 10507-2400

Dear Caitlin,

Wow! You're off to a great start. Take your time; don't rush things. Proof your work aloud (quietly, so as not to draw attention). You'll catch errors that you wouldn't ordinarily see with the naked eye. I tell students of writing that there's a short circuiting between the brain and the hand. Reading your work aloud helps nip this in the bud.

I've touched base with Mary Jennings and told her what a nice job you've done for openers. I'm going to take the next step right after the holidays, meaning I'll query a few literary agents and publishers referencing the Son of Sam law. If it's too involved and/or costly, I'll tackle it as fiction. I'll see what happens and certainly keep you posted.

Continue the way you're going. I'm sure you'll have other thoughts you may want to address that happened back in time as well. Feel free to fill in any gaps as you move ahead to the present. I'll put everything in the proper order when you've finished telling me your story. Tell me about prison life at Bedford Hills Correctional Facility. Tell me the good, the bad, and the ugly. And please don't concern yourself too much with spelling, punctuation, and grammar. It's important that I copy your letters as you have written them; however, for the sake of clarity, I'll only alter syntax where it tends to lead to confusion. Your handwriting is what's important. You're not that bad. I wish I had you as a student in my English classes. English would not have been your worse subject. Believe me.

I'm happy to hear that you received a receipt re the money order.

Take care. Madeline says hello. Merry Christmas from both of us.

Very best regards,
Charles

****

Dec. 29, 2010

Dear Charles,

Thank you for the Christmas greetings from you and Madeline. Hope you had a good one.

I know I left out more then a few things about the first 15 years of my life. I don't remember the exact years that things happened because they happened very early on.

My Mom and Dad were having a very big arguement. Mom didn't argue with him often. He threw a bag of hard candy at her face. The candy hit her glasses and the glasses broke. I thought at first that one of her eyes was bleeding. I started crying, thinking now, my Mom will be blind. When this happened, all 4 of us were sitting in the living room watching T.V. When my Mom went crying in the bathroom, I cried to and went with her. The broken glass had cut right underneath a eyebrow and not the eye itself, thank God.

During my early childhood, there were times you wouldn't know why my dad was mad at me. I would walk into the room and he would stand up and hit me. I would be on the floor but didn't know why. I guess he was just drunk, don't really know. One day he took my brother Shawn into the garage to beat him. Dad beat Shawn so bad he had to carry him back into the house in his arms.

I can't remember if I wrote you or told Mary Jennings about going coon hunting with my Dad. Shawn got tired of going with him. I begged to go, thinking Dad would like me better. That's how I learned to shoot so well. During grand jury or trial, the prosecutor said I shot Jimmy with the precision of a sniper. I remember closing my eyes when I shot Jim.

I almost forgot to tell you that Mary came to see me last week. She's been a good friend and came to see me many times through the years. Visits last two hours, with me doing most of the talking. Years ago whenever Mary left here, she would only ride away from the prison a few short blocks, pull over and make notes on everything I have said. I keep forgetting to ask her if she gave those notes to you. Please let me know.

In my last letter, I didn't tell you exactly how I left Bobby Lee. His stepbrother Frankie tried to rape me a second time. I held him off with a knife that I kept by the bed because I knew he would do it again if I didn't defend myself. If I told Bobby Lee that his stepbrother tried to rape me like he did rape me the week before, one of two things was going to happen, neither of them good. Bobby Lee would believe me this time and get into a physical fight with Frankie. I told you that Frankie was big and very strong. Bobby Lee was no match against Frankie, and Bobby Lee knew it. Bobby Lee would either have to shoot Frankie to stop him from attacking me again, or Bobby Lee would believe Frankie again and probably want to kill me. To say that our marital relationship was strained after what happened only a week before was what you would call a understatement. At the very least, one of the three of us would wind up in the hospital or in the grave.

I thought about returning home to Georgia, but that might be like going from the frying pan into the fire. There were very good reasons why my Mom wanted me away from my Dad. I put a few clothes in a bag and decided the best thing to do was to leave Bobby Lee and

North Carolina. I looked eighteen and even had a driver's license that said I was eighteen, but no car of my own. That's a whole other story. Anyhow, it was summer time and school was out. I thought maybe I can make it on my own. The next day was Sunday and Bobby Lee went to work, Frankie wasn't home, and their grandparents were not yet back from their trip. I walked to the bus stop, rode to Main Street, got off and went to the service station to use the bathroom. I started talking to a lady that was washing her hands at the sink. She said she and her husband were going cross country to Los Angeles, California. She said it was going to be a hard trip because she didn't know how to drive and that her husband was doing all the driving. I told her that I wanted to go to a new place and start my life all over. I showed her my driver's license and told her if she and her husband would let me ride with them, I would love to do half the driving. We went outside and talked to her husband. He agreed. I was so excited and happy. I was going to have a new life. The only thing I felt bad about was that I didn't leave my husband a note because I didn't know what to say in it. Also, I didn't call my Mom and tell her anything. To this day, Bobby Lee doesn't know why I left him.

It took us about 10 days to get to California, but I sure got to see alot of the country. We spent some nights in hotel rooms. We ate 3 times a day! We enjoyed talking to each other. They never knew I was raped or married. This couple helped me get a job in a restaurant on the outskirts of Los Angeles that was open for lunch and dinner. My uniforms were furnished, clean and fresh and black and white. I also got a garage apartment. One room with a bed in the wall, table and chairs, alcove kitchen, couch, and bathroom with shower—all in the same room. I guess you would call it a efficiency apartment, except the bathroom was not another room, just a large piece of plywood up beside the toilet and sink. One large window was close to the floor, and one door.

The restaurant had a lot of customers in their 20's and 30's come in and eat alot. I made friends easily. Because of my Southern accent, people would ask me to talk and talk some more. At first I thought they were making fun of me, but they said they were not. This one group went skydiving every weekend. They invited me to go. I asked my supervisor if I could be off on a Saturday or Sunday so that I could go skydiving, and he said yes. My apartment was only 2 blocks from the restaurant, and one of the girls in the group picked me up that Sunday morning. We met the others at a small airport. I'm now 15½ years old and never been in a plane. These new friends want me to jump out of a plane with a parachute on. One of the men speaks up and said, Caitlin, you have to learn how to pack your own parachute first. I said like forget it. I'm to afraid. I can't do this. Another man speaks up and says I'll pack her parachute, give her a beer. I had never tasted any beer or any kind of alcohol before. I take the beer, thinking this may help me calm down. The beer tasted like some kind of bad, bad medicine. But I drank it anyway, just wanting to fit in with my new friends.

They are telling me how my legs have to be before I hit the ground. One of the guys is packing a T-10 type parachute for me, explaining that the rip cord pulls itself when you jump because it hooks to the plane. I am so afraid! After 3 of us are in a small plane at 3,000 feet, I am told to get on the wing of the plane. I do. All I can see are lots of white clouds that look so soft. All of a sudden, there are no more clouds. I am told when I see a large white canvas on the field to jump. Well, I saw it and said let me get back in the plane. I don't want to do this. A man at the door of the plane said you can't get back in and he pushed me off the wing. I started saying the Lord's prayer. I didn't even know I was peeing in my pants at the same time. I had on someone else's jumpsuit, someone else's boots, and here I am peeing and praying. The wind was only 5 miles an hour. People on the ground were screaming at me to bend my knees, and I did. I hit the ground real easy and kissed it before I got up, thanking God for saving me. This will not happen again I promised myself.

After a few minutes, I realized that the jumpsuit was wet. I was so embarrassed and kept telling the person who let me use it how sorry I am. They were all laughing like it was so funny. I went with these friends only one more time, but didn't even get in the plane. No way was I ever putting on a jumpsuit or parachute again. But I did enjoy watching the other girls jump, like it was nothing.

Everything was going well for the next few months. It was September, and I am in my bed. I can hear lots of motorcycles coming down the street. I had not seen any motorcycle gangs where I lived in that neighborhood. All of a sudden, a rock came in the window and glass was in bed with me. I didn't move. No lights were on. I was waiting to see if some big man was going to come through the window. No one did. I have no idea why someone broke that window. I didn't have a phone, so I couldn't call the police. I heard all the motorcycles ride away. I layed there until it started getting light outside to make sure I didn't cut myself with glass getting out of bed. I got dressed and waited until I knew my Mom would be home alone, knowing the time was different in California and Georgia. I wanted to go home. My Mom was so happy to hear from me. She started crying, and of course I was crying to.

Another thing I just remembered about my childhood. Years ago, our family went to Washington D.C. I do remember we were in that new 1949 car. As my Dad was making a turn, I thought I was holding the handle to roll down the window, but I turned the wrong handle and fell out of the back seat of the car. I got out of the middle of the road and ran after the car. Shawn told Dad, Caitlin fell out of the car. Shawn told me later Mom was screaming turn around and get my baby. Dad said if I do I'm going to beat her for opening that door. He didn't turn around, he finally pulled over and let me catch up with the car. When I got back in the car, I had blood on my legs and arms along with many scratches from hitting the blacktop. We went to a gas station bathroom so Mom could clean up my blood and scratches. Dad didn't beat me that time, but he was so mad at me for getting blood on the backseat.

Next letter I'll write about prison life like you asked.

Happy New Year to you and Madeline.

Caitlin

****

January 4th, 2011

Caitlin Fitzgerald
#00G1442
Bedford Hills Correctional Facility
247 Harris Road
Bedford, New York 10507-2400

Dear Caitlin,

You might say that, vicariously, I spent the holiday season with you. Piles of material relating to your case cover every table, countertop, couch and chair. A path of papers line the periphery along the walls of our home. It's just easier to find what I need rather than go through prodigious stacks. Sorry that we cannot work together side by side and under better circumstances.

On another note: The weather. You know that first line from *Let It Snow*? "Oh, the weather outside is frightful . . ." Well, it is! I don't know whether or not you unload trucks in or out of doors re your responsibilities at the commissary, but if it's the latter, both Madeline and I hope you keep warm. Mary told us a little bit about your job at the commissary. Tell me more when you get the chance.

Best to you (as best as can be expected) for the New Year.

Very best regards,
Charles

****

Jan 15, 2011

Dear Charles & Madeline,

Happy New Year.

I am so sorry I haven't written you sooner. There just isn't enough hours in a day. Mary Jennings came again to visit me over the holidays. She says she no longer has the notes she wrote after leaving here on visits. She said that she wanted to write my story but knew she was no writer. She wanted to give them to you when she first spoke to you. When she thought you weren't interested, she tossed them. When she later learned that you were interested, she wished she had kept them to give to you. Anyhow, I don't think I missed telling you anything up until the time I arrived here at Bedford Hills prison for women. And that's what I'm going to start telling you about. Mary did not take any notes about my confinement here. Just my childhood and the trial. As a matter of fact, I told you so much more because I remembered so much more because I was writing things down for you. It jogged the memory

149

more then just talking to Mary about things.

I'm just so tired from working through the holidays at the commissary. I promise to begin my next letter about prison life here. I just want to put down pen and paper now and go to sleep. No need to write me back until my next letter to you.

Sincerely,
Caitlin

Chapter Seventeen

Prison Life for Women at Bedford Hills

Jan. 21, 2011

Dear Charles,

As you know, Bedford Hills Correctional Facility is a maximum security prison for women up here in Westchester County. I work in the commissary all week. Also I unload trucks. Its a very hard job, but I love it because it makes the days go by really fast. I've been a seamstress and dressmaker all my life. I knew if I can cut material to exact measurements, I can cut hair. As a matter of fact, I use to cut my brothers hair. Anyhow, the correction officers were not going to put a pair of scissors or shears in my hands. So I cut inmates hair on weekends with toe nail clippers. Inmates here can get a haircut for $5.50, but you could wind up with a trainee, so you don't really know what you will look like when that persons finished with you. The beauty school here really sucks. Believe me. I actually give the best haircuts of all the girls and women here. In fact, I had more than a bit of training when I was very young.

At 10 years old my brother started making me cut his hair because once a month he was given 50¢ to get a haircut at the barber shop. He would use that 50¢ to play the pinball machine at the gas station. Mom always had good scissors around because of her sewing. The first time I cut Shawn's hair I was really afraid that I would cut him when I was shaving his neckline, but I didn't. At the dinner table that afternoon, Mom said to Shawn, Why didn't the barber cut your hair shorter? Shawn said, I don't know, Mom. Mom said, well next month you tell him I want your hair alot shorter like a G.I. Well, I'm thinking, Oh, my God! I sure hope Shawn goes to the barber. Of course he used me again to cut his hair and used the money to play the pinball machine. This went on for about two years. One day Mom got up at 4:00 A.M. and caught us. She said how long has this haircutting been going on? I said about 2 years. She said well if you can cut your brother's hair, you can cut mine and your Father's hair. Within months I was cutting Aunts, Uncles, 12 cousins, every 4 to 6 weeks and no one paid me a dime.

In my next letter, I'll talk more about prison life here. I know my spelling, punctuation and grammar is very bad, even though you said it was alright. I get really confused with those apostrophe words. You have no idea how long it took me to look up the correct spelling of apostrophe. Also, I'm beginning to get a bit of help from a schoolteacher here who murdered her three children. I don't let her see what I'm writing, but I'm starting to ask her lots of questions about the possessive case and contractions. You may even see a <u>*marked*</u> *improvement in my writing. Get it? My next letter will take a bit longer because of editing, but it will be worth it in the end. You'll soon see.*

Sincerely,
Caitlin

****

February 6, 2011

Caitlin Fitzgerald
#00G1442
Bedford Hills Correctional Facility
247 Harris Road
Bedford, New York 10507-2400

Dear Caitlin,

I'm updating you with a copy of the enclosed letter that I sent off to Simon & Schuster. Don't hold your breath. I'm just going through the motions with similar letters sent to literary agents and publishers. We'll eventually decide, together, which tact to take: nonfiction or fiction.

In your next letter, tell me more about your appeal and how you got your sentence reduced from 30 years down to 15 years.

Very best regards,
Charles

enclosure

copy

Charles Winfield
72-61 113 St.
Forest Hills, N.Y. 11375

February 6, 2011.

Carolyn Reidy
CEO & President
Simon & Schuster
1230 Avenue of the Americas, 11th Floor
New York, N.Y. 10020

Dear Ms. Reidy:

I have been asked to write a true crime story about an abused woman, Caitlin Fitzgerald, who murdered her husband. The crime occurred in Flushing, New York on August 15th, 1998. Mrs. Fitzgerald was interviewed on *20/20*, and her case was broadcasted on *Court TV.* I am presently reviewing those tapes, grand jury and trial transcripts, as well as communicating with Mrs. Fitzgerald. The woman is documenting her life through letters that she is writing to me from the Bedford Hills Correctional Facility in Westchester County where she is serving a 15-year sentence, appealed from a 30-year sentence. Mrs. Fitzgerald is expected to be released in March of 2015 at the age of 73. Mrs. Fitzgerald wants *her* story—a tragic one, which begins in early childhood—to be told.

My concern is the Son of Sam law, which mandates that all profits obtained from selling a book based on a crime go to the victim's family. In 1987, Simon & Schuster challenged that law regarding a book written by Nicholas Pileggi. As I'm sure you are aware, in 1991, the court ruled in Simon & Schuster's favor, declaring the Son of Sam law unconstitutional. Any knowledge you may have pertaining to the Son of Sam law referencing this book project would be greatly appreciated.

My writings have been mostly in the area of fiction, having published three novels (two of which are award winners) by a small, royalty-paying publisher. My nonfiction work had been for the *Towers Chronicle* (Douglaston, Queens) as an investigative reporter. Presently, I freelance for outdoor magazines regarding fishing and hunting. Additionally, I had attended a high-profile serial killer trial in Riverhead, New York, five days a week for 15 months then wrote a fictionalized account of that case. Please take a moment to visit my Web site at www.CharlesWinfield.com for a more detailed account of my writings.

I look forward to hearing from you.

Most sincerely,
Charles Winfield

****

Feb 27, 2011

Dear Charles,

Received the copy of your letter to Simon & Schuster. I am sorry I didn't write sooner, but there has been a virus going around. Over half the compound is sick, including c/o's. Also, I received a letter from Mary Jennings. She is sick too. Sounds like the same virus is really going around. In addition to the virus, I hurt my hand and thumb in the commissary again. I didn't tell my supervisor about it because I would lose my job. Before you can work in the commissary, you have to sign a contract that says if you hurt your back or any part of your body, you are out of work—with no pay. My hand and thumb hurts like hell, so I limit my writing to a page a day. I could write with my left hand because I am ambidextrous, but the handwriting is not as neat.

I edited this letter many times before sending it to you. You wanted to know about the appeal, which is a story in itself. Here goes.

I tried to fire my attorney, William Baxter, before my trial was over. I could tell Baxter had never done a murder case before. He didn't exactly lie to me, but he did lead me to believe that he had. Baxter wanted to put in paperwork for my first appeal. He came here a few days after I was driven here in Jan. of 2001. I was so angry with him. I told him I had put in for my appeal and did not want to see him anymore. He was only here maybe 15 minutes. Actually I wrote to my first attorney Anthony Sileo who I stupidly got rid of. I asked if he would handle my appeal. He never wrote back. I had done the paperwork to get a public defender. However, I lost my first appeal.

When you do a second motion on appeal it's called a P.C.R. (post-conviction relief). I did the paperwork again for a second public defender and lucked out. At the same time I had become friends with an inmate here, Lacrishia Jones. She is the best 'jailhouse lawyer' anyone could have on their side. She worked on my case for about six months. She read all the trial transcripts you have now. She did my pro se briefs. I think you may have a copy of that too. She didn't leave alot for my new public defender Kelly Kehon to add to. She's that good. I studied law in our library 5 nights a week for 1½ years, but I can't compare myself to Lacrishia. She is unreal. Lacrishia can read any law book and memorize it because she has a photographic memory. She got herself off death row twice.

Kelly Kehon was a hot-shot criminal lawyer that semiretired, working as a public defender for the state of New York. I was taken back to Queens County Court House 13 times before I received my reduction of 11 years and 5 months off my 30 year sentence. Kelly Kehon doesn't give up and neither do I. I even promised the judge on the stand I wouldn't be back. As I said in one of my earlier letters to you, I'll be out of here in March of 2015.

Both Kelly and Lacrishia were trying to get back the prosecutor's one and only plea bargaining offer to me, which was to serve 85% of 12 years. Boy am I sorry I didn't take it. In Jan. of 2009, Kelly came to see me and said Jimmy's daughter Evelyn was asked how much time she would be satisfied having me serve. I was offered 20 years with 85%. I wouldn't take it. That was back in Jan. 2009.

In Feb. of that year, the judge allowed me to take the stand. He said, Mrs. Fitzgerald, at the rate you're going you could get a new trial, but you would be sitting in a county jail for a year or two waiting for it unless someone bails you out. You could go to trial and still end up with 30 years with 85%. So I'm offering you 17 years with 85%. I discussed it with Lacrishia and the man I work for here and decided to take it.

You get very tired, Charles, of being woke up at 4:30 A.M. for a strip search, getting dressed, offered breakfast that you never eat when you go to court, stripped searched again by c/o's that you are riding with, put in shackles and handcuffs that are way to tight, not being able to use the bathroom all day, spending one night each way in a dirty cell that hasn't been cleaned in months, no shower, no nothing. I could have kept going back to court until I won a new trial, but 2 of my witnesses are already dead and my brother Shawn is not physically able to make this trip again because he's pretty sick.

My hand is hurting bad, so I have to stop for now. Sorry. Will try and write more next weekend. Hope you see a improvement in my punctuation.

Sincerely,
Caitlin

****

Charles Winfield
72-61 113 St.
Forest Hills, N.Y. 11375

March 4, 2011

Mr. Anthony Sileo
229 7th Street # 300
Garden City, New York 11530

Dear Mr. Sileo:

I'll begin this missive by taking you back in time to August 15th of 1998. Caitlin Ann Fitzgerald shot and killed her husband and was a client of yours until she made the second biggest mistake in her life—dismissing you and hiring William Baxter, Esquire. Actually, before you had initially agreed to represent Caitlin, you helped the woman get her car back from the police impound when she was out on bail. Caitlin did not heed the advice of the family she was staying with during that period, Enzo and Janine Margola. Caitlin is godmother to one of their two daughters. Enzo is owner and publisher of a fishing magazine from Bayside, Queens and highly recommended you to Caitlin. For purely monetary reasons, Caitlin took the advice of an acquaintance and hired Mr. Baxter, who proved to be an incompetent attorney and who has subsequently been disbarred.

As a spectator, I had sat in on Caitlin's trial as well as having read the entire court transcript. I was nonplussed at the number of times that the presiding judge, Judge Hershfield, had called Mr. Baxter to sidebar, chastising him mercilessly for failing to understand court procedure as well as the law as it pertained to a capital case. Amazing!

Now, a bit about me and how it pertains to the above. I'm an award-winning novelist. After Caitlin's sentencing, a good friend of hers wanted me to write her story, which I'm in the process of doing. I made it quite clear that there were no guarantees that a literary agent and/or publisher would bite. The fly in the ointment is the Son of Sam law if the book is written as nonfiction, which I would prefer.

In 1987, Simon & Schuster challenged that law regarding a book written by Nicholas Pileggi. As you might be aware, in 1991, the court ruled in Simon & Schuster's favor, declaring the Son of Sam law unconstitutional. Has any precedent been set in that regard, or is there one on the horizon? I would appreciate any insight.

In closing, I would like you to know that on more than one occasion, Caitlin, in her letters to me, says that she deeply regrets not having followed through with you as her trial attorney. She has subsequently learned that you get what you pay for and that you are one of the best criminal defense attorneys in Queens. A good example of shoulda, woulda, coulda.

I certainly look forward to hearing from you.

Sincerely,
Charles Winfield

****

Charles Winfield
72-61 113 St.
Forest Hills, N.Y. 11375

March 5, 2011

The Honorable Christopher Drew
Governor of the State of New York
New York State Capitol Building
Albany, New York 12224

Dear Governor Drew:

Thank you for referring my request to the New York State Parole Board referencing clemency for Caitlin Fitzgerald, inmate #00G1442, confined at the Bedford Hills Correctional Facility, 247 Harris Road, Bedford, New York 10507-2400.

I have received instructions from Carol Norris, Hearing Officer 2 and Supervisor of the Executive Clemency Unit of the New York State Parole Board, on how to proceed re Caitlin Fitzgerald. I have written to the prison administrator today requesting the application(s).

I have enclosed the following editorial (one of nine extensive articles) that I wrote for the *Towers News*, many a year ago. There are a few reasons for my sending you this piece. I will be succinct. I did not know the fellow, mentioned below, whom I helped get out of prison, assisted by Barry Slotnick (renowned Manhattan attorney), his associate, Mark Baker, and Mike Taibbi, then with CBS News. I simply read the court transcripts and knew that Richard Tchilinguirian was innocent and that he was railroaded by the police. The long and short of it was that the presiding judge, Judge Ralph Sherman, overturned the guilty verdict, and Richard Tchilinguirian was set free.

Similarly, I did not know Caitlin Fitzgerald. Again, I simply attended her trial, read the court transcripts, and learned that the police had dropped the ball. I firmly believe that Ms. Fitzgerald acted in self-defense and, in fact, had an inept attorney. The long and short of this injustice is that the system failed her: both the police and her attorney, William Baxter (who has subsequently been disbarred).

My sending you the enclosed editorial, along with an explanation, serves to illustrate that I am not coming to the aid of these defendants out of any sense of loyalty, but simply to right a wrong. It also keeps my name in front of you so that when the matter of Caitlin Fitzgerald's clemency comes before you, you will know that I support her in only the strictest sense of an investigative reporter and a concerned citizen.

So that you do not begin to think that I am some sort of a crusader with a bent to assisting the incarcerated, I feel it is worth mentioning that I also *helped* put a guilty person behind bars (50 to life).

Note: Realizing that the governor is a busy person, I will keep this letter to one page. At the risk of behaving presumptuously, I'll respectfully state that if an assistant is screening this letter, that he or she makes it his or her business to hand you this missive. Caitlin Fitzgerald is my swan song . . . as in <u>retired</u>.

Sincerely,
Charles Winfield

Enclosure: *Police Prevarication: The Long and The Short Of It*

****

Bedford Hills Correctional Facility
Administrator
Ronald P. Townsand

March 15, 2011

Charles Winfield
72-61 113 St.
Forest Hills, N.Y. 11375

RE: Caitlin Fitzgerald, #00G1442

Dear Mr. Winfield:

I'm in receipt of your letter of March 5th requesting Executive Clemency forms on behalf of Caitlin Fitzgerald. Be advised that I will meet with Ms. Fitzgerald and instruct her that she can obtain the Executive Clemency forms herself through the Classification Department.

Very truly yours,
Ronald P. Townsand
Administrator

cc: Caitlin Fitzgerald #00G1442
     Inmate Class File

****

Charles Winfield
72-61 113 St.
Forest Hills, N.Y. 11375

March 22, 2011

Mr. Ronald P. Townsand
Administrator
Bedford Hills Correctional Facility
247 Harris Road
Bedford, New York 10507-2400

Re: Caitlin Fitzgerald #00G1442

Dear Mr. Townsand:

    I am responding to your letter of March 15, 2011 and have enclosed letters sent to Governor Christopher Drew and the New York State Parole Board. The letter from the New York State Parole Board instructed me, as you will note, to contact you.

    I did not inform Ms. Fitzgerald of my letters requesting clemency because I did not want to raise false hope. However, at this point, I will send her all correspondence relating to this endeavor.

Sincerely,
Charles Winfield

Enclosures

****

March 31, 2011

Dear Charles,

Wow! You have really been a very busy man. I thank you from the bottom of my heart. I have written the Classification Department asking for the Executive Clemency forms. I hope to receive them in the next few days.

Charles, our c/o opened my door the other day and said Ms. Fitzgerald you are wanted in the Administration Building. I was led right to Mr. Townsand's office. Mr. Townsand said, Caitlin, do you know Charles Winfield? I said yes. He said, well he just wrote me a letter. He handed me the letter, but I went to his office so fast I didn't take my glasses. So I couldn't read it. So Mr. Townsand read it to me. Then he said to me that I <u>can not</u> apply for Clemency nor will the forms be sent to me because he found out from someone that in my case, Executive Clemency <u>can not</u> be considered because the law says that I have to do all my appeals before I can even try to get Clemency. I told Townsand I did my appeals and won my P.C.R. and had 11 years and 5 months taken off my original sentence. He said, yes but on the stand and under oath you promised the judge you wouldn't be back in any courtroom. I tried to explain that meant I wouldn't be back in any courtroom for being in any kind of trouble. He just shook his head and said that Governor Drew won't soon be doing any Clemency any time soon. Plus he said that even if I did apply for Clemency, by the time the Governor got around to it and before all the court dates went through the system, I would be out of here anyway.

I'm just hoping this doesn't make Mr. Townsand interested in reading any of our mail. I am writing this very slow because my hand hurts but I will write more this weekend. Last week I put in a medical slip and was called in to see Dr. Malone. She has ordered me a brace. That will take two weeks to get. My supervisor still doesn't know. I don't want to lose my job at the Commissary.

Thank you again for all you are doing.

Best regards,
Caitlin

****

April 8, 2011

Caitlin Fitzgerald
#00G1442
Bedford Hills Correctional Facility
247 Harris Road
Bedford, New York 10507-2400

Dear Caitlin,

First off, I'm sorry to hear about your hand. Take your time and don't push the writing. You're doing fine. What you told me in your last letter about your plea bargain ordeal is absolutely remarkable, including the insight I gained referencing Kelly Kehon and Lacrishia Jones. It's soooo important that I know these facts.

Referencing those pro se briefs you mentioned, no, I <u>do not</u> have a copy; I double-checked. No big deal. It's the result that's important.

Secondly, I was quite surprised to learn that Administrator Townsand summoned you to his office and gave you that response. I was hoping that the governor himself would view and consider my correspondence carefully, but I'm sure that an underling simply passed it on to the New York State Parole Board.

As you now know, I have been and am still very busy with correspondence concerning your matter. However, Madeline and I needed a bit of a break, so we drove down to Delaware, looking at boats. As we get older, we're beginning to downsize. We started out in the late eighties with a 25.5 foot cruiser, 9.5 foot beam; down to a 22-foot pilothouse, 8.5 foot beam in 2000; now we're down to an 18 foot, 7.6 foot beam center console (open boat). It's fine for the bays; we're into fishing, crabbing, clamming, et cetera. Good to go.

Write when you're up to it. When you do, let's switch gears again before you continue writing about prison life at Bedford Hills Correctional Facility. Go back in time again and tell me about your other marriages and your child, Billy, Jr. Until then—

Very best regards,
Charles

Chapter Eighteen

Caitlin's Marriages

April 17, 2011

Dear Charles,

    This is a painful subject for me to write about, but I will do as you ask. I'll start where I left off when I left my first husband Bobby Lee Reynolds and returned home from California. Here goes.

    Bobby Lee heard that I was back home. One evening he comes to the house in his car. Mom goes to the door and invites Bobby to come in. All I say is hello. He hands me divorce papers and asks me to sign them. I do. Then Bobby asks me if he could have the wedding ring back. I go get it and gave it to him. Bobby leaves. Mom and Dad never asked me what California was like or how I got there. They never even asked why I left Bobby. My brother Shawn had already moved out, gotten a girl pregnant, and got married. So it was just me, Mom and Dad. Dad is pretty sick. I'm back in school and have a part-time job on Friday and Saturday evenings in a department store. I did not ask to be placed in the men's department, but that's where they put me. I planned on working 5 or 6 days a week in the summer when school is out.

    I'm working maybe eight months when one day this man comes in looking at suits. He asks me if I'm Jake Reeves daughter. I said yes. He said I used to date your Aunt Margret after her divorce. He said your Dad and I are friends. I'm a supervisor at a furniture warehouse the next town over. Do you know you look so much like your Aunt Margret? I said yes, alot of people tell me that. Anyway, he buys 2 suits, tells me his name is Billy David Hendrickson, and asks me for a date. I said I don't date. He's like, You're kidding me! As pretty as you are, you don't date? I said no. I'm only 16. My dad won't let me. Billy said I look like I'm 19 or 20. Well, I'm not, I told him. He finally leaves the store.

    I don't remember if it was a week or a month. But my Dad asks me if I would like to go to the car races with Billy Hendrickson. I said yes. Billy comes to the house in an older but big yellow Cadillac. I'm very impressed. I enjoyed the races. It was great to go somewhere different. I'm 16 and Billy is 36 years old. He had been married twice and still lived with his parents, brother and sister-in-law. I didn't even think about that because I am to young and stupid.

In the summer, Billy would go to Pine Lake with my Mom, Dad and me on Sundays. He ate dinner at our house at least 2 times a week. My Mom and Dad really liked him. I turned 17 and Billy asked my Dad if he could marry me. No one asked me. My Dad said yes. No one bothered to ask me. When Billy left after dinner, I protested. But both Mom and Dad said that marrying a mature man was the best thing that could happen to me. Mom said that Billy and me could be married in the house. Sick as he was, my Dad gave me away at the wedding.

Billy and me went on a honeymoon for a week to the beach. It was nice. I didn't know that Billy had made some kind of agreement with my Dad where to live. I find out we're going to live with my Mom and Dad until Billy and me found a place of our own. I quit school because I wanted to go to fashion school which I did. I was tired that I was back to cutting everyone's hair for free. Two months later, I find out I'm pregnant. The baby is due in September, but I can finish the 9 month fashion school course given at a nearby college by the end of August. I am the only person in this college course married and pregnant. I can't wait to finish. I finish and get an appointment to take a 8 hour test. I take a half day oral exam. The other half day was written. The next day was a hands on full day of making a pattern, transferring material, cutting material, basting and sewing. I had to wait six weeks for my grades. I got all A's.

My son Billy Hendrickson, Jr. was born on Sept. 15, 1961. I'm 19 years old.

I'm going to stop for now. I'll write more next weekend. No need to write me until I continue and finish what you asked me. You've written to so many people and again I thank you. Take care.

Sincerely,
Caitlin

BATTERED

******

Dear Charles,
(continued)

I'll begin with my third husband Otto Ober. After my second husband Billy Hendrickson was killed in a car accident, about 2 years later I started dating again and met Otto Ober. Otto was wonderful with my little boy Billy Jr. Otto would take him to the park and get him ice cream when I was working. He'd take him to playgrounds and push him on the swings. Otto was a self-employed electrician and could make his own hours. He was 2 years older then me. I thought he would make little Billy a good Dad. I married him and he moved in with Mom and me. Dad had died by then. Some weeks Otto would take a job 40 to 50 miles away and be gone for a few days. A few months went by when he took a big job up in South Carolina. He didn't call me every night, but usually 2 times a week. One week he didn't call at all. I was worried maybe something had happened to him on the job. I knew the name of the motel he was staying in, so I called my babysitter and asked her if she could come and stay with Billy Jr. while I drove to South Carolina. She said she'd be happy to, so off I went to look for my husband Otto.

To make a long story short, I saw Otto's car parked right in front of the motel room he was staying in. As I'm his wife, I had no trouble getting a spare key from the motel manager. I opened the door to the room and found him in bed with a girl. Otto jumps up and starts telling me how sorry he is. He says he had been out drinking with some guy he worked with who had a big fight with his girlfriend and this poor girl had no place to stay that night. I told Otto to go to hell and left crying. I drove back to Macon.

Two days later, Otto comes home and begs me to forgive him. I took him back but not for long. One night we're making love and little Billy starts crying in his room. I got up to see what was wrong. He wasn't wet or hungry so I rocked him in a rocking chair until he went back to sleep. Then I went back into the bedroom and Otto and I started making love again. Suddenly, Billy Jr. starts crying again. Otto gets out of bed mad and says he'll take care of this. He goes into the *baby's room and hits my child very hard. I start screaming at Otto. I couldn't believe he hit Billy, Jr. hard like that for crying. Not in the butt but in the face. Otto went back to bed. I picked up my baby and sat in a chair holding him for the rest of the night.*

I don't know if I told you that sometime after Dad died, Mom remarried and had moved out of the house. So it was only me, little Billy and Otto living there in my Mom's house. I didn't have Mom to watch Billy Jr., and I had to be at work every morning. My friend who babysits for me called and said she was sick and couldn't come that morning. I told her what Otto had done to little Billy. She and I both agreed that after the motel incident and now the hitting incident, Otto had to go. Otto went to work that morning like nothing had happened last night. I wanted him out of the house for good. I called work and said I wouldn't be coming in that day. Then I called all 3 of big Billy's brothers and told them what Otto had done to their baby nephew and could they be at my house before 5 o'clock that afternoon to throw Otto out with his belongings that I had packed. The house still belonged to my mother. Nothing there belonged to Otto but his clothes. My brother-in-laws couldn't wait to see Otto. I made them promise not to beat Otto up unless he wouldn't leave peacefully.

When Otto came home that afternoon and saw all his clothes packed and realized he was being thrown out, he went crazy. Billy Jr.'s uncles told Otto to cool his heels or they'd beat him to a pulp. As Otto was driving away, he screamed at me and said he'd get me for this. I was glad that he and his clothes were out of the house. Billy Jr. and I stayed at one of my sister-in-laws house for the next few days for fear that Otto might come back and make good on his threat. As far as I know, he did not.

Shortly after Otto was gone, I was in a terrible state. I needed money badly. Bills were mounting up from Billy's deadly car accident. I was still paying off hospital bills and funeral parlor bills because we had no insurance. Billy's family promised to help pay these bills because they pushed me to have the very best of everything when we buried him. I never saw a dime. You could buy a small house for what the funeral and flowers cost. Now my gynecologist bills were mounting because I was bleeding inside. I needed money for a divorce lawyer to properly get rid of Otto.

I met a friend of one of my cousins, Richard Barradale. He was from a very large family, lots of brothers and sisters. We fell in love and Richard wanted to get married. I told him I couldn't because I was still legally married. He not only gave me the money for a divorce lawyer, he insisted on wiping out all my debts. I had the best medical care. Money was not a problem for Richard. He told me we're wiping the slate clean and starting over. A fresh start. Everything in the past stays in the past he said.

We drove up to South Carolina and got married at a courthouse. No waiting period after the blood test. We found a new apartment building just outside Macon, Georgia. We got along great and had great fun together. Sex was fantastic. We went dancing every Saturday night.

Richard was not a showoff with money. But it was always there when we needed it. Babysitters, great food, nice clothes for Billy Jr. and me, and my own late model car. I started thinking, where did all this money come from? He worked from home on the phone and told me he was an investor. Real estate properties around the country, overseas import export. He said he had people all over the world handling things for him.

One evening he said he had to go out and that he'd be back late. My thinking was, Oh, no! Now this new husband of mine is going to run around on me like Otto did. So I take Billy Jr. next door to the babysitter while Richard's in the shower then follow him to the outskirts of town. He turned off on a narrow dirt road, slowed down and stopped. I pulled over and turned off my headlights. I saw him get out and head into a house or building. I sat there waiting for maybe 20 to 30 minutes to see if he'd come back out. He didn't, so I continue down this narrow dirt road that has only room for one car at a time. As I came closer, I see lots of cars and a big log cabin. I park my car and get out, and go up and knock on the door. A man comes to the door, looks very surprised and says, Yes? I said I'm Richard Barradale's wife and I would like to see him. This man didn't invite me in but he didn't tell me to leave either, so I follow him through the house. He opens a door to a large room. It's full of smoke and large round tables with six men playing cards. The man says, Richard your wife is here. Richard looks up then stands up and says, What the hell are you doing here? I say I'm checking up on you. Richard says get out! Go home. I'll be home later. This is the first time I've seen him mad. I leave very quickly. I get home but can't sleep, so I sit up watching T.V. until Richard came home about 2 A.M. He smells like beer and smoke. He takes a shower, brushes his teeth, then sits on the couch to talk. Richard said how did you find me? I told him I followed him. He said I didn't want you to know the kind of work I do. And no women are ever allowed in a gambling house. I asked him who's house it is. Richard said he rents it, runs the gambling operation, and get 10% of the take.

I was so happy I didn't find him with another woman that I really didn't care what kind of work he did. So everything is o.k. between us. I promised Richard I would never go back to that house again. Richard even had a real part time job selling cars as a cover. I became pregnant but miscarried. Richard and I were very sad about that, but our life was going well. Not long after, it all goes to hell. Richard is arrested for gambling, prostitution, racketeering, armed robbery, and I don't know what else. He went away to prison for a long, long time.

I want to back up and tell you more about my second husband who was killed in that terrible car accident. He was the very best of men I had met and married. I want to tell you about that horrible accident.

I had just finished work and come into the house when Mom tells me the hospital called and that Billy was just in a car accident and to go to the hospital immediately. I ran out the door and drove to the hospital. I parked as close as I could to the emergency area. I ran inside, opening double doors. There were doctors and nurses all around a gurney. I saw blood shoot up in the air. I just knew that person lying there was Billy. He had just given his younger brother a ride home from the beverage company where he worked.

When I finally get to see Billy, his head was shaved and he was hooked up to all kinds of machines. They were keeping him alive with a respirator. I went to the hospital 3 times a day. Before work, during lunch hour, and after work. I had to hire a second baby sitter to look after little Billy. I'd sit in the hospital a good part of the evening holding big Billy's hand. Billy's younger brother Greg was not hurt in the accident. But a lever of the car had gone through part of Billy's neck and shoulder. The jugular vein had been cut. Greg said he held that together by applying pressure when the accident happened.

I talked to Billy each day while I held his hand, but he could say *nothing. Only one time did he squeeze my hand, but the nurses and doctors told me that it was some kind of reflex, that he was paralyzed from the neck down. His neck was broken. Weights were hanging on the floor in case he did try and move his neck. His head and upper body were swollen almost twice in size. I did a lot of crying and praying for 13 days.*

It was late in the evening. I was home with our son. I had just left the hospital around 8 P.M. I was in bed with the baby when the phone rang. I knew it was the hospital and was sure Billy had died. The caller said, Mrs. Hendrickson, please come back to the hospital immediately. I put on some clothes, took Billy to a neighbor then drove to the hospital as fast as I could. But Billy was already dead. Something about a blood clot to the brain that they couldn't remove. It was like I was suddenly paralyzed. I couldn't move. Greg was there and had to help me to my car.

I carried little Billy to the church for the funeral, but during the service I was crying so bad that one of my sister-in-laws took him out of my arms until we left the church.

Of all the Hendrickson family, Greg was the only one I saw visit Billy in the hospital. Mr. and Mrs. Hendrickson had 10 children, 5 boys and 5 girls. At the funeral home, the family picks out a mahogany casket, the best vault money could buy. One of Billy's sisters insisted on all yellow roses for a blanket and pillow to lay on top of the casket. I went along with everything they said because the family said they would all help me pay for this. I think I told you I never saw a dime.

Keep in mind that Billy and I had no health insurance, no life insurance, and no car insurance. Billy was buried like we were very wealthy.

During the whole time Billy lay in the hospital, right up to the time he was put to rest, I slept with Billy's favorite sport coat. The next day I went back to the cemetery to take the ribbons off some of the flowers. When I was gone, Mom had 2 of Billy's brothers take all his clothes and shoes out of the house so I would stop looking at them, crying, or sleeping with his coats. When I came back to the house and opened up his closet to grab his favorite sports jacket, I went nuts. Nothing was there. I didn't think I could even cry anymore. I yelled and cried and screamed at Mom so bad. She kept saying she thought she did the right thing for me. She did not as far as I was concerned.

Not at all! I raised my son by myself till he was grown up and went into the Marine Corps.

Bobby Lee Reynolds, Billy David Hendrickson, Otto Ober, Richard Barradale, James Fitzgerald. Five Husbands and one child. I don't think I need go into Jimmy's history. That's pretty much been covered in the courtroom except for the extent of my beatings over twenty eight plus years that would fill many volumes. I think I pretty much covered what you asked me to do. Very painful to tell these stories.

I hope you noticed that my punctuation is getting a little bit better in terms of the possessive case. Yes? I'm all about self improvement. I want to better myself, Charles. I want to be happy again. I don't know if that will ever happen but I hope it will.

Chapter Nineteen

Back to Daily Prison Life at Bedford Hills Correctional Facility

April 23, 2011

Dear Charles,
(continued)

    I'm including this letter along with the other two about my husbands and child. My hand is feeling much better so I'll continue on with prison life here at Bedford Hills Correctional Facility as you asked.

    Back in Feb. we had an emergency shakedown. A maintenance man's key to his truck went missing. It was later found behind a set of wall lockers. Of course some dumb ass inmate put it there. But every one in this building had to suffer for it because no one said they know who did it.

    Prison life here in a maximum security facility is pretty bad. One day I'm sitting in the mess hall with another inmate, Jenny Frohnhofer, sitting in front of me. Suddenly she says, Caitlin, get up fast! All along long steel tables sit 8 inmates. Some of the tables are connected together. I stood up fast as trays of food and two bodies on their stomachs come sliding along the table in front of me. Both girls hit the floor at the end of the table we were sitting at. The girls got up and kept hitting each other. The alarm is going off. A correction officer is in what we call the bubble. It's actually a plastic dome. He's with a lieutenant. They are screaming at all of us to get out of the mess hall through an exit door. Over 300 of us inmates are trying to go through that door. A task force of about 18 was now coming in from the other side of the room with fighting gear on, all wearing plastic helmets that protects there face. It takes 6 or 7 c/o's to pull the two girls apart and put their hands behind their back to be handcuffed. Both girls are taken to the hospital for body assessment. They are then taken to lockup. Both are given what is called blue sheets. In a few days they go to what is called Ad Seg. That's Administrative Segregation. Extreme isolation. It's also called the box. You do not want to go there. It's a 7 x 13 foot cell. Bed, toilet and sink. The single overhead light never goes out.

From there the two girls were taken to a very small courtroom with two people that decide what their punishment will be. Cameras in the mess hall have the videos. The cameras also have the video of the inmates who stood on tables to watch the fight instead of getting out of the way as fast as possible. Whichever girl hit first is going to get the most time. Girls who start the fight generally get one year in the box. Even the girl who didn't start the fight will get six months.

Another time in the mess hall, Sandra Smith knocked her girlfriend to the floor. The girl on the floor rolled herself up like a ball to protect her face and stomach. Sandra kept kicking her in the head and back with big boots. Sandra looks up and sees the Task Force coming. Sandra goes to a wall and faces it with her hands up on the wall. But the task force had already seen Sandra kicking the other girl. One of the c/o's grabs Sandra and throws her to the floor really hard then kicks her in the head with his steel toe boots. Sandra deserved that big time. The girl that Sandra beat and kicked was taken to the hospital. Sandra got a year in Ad Seg. There are two kinds of Ad Seg. One where you're allowed personal belongings such as books and magazines. The other where you're declared R.F.P. Removed From Population. You are allowed nothing but the clothes on your back. Sandra was declared R.F.P.

There is also something here called "Gay for the Stay." About 1/3 of the women who come to prison turn "gay for the stay." You can only find a few that were gay before they got here. When I first got out of "reception" and got my own room, on weekends 2 different girls approached me while I was walking alone in the yard. At first I thought they were being friendly or maybe they didn't want to be walking alone. After walking and talking about the prison or whatever, they asked me if I was gay. And I asked them if they were crazy. About 95% of all the fights you see in here are over another girl. Coming to prison is like being in a world that you know nothing about.

You never get use to being strip searched. You do not get use to shakedowns, when a c/o comes in your unit and messes up all your stuff while looking for drugs or other stuff you are not supposed to have, like cigarette lighters or food stolen from the kitchen. Now we can not have a magic marker anymore. If you need one, you get it from the c/o in your unit, mark your bowls and plastic cups, then give it back.

I'll write more later.

****

May 8, 2011

Caitlin Fitzgerald
#00G1442
Bedford Hills Correctional Facility
247 Harris Road
Bedford, New York 10507-2400

Dear Caitlin,

You mentioned that you and James were married at the Playboy Club in New York, and that it was a "fake marriage." So of course there is no certificate. Your cousin Wallace and his wife Rose had either forgotten that fact or didn't know that the marriage was bogus. Actually, you didn't know either because Jim had pulled the wool over your eyes, flat out deceiving you. Madeline is primarily working with Wallace and Rose in obtaining the necessary documents and other paperwork for clemency, regardless of what officials say about your chances. We'll need the legitimate marriage certificate from Las Vegas. As Wallace resides just outside Macon, he already has most of the information needed referencing the marriages, divorces, and deaths for your clemency application, so you need not notarize anything for us at this point. Should we need you to notarize papers, are you permitted to do so? I had asked for your date of release from the facility. There was some confusion as to whether it is 2014 or 2015. Believe that? Please give me the exact date.

Wallace and I had a nice long chat on the phone the other day, and he said that he would be sending me copies of everything he has gathered. We'll go from there. While Madeline and I are gathering information up here, Wallace has been driving to courthouses and several agencies below the Mason-Dixon Line, searching for vital records. He's certainly a good friend to you, but I don't have to tell you that. Nor do I have to tell you that even though you see little hope, we're all plugging away. You never know. We all have our fingers crossed. We're hoping that your exemplary conduct as a model prisoner will carry significant weight in the eyes of Governor Drew.

Your description of prison life is certainly an eye-opener. Keep going, girl.

Very best regards,
Charles

****

May 15, 2011

Dear Charles,

I can't begin to thank you, Madeline, Wallace and Rose enough.

I'm going to tell you another couple of stories now that happened a few years back.

One day I was called out of work to go to the South Hall building for a talk. A sergeant and a correction officer were there waiting for me. The sergeant takes a copy of a letter out of a folder and said, Mrs. Fitzgerald is this your letter? I looked at it and said yes it is. Then he takes out an x-ray of a razor blade. He said Mrs. Fitzgerald, this was in your letter. I said it's not mine. Then the sergeant said, Mrs. Fitzgerald, I don't know you. That means you are a good inmate. But I have to do my job. Put your hands out. He handcuffs me and took me to Lock Up. In Lock Up we have what is like a small court. After 2 days, Mr. Townsand the Administrator came to see me in Lock. He knows it's not in my character to do something like that. I had never had a charge before. They take me to this little court. We all had a little chat. I told them I would sometimes give my mail to anyone on my wing to mail for me before breakfast because they had to pass the mailbox. I don't ever go to breakfast because I spend that time taking a shower and getting ready for work at the commissary. If you go to breakfast you don't get to take a shower before work.

I know people on my wing were jealous of me because I had gotten 11 years and 5 months taken off my sentence. But I never thought any one would open my mail and put in a razor blade. For that charge I could have gone to Ad Seg for a year. I also could have lost 60 days off the 15%. It was the worse 10 days I ever spent in my life! And I couldn't believe they made me do 10 days in Lock Up because they all knew that I would never do anything like that. But I couldn't prove that it wasn't mine. I even offered to take a lie detector test and begged them to get finger prints off the razor blade. They said that would cost to much money.

Charles, I don't know if you or Madeline knew about the ACLU action taken several years back. But this prison picked 40 of us who don't take any psyche drugs to be sent to the Downstate Correctional Facility in Fishkill, an all men's maximum security prison, because of over crowding here at Bedford Hills. Over half the inmates here at Bedford Hills take psyche drugs because they like getting high then going to sleep. Anyhow, we got 4 free lawyers through the ACLU, sued and won, but it took us 18 months to get back here. The 40 of us were not put in Ad Seg, but in another Unit that was almost as bad. I know the difference for a fact because it was part of my job to go into Ad Seg to cut women's hair with toe nail clippers.

No sooner then I stopped at this point in the letter, there was a big fight in the mess hall this afternoon. I'm sitting in the middle of the mess hall as the last person was getting her tray at the window. Suddenly a women jumps up, grabs the girl's head, then starts smashing it hard on the stainless steel table. About 12 feet away to my left another fight breaks out. Another 12 feet away to my right a third fight breaks out. It's all surreal. You can't believe this is happening. Your eyes don't know which fight to watch. You don't need to move your head, just your eyes as 6 people are fighting. All of a sudden another person jumps up to help the first girl who was getting beat bad. The lieutenant and a c/o do not come out of their bubble dome. They are screaming for the rest of us to get out the exit door while many c/o's are in the front door of the mess hall. It takes a few minutes for the rest of us to get out the exit door. Plus no one seems to be in a hurry because many want to watch the fighting because it's better then watching T.V. If you haven't been in this prison long, you don't know that a video is being made of you also watching the fight. The administration watches this video to see who started the fight and who's standing on the stainless steel tables and benches. It won't matter that you were not in the fight. You will get a blue sheet and be sent to Lock Up. But this won't happen until the next day. All girls and women in the fight will first be taken to the hospital before being put in Lock Up. I think I told you about what happens there before.

The first shakedown I had in here, the c/o's come in the South Hall, South wing and told us all to go to the T.V. room. It was 8:30 P.M. on a Saturday. I had just come in from Bible study. It was also count time, making sure everyone was accounted for. All names and numbers are on our doors. You are locked in at 9:45 P.M. You never know what the c/o's are looking for. At least 6 c/o's will come in to cover one wing. Many times they throw your mattress and sheets in the hallway. My first 3 shakedowns in Max I spent most of the night crying while putting the tiny room back together. After that I got used to it . . . sort of.

You have many people in here who will lie about their crime. They are so stupid because they don't know all you need is their full name and state number, send it off to a friend and ask that friend to look it up on a computer then send the information back to you.

This place is about 60% black women, 15% Spanish, 2% Asian, and 23% white. It's not good to get real friendly with a lot of people. They will try and use you for favors in the commissary. They make you feel very sorry for them. It took me years to learn this. I had a hard time saying no. But not any more. There are people in here who have been back 4, 5, and 6 times for drugs, shoplifting, etc. I know one woman who is back here for her third bank robbery. I don't know if she will ever get out this time.

I don't think I told you that I also work in the upholstery shop. Our beautiful work is shown to people on the outside for them to see how the shop is run.

Wishing you and Madeline the very best,
Caitlin

****

Charles Winfield
72-61 113 St.
Forest Hills, N.Y. 11375

May 30, 2011

The Honorable Christopher Drew
Governor of the State of New York
State Capitol Building
Albany, New York 12224

Dear Governor Drew,

I had written to you on March 5, 2011 with regard to clemency for Caitlin Fitzgerald, Inmate Class File #00G1442, incarcerated at the State of New York, Department of Corrections, Bedford Hills Correctional Facility, 247 Harris Road, Bedford, New York 10507-2400.

This petition is respective to the murder trial of Caitlin Fitzgerald, I.D. #00G1442. Mrs. Fitzgerald was convicted of killing her abusive husband (James Fitzgerald) in 2000. She is presently serving her sentence and is scheduled to be released in March of 2015. The Honorable Judge Hershfield presided, and the prosecuting attorney was Philip Murrow; the defense attorney was William Baxter. I had recently completed reading the court transcripts re Mrs. Fitzgerald's trial at the time that I initially wrote to you, in which I stated that I was appalled that the state of New York would have allowed such an inept attorney as William Baxter to represent Caitlin Fitzgerald. I found it interesting to note that Mr. Baxter was subsequently disbarred.

I am seeking an early release for Mrs. Fitzgerald. On an inquiry into her case, I am sure you will find that her trial was handled inadequately. It is unbelievable that the state would ever allow an incompetent attorney such as William Baxter to represent a defendant in a murder trial. Judge Hershfield, many times at sidebar, sent Mr. Baxter off to 'consult the law.' Amazing!

In brief, Caitlin Fitzgerald was a battered woman [this is documented re past orders of protection] who had asked the 107th precinct to intervene on her behalf, asking to be escorted home, for the woman was in fear of her life. The police failed to do so. Instead, one of the officers called her husband at home, had a conversation with the man then told Mrs. Fitzgerald that it was safe to return home. It was anything but safe. James Fitzgerald went after her with the intent to cause bodily harm as he had done on other occasions. Caitlin shot her husband in self-defense, immediately surrendering herself to the police precinct. Had the police followed procedure and escorted Caitlin home, this unfortunate event could have been averted.

I certainly do not condone murder but have come to realize that there are, indeed, extenuating circumstances. I truly believe that this was one such situation. Jim Fitzgerald was an incorrigible bully with a well-documented history of violence, not only toward his wife, but directed toward others as well. Still, Caitlin Fitzgerald had to pay for what she had done. She has paid that price with better than a decade of her life to date.

During Caitlin's confinement, the woman has been a 'model prisoner' in the true sense of that term, receiving many certificates of achievement and recognition as documented throughout the enclosed packet. It should be of interest to note that Caitlin had an outstanding work ethic *before* her conviction, as attested to by many of her long-time friends and customers who wrote on her behalf to Philip Murrow, Judge Hershfield, and you; my point being that she would *not* be a threat to society upon release. Too, she has the support of family and friends, several of whom I contacted re research and verification.

Case in point: Caitlin's cousin, Wallace McKenna and his wife Rose of the Macon, Georgia area, worked indefatigably in securing the paperwork necessary to filling out the forms for clemency (marriage, divorce and death certificates). It wasn't always a matter of obtaining the necessitous information via the mails because the man was given incorrect and/or misleading information in two instances, having to drive hundreds of miles in order to nail down and collect the correct copies of record. In another instance, Mr. McKenna had a relative track an ancestry site in order to successfully obtain a missing piece of information so as to complete *all* the required paperwork. This will give you some idea of the support system behind Caitlin Fitzgerald. As I am here in New York, and the McKennas are in Georgia, where most of the *footwork* was needed, this facilitated matters. Additionally, Mr. and Mrs. McKenna often visit Caitlin at the correctional facility. I had to smile when Wallace told me that visiting a women's prison was not exactly on his "bucket list." Wallace and his wife, along with many other caring family members and friends, will be there for Caitlin when she is released.

I ask you, Governor Drew, to please consider this petition for clemency.

Sincerely,
Charles Winfield

Enclosures

****

June 7, 2011

Caitlin Fitzgerald
#00G1442
Bedford Hills Correctional Facility
247 Harris Road
Bedford, New York 10507-240

Dear Caitlin,

Your cousin Wallace secured the last document; that is, James' and your legitimate marriage certificate from Las Vegas. Wallace set up and sent me spread sheets showing all data for your clemency application.

Quite busy. Sorry for the brief correspondence.

Best regards,
Charles

****

Robert Banfelder

June 15, 2011

Dear Charles,

    Thank you again for what you Wallace and Rose are doing, and everyone else for writing letters to the Governor on my behalf. I'm blessed with very good friends. You really get to know who your friends are when the chips are down. I received the large envelope you sent with all the necessary paper work for clemency and had everything notarized. Your cover letter to the Governor was EXCELLENT. Thank You! Thank you!

    What happened first is that I had to put in a request slip to see a notary public here as soon as possible. So the next morning I was called out of work to see Mr. Newman, then ran back to unit to get all these papers. Nothing has ever been done for me this fast here. I just couldn't believe my luck. After reading all these papers, Mr. Newman asked me if I had copies of everything. I said no. I then have an appointment to get copies made of all these documents and your letter to Governor Drew.

    Next Mr. Townsand the Administrator looks these papers over then sends them to Governor Drew. He didn't seem happy for me. Remember he said that by the time everything was done I could be out of here. This time he said it could take 1 to 3 years to be answered. I'd be very happy if I got 1 or 2 years knocked off my sentence.

    Thank you again for all your help on Executive Clemency.

Sincerely,
Caitlin

****

June 22, 2011

Caitlin Fitzgerald
#00G1442
Bedford Hills Correctional Facility
247 Harris Road
Bedford, New York 10507-2400

Dear Caitlin,

I am in receipt of your June 15, 2011 letter explaining that you received the envelope re executive clemency and that you had all the necessary papers notarized. I'm happy to hear that everything is moving along nicely for you. Madeline and I, as well as all concerned parties, pray that Governor Drew's response is positive and that you are released early. Again, this is a long shot; however, with the mitigating circumstances surrounding your case, many of us remain hopeful. All you can do at this point is to remain cautiously optimistic. Also, I wouldn't broadcast what is in the works. I'm sure there are jealous inmates who would just love to undermine our endeavors. Therefore, remain a good girl, maintain that work ethic of yours, and hope that Governor Drew, along with prison administrators, view matters the way that we do on this end.

The theme of the book will be what battered women must do in order to get out of such horrendous situations—not to take matters into their own hands the way you did because you saw no other way out. Of course, there are extenuating circumstances. Here, within, lies the rub because I wouldn't be positing those points in terms of nonfictional prose. In terms of fiction, however, I could put another face on this matter in order to sensationalize the account, for I'll need some sort of dramatic climax.

To reinforce what you said in your last correspondence: Yes, you have good friends in your corner. You have a supportive family, especially concerning Wallace and Rose.

Very best regards,
Charles

****

August 3, 2011

Dear Charles,

Our electric went out last night at 9 P.M. There is no T.V., no showers, and we cannot be taken from our cells for work details or anything except when mess is called out. Mess hall in Max, and what is called Grounds, have generators. All the other buildings that house inmates do not.

I don't think I told you about the trip from here at Bedford Hills to Downstate Correctional Facility in Fishkill. It was done in two loads of 20 women. Our bus got stuck in the mud and we were all sitting there for quite a while. Then we were all told to move up toward the very front of the bus to distribute weight. That didn't help. Finally another bus was brought in and we were on our way.

We all thought Bedford Hills prison for women was bad until we arrived at the Downstate all men's prison in Fishkill. Once all 20 of us were in our cells, and all the steel doors were slammed shut, it was the worst day of my life. For five straight weeks I cried. When I received my property, the only two things I got back were my underclothes. Bedford Hills had not sent my uniforms, towels, wash cloths, or nightgown. They did pack my watch, fan, hot pot, comb, brush, blow dryer, curling iron, and T.V. However, the prison would not let me have any of those items. It was unreal; 40 women on one tier. Correction officers went through the few personal items we had. To make matters worse, we were in Lock Down 24/7.

Finally, one morning, they let us out of our cells and march us off to breakfast. When we got there, there were only 28 stools. If you didn't get in line fast enough, you had to take your food back to your cell. When we got back to our tier, not all of the cell doors opened at the same time. So whosever cell doors were opened, those were the ones who sat and ate. The rest of us stood and ate our breakfast. These were the mind games the c/o's played with you.

When they finally started giving us yard time, Lacrishia Jones and myself had a chance to talk to each other. She was already writing a motion to sue the Department of Corrections. We did not have a law library. Lacrishia did all this from memory. Remember I told you she can read a law book and memorize it because she has a photographic memory? She is one of the smartest persons I have ever known.

I had told Lacrishia that maybe my girlfriend's neighbor's husband, a civil rights lawyer, could take this case. His name is Marco D'Angelo. He came to visit me at Fishkill but would not take the case because he was retired. He recommended someone who recommended someone who finally hooked us up with the American Civil Liberties

Union (ACLU) of New York's Woman's Rights Project. This took a few months.

Anyhow, when we got back here to Bedford Hills, the 20 of us put together a Inmates Survival Guide for women on how to exist locked within 3 walls and 1 door. Each woman wrote a page or 2 expressing their feelings. I asked Mary Jennings to send you a copy of the pamphlet that I gave her when she visited me here. She said she would be happy to. Please let me know when you get it and what you think.

I got my hands on a grammar book here, and I see that I have a problem with compound words and some misspelled words like alot, when it should be <u>a lot</u>. You should see an improvement in my next letter.

Sincerely yours,
Caitlin

****

August 15, 2011

Caitlin Fitzgerald
#00G1442
Bedford Hills Correctional Facility
247 Harris Road
Bedford, New York 10507-2400

Dear Caitlin,

Yes, I received from your friend, Mary Jennings, *A Woman Inmate's Survival Guide: How to Live Within 3 Walls and 1 Door.* I perused the pamphlet; it provides invaluable information. The thesis of the work is, and I'll quote your group: "The sole intent of this literary work is to help the next female prisoner survive and thrive under the circumstances."

Take comfort from part of *your* last sentence in the pamphlet: ". . . keep your faith and know that you are not going to be here forever." But, of course, some of you are.

According to your wishes, I am writing your story as fiction. Again, it's going to be a tough sell.

Oh, and good luck with your grammar book. It's a bit tough without a tutor as most texts tend to be confusing. A grammar book combined with a private tutor or classroom instruction is the way to go, but I'm sure you'll do fine. One day, I plan to write a comprehensive grammar text that clears away the cobwebs and will assist new writers without the aid of a tutor or classroom instruction.

In your next letter, tell me more about your confinement at the Downstate Correctional Facility in Fishkill before continuing with life at Bedford Hills.

Very best regards,
Charles

Chapter Twenty

Caitlin's Transfer to an All Male Prison ~ Fishkill, N.Y.

Sept. 24, 2011

Dear Charles,

I'm so glad that you're going to write my story as fiction.

You asked to hear more about Fishkill State Prison. As I told you earlier, I was made Haircutter/Hairdresser for the women confined to Ad Seg (Administrative Segregation). Better known as solitary confinement or the hole. Those from other prisons were sent there for a minimum of 30 days. Most got 1 year. The cell is not well lighted for cutting hair, especially with toe nail clippers instead of scissors. I think there are about 30 cells. The c/o's would handcuff one girl at a time to get their hair washed and cut. No curling irons or blow dryers are allowed.

We should never have been sent there. That place should have taken the gang members called the Bloods and the Crips. I have this girl right across the hall from me here at Bedford Hills. Monisha Washington. Bad to the bone, Charles. It was her fault we had 2 shakedowns this week. My little cell looked like a tornado hit it. It took 2½ hours to sort and put everything back together, mostly my papers, books and magazines. I could only do part of it because I had to go to work at the commissary. When I got off work at 3:00 P.M. I finished straightening out the cell. At 6:00 P.M. the c/o's made us go outside. When we returned, the c/o's had tore up the place again. I even started to cry and curse, something I haven't done in a very long time. I just couldn't take anymore mess.

My wing can only do laundry on Monday, Wednesday, and Friday. When you do your clothes and bedding, everything takes 4 loads because of blankets. You cannot wash or dry between 9:00 P.M. and 6:00 A.M., so there is always a long line waiting.

Mr. Townsand, the Administrator, has promised Monisha Washington he wouldn't send her to Ad Seg (Administrative

Segregation). Let me tell you why I think that. Because while I was in Fishkill State Prison, 22 gang members rioted in the mess hall. The ones that didn't wind up in the hospital, they put in Lock Up while waiting for cells in Ad Seg. They even let some people already in Ad Seg get out early because they needed those cells. I'm sure Mr. Townsand didn't want something like that to happen here, which probably would have happened if Monisha Washington had been moved to Fishkill. Who's running the asylum, Charles?

Tell me what you want me to write about next.

Best regards,
Caitlin

****

October 1, 2011

Caitlin Fitzgerald
#00G1442
Bedford Hills Correctional Facility
247 Harris Road
Bedford, New York 10507-2400

Dear Caitlin,

As you had asked what to write about in your next letter, why don't you cover a typical day concerning the commissary to which you are assigned? Explain exactly what it is that you do. Tell me how long of a day you have, your duties, and about the women who work with you, et cetera.

Madeline and I spent a few days fishing in our area. As the weather gets chilly, the fishing gets better. The fish are on the move, traveling to warmer climes, so they have to eat a lot along the way. We usually go out on the boat three days a week for an hour or two. Bluefish and striped bass come into the river to feed on baitfish. In past years, the stripers and blues have been big, but this year, we're only seeing very small ones; i.e., snappers—not even cocktail size. However, we limited out on BIG porgies. Great eating—filleted medallions coated with flour, egg, and bread crumbs then fried. They're also great cooked whole upon the grill. If you're allowed to have pictures, I'll send you one of Madeline and me in my next letter. Let me know. Madeline sends her best.

Very best regards,
Charles

Chapter Twenty-One

Bedford Hills Commissary

October 8, 2011

Dear Charles and Madeline,

You will never know how long I've been wanting a picture of you and Madeline. I just didn't know how to ask for it. Yes, please send me a picture of the 2 of you.

While I was in Max here, working in the upholstery shop all those years, except the 18 months I was in Fishkill, I knew all about the jobs on Grounds detail. I was told about a week in advance that I was going to be moved from Upholstery to Grounds. I told my boss that I wanted to work in the Commissary. He said, Caitlin you are to old to work in Commissary.

Well, I went off on him. I said who the hell do you think has been lifting that heavy furniture all these years? The good fairy? He said, But you are getting older now.

I've never spoken to anyone here in authority that way before but I was really mad. About 2 days later, his boss comes in. Mrs. Moorman. I ran to her, not caring that she had an important looking man with her. I said, Mrs. Moorman, I want to work in Commissary. Please get me a job in Commissary. She smiled and said, Caitlin, I already have. The first day you report to Commissary, you will sit in front of the boss's desk, and he will give you papers to read and sign. If you hurt your back or drop a case of soda on your foot—whatever— you will lose your job and you will not be paid. They have back braces of every size and I suggest that you wear one. You must have your uniform on and wear good boots. Anytime you have to see a doctor, $5.00 plus the cost of your meds will be taken out of your pay. Are we clear?

I of course already knew all this and thanked her very much for the job. In Commissary you must learn every job. We start at 7:30 A.M. but must be there at 7:10. We break for lunch at 11:30 and go back to work at 12:30 sharp. We work until 3:00 P.M. Sometimes it's 3:30 but not often. We do not work on weekends or 14 holidays a year. And of course we aren't paid for those day off holidays.

The only inmates here that work 7 days a week are Kitchen workers working three shifts. They never get a day off. The only way they get time off from Kitchen Duty is to be sick. They're out on a medical with no pay of course. After you've been in the Kitchen about a year, you can make $80.00 a month.

There is another shift for c/o's in another mess hall where they can eat in the middle of the night. They get different food then we get. By the way. Our food is awful. A dog wouldn't want some of the food they give us. I only go to lunch. I do not go to breakfast or dinner. That's why I gain weight. I live mostly off of milk, bread, potato chips, cookies, candy bars and soda. All the junk food. If you don't get any infractions for a year, you get to order a food package twice a year. But we can only order from certain vendors. We have 2 large refrigerators and microwaves for cooking. All the prices are unreal. Like 2 pounds of small cooked shrimp is $22.00. A small piece of cheesecake is $4.75. You can order up to 40 pounds, but most of us do not have that kind of money. We can only order from certain vendors.

Well, I'll get back to the Commissary. Every Tuesday we all help unload a food truck. Every Wednesday, we unload a soda truck.

Two people here take care of the clothes. They have to put your last name and I.D. number on all clothes. We can order men's boots, men's sneakers, green T shirts and shorts, green sweatpants and sweatshirts—all for men. Even the pajamas are for men, but they do sell us bras and women's underpants. They only give us two used uniforms every year.

There are 14 inmates working in Commissary that are in charge of such items as stamps, cigarettes, batteries, headphones, cards, shampoo and hair removal products, Lubriderm lotions, toe nail clippers, bagels, candy bars, vitamin pills and aspirin. All cups, bowls, forks and spoons are plastic. One girl is in charge of a control cart. She has a pick sheet for each unit. Another girl has a box cutter who cuts, sizes, and tapes the bottom of boxes that cases of food comes in. There are two girls called checkers that stand inside a large square area before large countertops. I am standing off to one side of the square when the different size boxes come around to me. I write with a black marker the Unit and person's name then walk it over to the sealer. On both sides of me, I have boxes of different size plastic bags that I have to cut; 9 sizes in all. I have to know what size bag will fit each box. The boxes cannot be over 5 inches high so that a person can see every item that is in the box before the plastic is ripped off. Anytime I'm not lifting and sizing and sealing everyone's Commissary in boxes and bags, I'm cutting more bags.

We can put 30 pounds of Commissary in one large box, but you have to make sure the box doesn't break open when you pick it up. You have to do this very fast because if you don't, the whole counter will fill up. The soda we carry and sell is called Big Red and comes in 20 fluid oz. plastic containers; 24 to a case.

One of the reasons I like my job so much is because we have 20 and 30 year old workers in Commissary who can't do my job. My boss knows how old I am and tells me I'm one in a million. I thank God I'm so healthy and strong, and I want to stay that way.

There are 7 girls that walk up and down 4 aisles of food and paper goods. They pick out toilet paper, paper towels, and soda. Kind of like shopping at a grocery store. The meat and fish we carry and sell comes in a pouch and is absolutely awful: mackerel, octopus, salmon, tuna, pepperoni and spam. I don't buy any of it. I do buy cans of beans because of its protein. I would send you one of our Commissary lists, but I only have one. None of our Commissary goods is a brand name you've ever heard of. If you boil the spaghetti over 5 minutes, you cannot eat it. It's like white mud.

We also sell T.V.'s, watches, hair blowers, sheets, towels, wash cloths, 4 kinds of soap, 2 kinds of laundry detergent, I don't know what else to write you about my job.

One of my friends badly wanted to work in Commissary, but she cannot because she has a bad back problem. She works in sewing where she sits down most of the day making 39¢ an hour. She works 7 hours a day, 5 days a week. That's $13.65 a week. That's the only job in prison that pays by the hour. All prison jobs are really slave labor, but there is nothing anyone can do about it because we put ourselves in here. There are lots of prisons that don't have enough jobs for inmates. They sit in a cell all day and watch T.V., if they even have one.

There is a women's prison in Florida where a lot of the inmates sew, making uniforms for the c/o's and don't get paid a dime. The prison gives them their bath soap, shampoo, toothbrush, toothpaste, laundry detergent, sanitary pads and toilet paper once a month. If they don't have family or friends sending money, they never get a candy bar, cookies, soda or popcorn.

After spending 18 months at Fishkill State Prison, this place here at Bedford Hills should be called 'Cupcake Convent.'

It's great you and Madeline both go out on your boat at least 3 days a week. Enjoy every day. They're precious. I can't wait till the day comes when I can just stand and look at the Ocean again. I can't tell you in words just how much I miss watching it. I'm sure I would run in the water and not even care what the temperature was. I enjoy swimming so much.

Well, it's 1:00 A.M. and I guess I better get some sleep.

Wishing you both the very best always,
Caitlin

P.S. I don't like a few of the 14 women that work in Commissary. It's their attitudes. But over the years I've learned to work with anyone. Most of the women here at Bedford Hills are drug addicts. One woman cooked her baby in the oven then served it to her husband for dinner. She was in a mental institution for 10 years before she was put in Max. After 10 years in Max, she was moved to Grounds 6 years ago. She has 8 more years to go.

P.P.S. I hope you will note an improvement in my punctuation and the use of compound words. Trying very hard. I look up every word I'm not sure how to spell in the dictionary. That's one of the reasons why it takes me so long to write a letter.

****

October 15, 2011

Caitlin Fitzgerald
#00G1442
Bedford Hills Correctional Facility

247 Harris Road
Bedford, New York 10507-2400

Dear Caitlin,

Enclosed are a couple of photos of Madeline and me.

The two of us were upstate in High Falls, NY, last weekend at a couple's home. Madeline got to ride on my friend's tractor, something she hasn't done since she was eight years old.

In the other picture, I'm holding a striped bass, which I caught in the Peconic River.

Yes, I'm seeing a marked improvement in your writing. You did a nice job in explaining the commissary.

Very best regards,
Charles

****

Oct. 23, 2011

Dear Charles and Madeline,

Thank you for the pictures. You are a very attractive couple.

Charles, I've seen you somewhere before. Were you on a T.V. fishing channel show, or in the Bayside Anglers fishing club? Jimmy's friend belonged to that club and we went to a seminar there. No, it wasn't that lying police officer Sergeant Dennis Phelps from the 107 Precinct. Anyhow, you certainly do not look 69 years old. I honestly don't remember you sitting in the courtroom as a spectator. Mary Jennings didn't tell me about you until the trial was over. She told me where you generally sat, but I was so focused on looking at the judge, jury, prosecutor and my defense attorney.

You didn't say what to write about next. But I'm glad you see <u>an</u> improvement in my writing. See? I'm learning about indefinite articles such as <u>a</u> and <u>an</u>. It can be a bit confusing but I'm getting the hang of it—I think.

In talking about Jimmy before, I left out parts where he once pushed me out the front door barefoot and down into the snow with nothing on but my bathrobe. I had just come out of the shower. I just stood there crying for a good hour before he let me back inside.

*Another time he came home drunk, falling **up** the steps and scuffing his new $400 Bally shoes. He stumbles down the hallway and into the bedroom, cursing while taking off all his clothes. He straddles me in bed and hits me very hard in the chest and stomach. I had not said a word to him.*

I know some people wonder why I stayed with Jimmy. Many don't know that I left the state four times to get away from him, but he always found me. The last time I agreed to take him back if he took his name off our home. Always starting life over after five marriages, you get tired of giving up what you've worked so hard to get.

Thanks again for the pictures. It's nice to see who you are writing to. Let me know what you want me to write about.

Best regards,
Caitlin

****

October 31, 2011

Caitlin Fitzgerald
#00G1442
Bedford Hills Correctional Facility
247 Harris Road
Bedford, New York 10507-2400

Dear Caitlin,

I'm glad you liked the photos. I gave you my best profile photo so that I wouldn't look 69 years old. ☺ ☺

No, I haven't been on a fishing show or a member of the Bayside Anglers club that you mentioned. There are, however, YouTube videos on the Internet of Madeline and me clamming in Great Peconic Bay with a couple of friends. Also, there is a series of YouTube videos of me giving a talk about my novels at a local restaurant here in Forest Hills.

My new novel has just been published as an e-book and is available online for various e-readers such as Kindle and Nook; computers such as PCs and Macs. It is not in print form yet; maybe down the pike. Madeline posted my novel on Kindle Amazon, and she will do the same referencing your story once it is written. So, the good news is that the book will be out there even if a traditional publisher does not bite.

As Madeline and I maintain a small home on the East End of Long Island, spending more and more time out here, we got involved with a Cablevision show and just finished our first interview, which reaches folks from Wading River to Orient Point on the North Fork, and Eastport out to Montauk on the South Fork. Originally, we were scheduled to tape only one show, but the host and director were so impressed, Madeline and I wound up doing three shows back-to-back in a single sitting, which will appear on consecutive Friday nights spanning three months. I told studio folks to expect letters and phone calls from viewers asking, "Don't these people have a wardrobe?" ☺ ☺ Had we known we'd be taping three shows, we'd have brought three different outfits. On one of the shows, I mentioned your situation, the facts of the case, clemency proceedings, and that I'll be writing your story as fiction. A little public relations never hurts.

As far as wanting to know what you should write about, you think and decide. You're doing great.

Very best regards,
Charles

****

November 12, 2011

Dear Charles,

That's very funny. Three shows and you and Madeline are in the same outfits. When 20/20 was taping me for two days I had on 4 different outfits in 4 different locations. My attorney, Mr. Baxter, didn't know I wasn't supposed to be on T.V. until the trial. Of course you remember that Judge Hershfield had a fit. I hope you didn't say my name on the show because people will know the story and book is about me.

By the way Charles. Whenever I send anyone a picture of myself I send only the good ones too. I'm trying to think of things I never told you.

When I was about 5 years old, my father had bought a beautiful mahogany coffee table with a thick glass top. I did a flip on the couch when practicing my gymnastics and landed on the top of the table and broke the glass. I didn't get beat for that but I should have. All my mother said to me was you won't be doing anymore flips inside the house. If my father was home at the time, he would have beat me badly. When he did come home, my mother took the blame. I thought he was going to beat Mom because he was so mad. I wanted to tell him that I broke the table but he probably would have beaten both me and Mom for lying and covering up for me.

Before my father died he was on oxygen. Mother took me aside and told me your Daddy wants to talk to you. I went into the bedroom and he asked to me to forgive him for all the times he beat me. Mom was standing next to me. I told my Dad that I could never forgive him. I hugged my Mom and left the room. When Dad died, Mom sold his boat, all the water skiing equipment and surf boards. I went to my father's grave and cried for a long time. I even told him that I forgave him.

People ask me if I'm sorry I shot Jimmy. I am not sorry and I tell them that. Jim did so many bad things to me. I have to go before the parole board before I leave here. I do not have to say I'm sorry. I only have to give them an address where I'll be living. They check the address out to see who lives there. I'll be on parole 5 years. A parole officer can check on me anytime he likes. But whoever checks on me they will see in my file that I never did any drugs—ever! So I really don't think I'll be checked on that much.

You and Madeline enjoy each day of your life together.

My best regards,
Caitlin

****

December 1, 2011

Caitlin Fitzgerald
#00G1442
Bedford Hills Correctional Facility
247 Harris Road
Bedford, New York 10507-2400

Dear Caitlin,

Sorry to have not written sooner, but Madeline and I have been bogged down with work. We have an unexpected major project with our new boat. When we pulled it for winter storage, we saw that the hull bottom paint had not been properly prepared. The primer and paint did not adhere. Madeline and I have been scraping the old paint off so that we can properly prepare the hull. If there's no paint, then the slime and barnacles stick to the hull and cause damage; as a boater, I think you know all this.

I want you to know that, yes, I did mention your name and situation on the Cablevision show, but not to worry. It won't have any negative effect on you or your story as the book is based on composite sketches of battered women as explained in the Author's Note at the beginning of the book. More on that when you see that note to the reader. If anything, the airing of the show(s) *might* help matters in a small but positive way.

Thanksgiving was spent at our friend's home as usual. I made clam chowder to contribute to the dinner menu. Prior to Thanksgiving dinner, their granddaughter was baptized. After the baptism, there was a breakfast. Too much food that day, for sure, but it was a joyous occasion. On that note, tell me what your Thanksgivings have been like at Bedford Hills. Too, please elaborate on what holidays such as Christmas have been like for you over the course of years. Unfold the good, the bad, and the ugly.

Would you be allowed to receive reading material from me; that is, one of my novels? As I am putting together your story in fictional form, I thought that you would like to see how I write. I could send you one of my award-winning novels. It is quite different from your story that I'll be composing; however, it will give you a good idea of my style. Additionally, I would hope that the book could serve as a bit of entertainment for you. Please let me know if the facility would permit you to have one of my novels.

Very best regards,
Charles

****

Dec 18, 2011

Dear Charles,

Sorry you had that problem with your boat hull and that I haven't written you until now, but I made 20 Christmas cards and bought 20, sending out 40 cards each year with a letter. In truth, it's a real pain. I would like to stop but can't because I get 40 Christmas cards each year and 19 birthday cards. Just can't give up on my friends. Plus a few friends put in $25 money orders, so how could I ever stop?

Mary Jennings came to visit me this month. She said she received a letter from the Governor's office saying her letter was put in with my clemency forms along with yours. Oh how I would love to get out of here early. But as you said before, it's a long shot. Still I appreciate what you and my other friends are doing writing letters to Governor Drew on my behalf.

Yes, Charles, I would love to have one of your novels to read. But the only way we can receive a book in prison is 'source of sale', meaning the book has been ordered from a book company and the invoice has to be inside the package.

Sounds like you and Madeline had a wonderful Thanksgiving. I hope your Christmas is just as wonderful. All holidays in prison suck! We try and be happy, but around Thanksgiving and Christmas a lot of us get very depressed. We are all glad when the New Year gets here because it marks one less year off our sentence; the light of freedom shines through a long dark tunnel.

You wanted to know what Thanksgiving and Christmas here in prison has been like for us. Well, here goes.

Thanksgiving: Lunch was 2 thin cheap slices of processed turkey lunch meat with a white tasteless sauce on it. 1 yam from a can. No brown sugar, white sugar, or butter. Overcooked mixed vegetables. 1 small lump of cranberry sauce the size of a quarter. 2 tablespoons of stuffing that was decent. 2 corn muffins. 1/8 slice of sweet potato pie. The small pie is cut into 8 slices, so 2 bites and it's gone. We will get the same thing for Christmas lunch.

Years ago in 2001, 2002, and 2003, it wasn't so bad. But now it gets worse each year. When I was in the Fishkill State Prison in March of 2007 for those 18 months, the food was much better there than ours is here. At least we got a piece of real turkey and a 1/6 slice of real pie. If I didn't have the job I have in Commissary, I wouldn't be able to buy junk food. Then again, I wouldn't be 20 pounds overweight. I would be skinny and hungry. The problem there is if I'm hungry, I can't go to sleep at night.

When Mrs. Blackman was our administrator during my first five years here, she let us have a Christmas decorating contest in each Unit, Max, and Grounds. If you won first place, you would get a piece of southern fried chicken, a roll, and soda. Second place would get you 1 piece of pizza and soda. Third place was a donut and juice. North Hall where I was housed won first place my first 4 years here. We had a girl here by the name of Kim Woo who could make anything out of cardboard boxes, 3 colors of paint, and a few brushes. That's the reason why we kept winning. The judges were the board of directors here at Bedford Hills. As the years went by, the board members were getting older and were having trouble walking to all the cottages. This place is tough to get from Max to Grounds because you first have to get on an old bus or a Department of Corrections van. In Max, once you are inside the gates, you have to walk to each Unit. And that's a lot of walking.

For the Christmas decorating contest, you could start making things on Black Friday, but you couldn't put anything on the walls or hallways until the day it was being judged. We only got to enjoy all these decorations we made but one day. Then they all had to be taken down. That's the part that wasn't fun. All your work was taken down before Dec. 20th so that the c/o's could see all us inmates better in the T.V. rooms, hallways, gates, wherever. If someone made a small Christmas tree in the T.V. room, that would be the only thing left for the 25th. By small I mean like 2 ft. high.

I got to come out to the Grounds in Aug. of 2009. You do have more freedom here. We would give small birthday parties in the kitchen of the cottage. Last Christmas Eve eight of us girls started singing Christmas carols, but the c/o's put a stop to that in 1 minute flat.

I have to say that since my long lost cousins from Georgia, the Carolinas and Virginia have found me this year, I am a much happier inmate. Wallace McKenna and his wife Rose made the trip here 3 times to visit me. On Nov., 4 my other cousins came to visit me also. These are relatives I haven't seen in 40 years. I feel like I'm getting part of my life back. It sure makes me happy. I even had c/o's ask me, Caitlin you are smiling all the time. What's up? And I tell them.

I am so thankful to have my family again.

We have some girls in here that have been back 3, 4, 5, and even 6 times for drugs and drug related crimes. Their families gave up on them. Some don't even get a visit or a card—ever! And it's really effected their brain. The sad part is when they do get out, they go back to living in drug houses.

My Very Best Regards to you and Madeline. Enjoy each day. May God always bless y'all.

Caitlin

****

Jan. 7, 2012

Dear Charles and Madeline,

Thank you so much for sending me the money order. It's greatly appreciated.

Charles, I've got lots of papers from the lawsuit that I helped put together with the American Civil Liberties Union against the State of New York, the Department of Corrections, and this Administration after 40 of us were transferred to the all men's Fishkill State Prison in March of 2006 until Sept. of 2007. You may find these papers very interesting for the book. Let me know if you would like these papers.

Have a wonderful New Year. Thanks again for the money and the Christmas card.

Caitlin

****

January 14, 2012

Caitlin Fitzgerald
#00G1442
Bedford Hills Correctional Facility
247 Harris Road
Bedford, New York 10507-2400

Dear Caitlin,

You're welcome. Madeline and I are glad you received the money order okay.

Yes, I'm very interested to see those papers that you have regarding the ACLU suit. I wasn't going to broach that subject until I met with you. Glad you brought it up. I didn't know that you have them in your possession. When you get the chance, please send those papers to me.

Regarding our boat hull issue, Madeline and I finally finished scraping last month. Brrr! Madeline did the sides at the waterline while I was scraping underneath the boat. Come spring, we'll have to de-wax the hull, lightly sand, apply 3 barrier coats of epoxy paint, then apply 2 coats of ablative bottom paint. The dealer made good for it—money-wise—but we will be doing the labor, which is certainly going to be a lot of work. At least it will be done properly, not only to protect the fiberglass from water absorption and blistering, but to retard barnacle growth as well. We had paid top dollar for the process and materials, but the boatyard crew dropped the ball. As the boat was purchased in Delaware, we're left to our own devices.

Very best regards,
Charles

****

Jan 28, 2012

Dear Charles,

I sent out the papers with a remit slip. Then 3 days later, the remit slip along with my large envelope of papers was returned saying they would not weigh the envelope and take the money out of my account for any mail except legal mail. I really couldn't believe this. But sure enough, we have another new rule. Anyhow, I put 10 stamps on the envelope, not knowing if it's enough or to much. I just hope you received those papers. Please let me know if you do.

Boy, you do have a lot of work to do on your boat. I sure didn't realize the work involved to do things the right way.

Back to the suit papers. I had forgotten I had sent out a lot of pictures that were in the newspapers to people. And I've forgotten who I sent them to. That's my short term memory catching up with me, I guess. Sorry. I make a joke that I have a very good memory but that it's short.

Best regards,
Caitlin

****

February 3, 2012

Caitlin Fitzgerald
#00G1442
Bedford Hills Correctional Facility
247 Harris Road
Bedford, New York 10507-2400

Dear Caitlin,

I received your letter and packet regarding the ACLU information yesterday. Madeline and I just returned from a vacation in Florida. Friends of ours rented a home in The Villages, just south of Ocala, for the month of January and invited us to come down for a stay. Before visiting them, we spent two days in Crystal River, which is on the Gulf Coast. We were overlooking King's Bay, which has many springs and where the manatees come in for the winter. The water temperature remains 72 degrees at all times in those waters. It's a mecca for divers.

We then visited Jean, a former creative writing student of mine, at her home in Inverness, about 20 minutes away.

The Villages is an interesting place. There are numerous pools, golf courses, club houses, et cetera. The people there, for the most part, are older and are enjoying themselves as if they were kids again. There's a lot to do socially. Any hobby you can imagine is represented by a group of active people.

On our way back, we stayed in Chestertown, MD on the Chester River. It's an historic town, dating back to the Revolutionary War. It's a very nice spot.

That's it for now. Take care.

Very best regards,
Charles

****

Feb. 15, 2012

Dear Charles,

Glad you got the packet. You won't believe this! I was called out to the mail house to sign for your letter dated Feb. 3, 2012 as though you were an attorney. I asked the c/o why? He said because it's legal mail. I said do you see attorney written anywhere on the envelope? He said no, but was told to give me your letter as though it was legal mail. So this place is reading all our mail.

I wrote and told you about trying to send you all those papers with a remit slip. I got it back saying it wasn't legal mail. Therefore I couldn't use a remit slip. Then I sent it with 10 stamps, got that back and was told to bring 2 more stamps to the mailing house which I did. Now I'm receiving your last letter as though it's legal mail. Go figure.

Anyhow, it sounds like you and Madeline had a wonderful vacation. I haven't heard of Crystal River, but 72 degree water temperature sure sounds great. I love swimming and diving.

Y'all take care.

Best regards,
Caitlin

March 3, 2012

Caitlin Fitzgerald
#00G1442
Bedford Hills Correctional Facility
247 Harris Road
Bedford, New York 10507-2400

Dear Caitlin,

I went over the packet quite thoroughly—every word, paragraph and page, and I must say I found it most disturbing. The so-named Defendants, et al., in finally satisfying the transfer issue of plaintiffs illegally sent from Bedford Hills to Fishkill's state prison for men, then returned to Bedford, while the Court brushed aside equally important matters of violations (by declaring those matters moot) is unconscionable. I'm surprised, no amazed, that the ACLU did not pursue those abuses under a separate class action suit. Damage was, indeed, done. Judge Burrows throwing plaintiffs a bone by saying that the women acted "courageously" and should therefore be "proud" by having "established a voice in making the prison system accountable to them and to the Court," addresses the matter only in part. The Court's declaration that everything remains moot is rather inane. It's analogous to authorities returning a bank robber's stolen money and having the thief escape punitive measures because those monies are now back at the bank.

In sum and substance, I'll say this: That packet will prove invaluable to our project. I'm glad you passed it along. Injustices are the bane of my existence, and I do what I can to alter the course of such events. For the wrongs that were committed at Bedford as well as the Fishkill Correctional Facility re the transfer of forty women for those eighteen months, half the time served at that institution should be deducted from their sentences. The abuses and their respective violations should have been further litigated by the ACLU.

As I can't, of course, speak for *all* parties concerned; i.e., forty plaintiffs re the class action suit, I can, however, do, and will continue to speak on your behalf, Caitlin, because of my having intimate knowledge of your plight. You deserve clemency, and I hope Governor Drew will agree, having hopefully perused the applications inclusive of the information that I and others who support you have sent to him and the parole board.

Very best regards,
Charles

cc: Governor Christopher Drew [please add to file re Caitlin Fitzgerald]
    ACLU (New York): Madeline Steinberg, Executive Director

****

March 11, 2012

Dear Charles,

Thank you for writing me so soon after reading all those papers and for copying Governor Drew and Madeline Steinberg, Executive Director of the ACLU in New York. I really like the example you used about the bank robber's stolen money. That's a wonderful idea that all us 40 women that served time unfairly in Fishkill State Prison should get a reduction from their sentence.

Mary Jennings is the only person that I know of who received a letter from Governor Drew's office saying that her letter had been put with my Clemency forms. I know that Wallace and Rose and a few other friends wrote letters also because they all sent me copies.

On March 1, 2012 I was called out of work to go to the Administration Building for what is called our yearly. They asked questions like, Are you happy with your job? Are you having any problems where you are housed? I'm given 8 pieces of paper. The last thing on page 8 is a paper that's dated 08/30/2011, stating that all the necessary materials for Executive Clemency investigation was sent out that date via interoffice mail.

I just wanted you to know that all those papers never left here until that date of 08/30/2011. You'll recall I had them notarized with Mr. Newman and that Mr. Townsand sent them to the Executive

Clemency investigators in the beginning of June of 2011. I don't know when the investigators sent them to the Governor's office, but I do know they are there because Mary received her letter.

Thank you for sending a copy of your letter to the Governor Drew.

After the suit started, the ACLU attorney kept coming to see some of us almost every other week. Fishkill State Prison gave us more time out of our cells, brought in law books, and even started letting us go to the men's gym a couple times a week. Of course the men prisoners were in Lock Down whenever we went to the gym.

Only a few of the 40 women wanted to stay at Fishkill State Prison because their families lived close by. I think I told you I cried the first five weeks I was here because I really thought God had forgotten about me. One of the happiest days of my life was getting to come back to this prison here in Bedford Hills. That's really pretty sad when you think about it.

What stays in my mind a lot was those 1,800 men in that prison. Some of them we were told had been in there for 40 years and longer. Some were sentenced to life with nothing to lose! I had horrible nightmares that they had taken over the prison and raped all of us until we were all dead. You have some of the worse men in this country in that prison. Some were even sent from other states because they broke out of the prison they were in.

For about 14 years Bedford Hills State Prison sent women from here to do a year in Fishkill State Prison because there was no room here. Another thing the ACLU was able to do besides returning us here was to make sure no other women will ever be sent to Fishkill State Prison for men. And as of Jan. 1, 2011 this prison here made room in North Hall for Administrative Segregation, which means that no matter what an inmate did here, they won't be sent to another prison.

I have never mentioned Harold Byrnes to you. Harold and his wife Julie are somewhere in their 90's. I used to do Julie's hair once a week and Harold's once a month when we all lived in Flushing, Queens. They had a home built in Nanticoke Pennsylvania since I've been in prison. Julie has been in a wheelchair since the early 1980's. On my birthday each year, Harold sends me a card from the both of them. In it he always writes, "Glad it's your birthday and not mine." Neither of them would ever tell me how old they are exactly. They followed my trial pretty closely through 20/20 and Court T.V. I remember now they're the ones that I sent a lot of newspaper clippings about the trial along with some of those other papers the ACLU gave me at Fishkill. I didn't think I needed or wanted them anymore because I thought my life was over. Maybe those other papers and the Byrnes couple could be of some help to you if they're still alive.

Tell Madeline hello from me. I hope one day I get to meet you both.

Best regards,
Caitlin.

****

April 8, 2012

Caitlin Fitzgerald
#00G1442
Bedford Hills Correctional Facility
247 Harris Road
Bedford, New York 10507-2400

Dear Caitlin,

I am in receipt of your letter dated March 11th, 2012. It's my turn to apologize for getting back to you late. There are so many things going on here.

Regarding your statement, "I hope one day I get to meet you both," there is no question about that happening. Shortly after your release (as I'm sure you'll be busy settling in at the beginning), Madeline and I would love to spend some time with you, here, on the East End of Long Island: boating, swimming, picnicking, fishing, dining, et cetera. You'll be sick of us in no time ☺ ☺.

In addition to my busy springtime writing schedule here on the East End, Madeline and I are chipping away at trying to get the boat ready for a May 1st launch. I'm sure you remember my explaining that the boat dealer's yard people failed to properly prepare and bottom paint the hull.

Well, that's about it for now. I've been asked to write a monthly report for a fishing publication. That assignment, along with my other outdoor article writing, will help pay for gas for the boat, which is almost up to $5 a gallon for high test.

Take care. Stay well.

Very best regards,
Charles

****

April 16, 2012

Dear Charles and Madeline,

Thank you for your nice letter. Do not worry about writing me back soon. I know you and Madeline have a busy life. And thank you for offering me a visit to your home and doing all those fun things you mentioned, but that will depend what state I'm paroled to. Mary will be moving to New Jersey shortly. If I live with Mary, maybe after a year I could get permission to leave the state for a week, but only if the parole officer says so. I'm hoping the parole officer gets to know me and realizes this old woman doesn't need to be on parole. God knows I wouldn't do anything wrong and have to come back here and do the other 15 percent of my sentence. It's great you have a way to make extra money to pay for your boat gas. I do hope you do whatever you have to do to get your boat launched by May 1. Enjoy.

Love,
Caitlin

****

April 28, 2012

Caitlin Fitzgerald
#00G1442
Bedford Hills Correctional Facility
247 Harris Road
Bedford, New York 10507-2400

Dear Caitlin,

Well, I guess Madeline and I will just have to visit you in whatever state you relocate to so as to do some of those things I mentioned. We'll look forward to spending some time with you. I didn't realize that you'd be on parole for such a period of time and not be able to leave the state that you relocate to. Whatever the situation, we'll be there for you.

Yes, we're chipping away trying to get the boat ready for May. Usually, we're in by mid-March; however, we've been very busy.

Take care.

Very best regards,
Charles

****

May 8, 2012

Dear Charles,

I'm not really sure where I'm going to parole out to just yet. Some friends of mine in Maine told me recently I could always stay with them. Don't know how these old bones would take the cold. We were freezing here with no heat at the end of April. The heat was turned off April 15, that's the law. It went down to 31 degrees. Brrr! Of course, Mary Jennings wants me to stay with her in New Jersey. We'll see.

Take Care.

Best regards,
Caitlin

****

May 3, 2012

Caitlin Fitzgerald
#00G1442
Bedford Hills Correctional Facility

247 Harris Road
Bedford, New York 10507-2400

Dear Caitlin,

Sorry to hear about those freezing temperatures with no heat. Sounds like an apartment my son and I lived in back in Bayside, Queens—many a year ago. Of course, I had the luxury of purchasing space heaters.

I'm sure by the time you are released that you will have decided on the best place to live. I'm glad you have options.

I've recently received correspondence from Wallace McKenna. He makes a good point about positing your age referencing clemency. I've written to Governor Drew and made this point, keeping your name before him as a constant reminder.

Best regards,
Charles

Enclosure

****

Charles Winfield
72-61 113 St.
Forest Hills, N.Y. 11375

May 3, 2012

(copy)

The Honorable Christopher Drew
Governor of the State of New York
New York State Capitol Building
Albany, New York 12224

Dear Governor Drew:

You presently have the clemency applications referencing inmate Caitlin Fitzgerald, I.D. #00G1442, of the Bedford Hills Correctional

Facility, Bedford, New York.

Caitlin Fitzgerald is among the oldest prisoners in her unit (69 years of age). Ms. Fitzgerald has been a model prisoner for over ten years, having taken numerous hours of classes and receiving certificates in upholstery. She is certainly no threat to the public. Years of unthinkable physical and mental abuse by her husband brought Ms. Fitzgerald to the breaking point. Yes, she made the wrong choice by killing him. However, Ms. Fitzgerald experienced a raw deal in that her attorney, William Baxter, proved inadequate in her defense and has since been disbarred for nefarious dealings. Additionally, Mrs. Fitzgerald had spent one-and-a-half years in the Fishkill all-male facility under horrendous conditions. A class action suit was filed and won by the American Civil Liberties Union on behalf of thirty-nine other women in that same predicament. Ms. Fitzgerald was then sent back to the Bedford Hills facility. Ms. Fitzgerald's relatives and friends are unconditionally supportive and would be there for her upon her return to society.

Governor, I request that you give serious thought to granting Caitlin Fitzgerald clemency. Your positive action in this regard would demonstrate your compassion and heartfelt leadership of the people of New York.

Additionally, I had written you two other letters (dated March 5 and May 30, 2011) referencing Caitlin Fitzgerald's clemency. I have not received confirmation that those letters were placed in Ms. Fitzgerald's file. Out of several friends, relatives, and supporters of Caitlin's, whose copies of letters I have on file, I know of only one person who has received notification that their correspondence was so placed. I would appreciate knowing whether my letters are, indeed, in Ms. Fitzgerald's file and are before you for consideration. If those letters were somehow misplaced or lost, I would be glad to resend them. Please let me know either way.

Thank you.

Respectfully submitted,
Charles Winfield

****

May 12, 2012

Dear Charles,

Thank you for your letter and for the letter you sent to the Governor. I am the oldest inmate in my Unit, but a Mildred Parks who is housed in another Unit will be 76 on May 13, 2012. That's tomorrow. I just found out today. I don't want the Governor or his people to think I exaggerate. I received a nice letter from Wallace McKenna and his wife Rose, sending me a copy of the letter they wrote to Governor Drew, too, asking that the letters be put in my file. You told me early on that it was a long shot. But I want everybody to know that I appreciate all the support I receive from everyone.

Mary Jennings and her friend came to visit me. They have a writing campaign going on my behalf, asking others in our circle of friends to write to the Governor also. I've also asked my brother Shawn and some other cousins to write.

Charles, I finally got the book Soul on Ice and read it last week while I was out of work with bronchitis. I didn't really like the book very much. I am now reading Never Seen Again by Jeanne King. This book is a lot more interesting. I'm also studying my grammar book and hope you see some improvement in my writing. Yes?

Very best regards,
Caitlin

****

June 18, 2012

Caitlin Fitzgerald
#00G1442
Bedford Hills Correctional Facility
247 Harris Road
Bedford, New York 10507-2400

Dear Caitlin,

It has been a whirlwind for Madeline and me these past five

weeks.

I've just completed editing a manuscript for an elderly gent who was involved in the French/Italian underground during World War II. The story is poignant. I had read the original manuscript in one sitting and decided to take on the project. Then the wife became involved, misplaced the original manuscript, and gave me three other versions plus a play she had written. I had to pull the best of the best from those other manuscripts. What a job! The manuscript is finally complete, and they want to self-publish the work. Madeline has uploaded the book onto the Internet to CreateSpace, which is owned by Amazon. CreateSpace is a print-on-demand publisher, which is the cheapest way to have a book self-published. I'm telling you all of this to let you know that your book, once it is complete, can be published this way if we have no traditional publishers interested. So you can rest assured that your story <u>will</u> be published—one way or another.

Next, Madeline and I were just approved for our own local television show on Cablevision Public Access Riverhead (Channel 20). The show is titled *Long Island Living with Charles & Madeline* and will air on Saturdays (for the entire month) at 12:30 p.m. The program reaches East End of Long Island viewers from Riverhead to Orient Point on the North Fork and Montauk to Eastport on the South Fork. We plan to cover a potpourri of topics: fishing, crabbing and clamming in our Long Island waters, hunting, consumer advocacy, the writing process referencing fiction and nonfiction, criminal justice, and many other subjects. We'll have expert guests in their respective fields join us. It's all very exciting. We have yet to learn how all of the studio equipment and procedures work.

I just received a letter from the New York State Parole Board stating that they received my correspondence re your clemency and that it is in your file.

I'm sorry to hear about your bronchitis and hope you're feeling better. Too, I'm happy to hear that your friends and family are writing supportive letters to the governor re clemency.

And yes, I do see continued improvement in your letter writing.

That's it for now. Take care.

Very best regards,
Charles

Chapter Twenty-Two

The Boss Chair

July 1, 2012

Dear Charles,

I received you letter of June 18 and am just getting over my bout with bronchitis. I guess as we get older, a cold or anything like that takes longer each time to recover from.

I don't remember if I've ever told you or not, but there is no air conditioning in this building, and of course we're having a heatwave right now. I really don't know how many more heatwaves I can take. There is only one building that houses inmates that has A/C. But I would not want to live in that building because you have to share one toilet and one small sink with 12 other women. My cell right now is 90 degrees!

Wow, you and Madeline really are busy. Mary Jennings had told me about Amazon and Createspace, but thanks for telling me more about it.

Congratulations on your own T.V. show. Wow!

Glad you received a letter from the N.Y. State Parole Board. A couple of my other friends did also. You may have pressed the right buttons, Charles.

I want to tell you what happened here on June 14, 2012. Special Operations Group (SOG) came to Grounds. They did one building at a time, starting at 7:00 A.M. with Castle Hall. Castle Hall is half a mile from Alpha Building. You can't see it from here. They went to a few other buildings before coming to us in Alpha Building. No one was at work. You just sit on your bed and watch T.V., read a book or whatever, just waiting until it was our turn. At 3 P.M. 2 doors open to Alpha and about 35 men and women in black uniforms come in screaming for us to get out of our cells and stand in the hallway with our hands on the back of our heads, facing the wall. Keep in mind that

June 14 was the second day of our first heatwave. There are 3 hallwaic in this building, 6 feet across each one. They kept making us move closer and closer together so we would only be in 2 hallways. All this time you could not take your hands off the back of your head. Most of us were in full prison uniforms, boots and all. One woman c/o told our c/o he had to leave the building while we were strip searched, 10 of us at a time; 10 female c/o's standing in front of us, all the other inmates watching us in the same hallway. We were told to start with our shoes, hand over one piece of clothing at a time to the c/o in front of us. She'd shake out our clothing then throw them on the floor. You're then told to turn back and face the wall again, raise one foot at a time, bend over, hold your anus open and cough. Next, you turn back around facing the c/o, bend forward and run your fingers through your hair. Sometime later, we were told to get dressed fast and go out the front door.

The BOSS (Body Orifice Security Scanner) chair was waiting for us; it's like a very large chair. First you put your chin on a part of the back of the chair and turn your face from side to side. Next, you walk around the chair and sit in it. This chair can tell the c/o's if you have something in your mouth or have swallowed something. Finally, you're told to stand in a straight line and put your hands back on your head until all the other inmates are checked out by the chair before walking single file toward the gym.

Inmates have hid handcuff keys up their noses and tape-wrapped razor blades under their tongues. Some have even cut slits on the inside of their cheeks to make small pockets to hide contraband like pills and other drugs. We even had one woman here who hid a cellphone up her butt. Cellphones are a c/o's worse nightmare because they can be used to make drug deals on the outside, or worse yet order hits on other inmates or c/o's in here or anywhere. It is believed that one c/o never made it home one evening because an inmate called her gang member friend on the outside who ambushed the officer in his car after leaving work.

This was my third time to see Special Operations Group (SOG) in 11 years. It's no fun being strip searched like that and having a total of fifty women and men looking at you on the Grounds. Talk about being humiliated. They speak to you like you are a piece of dirt.

If you ever want to hear about the other two times, just let me know.

Will your T.V. show be on 5 days a week? I know some people on Long Island that I will write to and tell them about you and Madeline's show. Again, that's wonderful.

Take care,
Caitlin

P.S. I just read your letter over and I see that I read it too fast the first time. Now I see you wrote each show will be aired on Saturdays for the entire month. 12:00 P.M. Channel 20. I will write the people I know on Long Island.

Wishing you and Madeline the very best,
Caitlin

****

July 12, 2012

Caitlin Fitzgerald
#00G1442
Bedford Hills Correctional Facility
247 Harris Road
Bedford, New York 10507-2400

Dear Caitlin,

Madeline and I have been crazy busy here, but we are taking time to have some fun fishing and clamming. We went out to the bay this morning and caught a few porgies and blowfish. We will grill them for dinner tonight.

We do not have cable TV, so in essence we do not have TV entertainment per se. But each year as a Christmas present, our son gives us a gift subscription to Netflix. Netflix is an online site where you can rent movies and receive them through the mail. You can keep them as long as you want without paying a late fee. It's really great for us as we receive two movies a week. We have a next-door neighbor who has a vast collection of DVDs and lends them to us, so we always have plenty of viewing. And, of course, I have those cassette tapes Mary Jennings sent of your trial coverage of *Court TV* and *20/20* that I view from time to time for the book.

Thank you for letting your friends know about our Cablevision show. The broadcast is pretty much limited to the East End of Long Island, but those who do receive Channel 20 make copies for their friends who are interested in a particular topic we cover.

As far as Amazon's CreateSpace is concerned, self-published authors have to market their book as best as they can by posting them on Facebook, blogging on the Internet, and joining groups online. It's also beneficial to give a talk at a library or other venue and have books available for people to purchase.

The weather has been hot here, too, and I'm sure it's unbearable for you. We're sorry to hear that you had to go through that shakedown. I know that you experienced this before.

Very best regards,
Charles

****

July 22, 2012

Dear Charles,

Glad to hear you and Madeline are taking the time to have some fun. I'm glad you have those tapes that Mary sent you. You'll be reminded of just how bad an attorney William Baxter is, or rather was, because he's been disbarred. Keep in mind that he begged me to take over my case. And that's after I had already paid my first attorney $1,000.00 as a retainer for that one visit.

I have friends that gave up cable T.V. and now have Netflix. They tell me they are saving over $1,000.00 a year. They get all their news from the computer and radio. We get 3 movies here a week on Friday, Saturday, and Sunday nights. They each play for 24 hours.

Yes, I've been through many, many shakedowns in the last 11 years, but the Special Operations Group (SOG) are the pits of hell.

Thank God I only experienced that 3 times in 11 years. It's bad enough the women c/o's look up your butt. Although our male c/o's are not present for that up close and humiliating examination, they still ogle us naked from a distance. Outside the building where the BOSS chair is, the scene is surreal. It reminds me of pictures I've seen of the Nazis marching a line of women off to what they thought were the showers.

I'm glad you and Madeline take time out for fun things to do. We only get to go around once in this old world. I have a cousin who always says this is not a dress rehearsal. I am thankful that I've been to 11 countries. I'm sure I won't be going to any more.

I had a wonderful surprise yesterday. My cousin Wallace McKenna and his wife Rose came for a visit. I had no idea they were coming. Wallace said he called the prison on Friday and told a lady who answered the phone to please call Alpha Unit and to tell Caitlin Fitzgerald they were coming. But this place never tells you anything.

Take care,
Caitlin

Chapter Twenty-Three

Dispelling Delusions

July 30, 2012

Caitlin Fitzgerald
#00G1442
Bedford Hills Correctional Facility
247 Harris Road
Bedford, New York 10507-2400

Dear Caitlin,

Referencing your last letter, I'll reiterate the didactic lines from my very first letter to you dated October 8, 2010:

"It will be a lot of time and work on our behalf. At the very least, your attempt may prove cathartic. If we succeed, you will be helping women who find themselves in abusive relationships."

I did not and do not want you under any misconceptions or delusions.

If a literary agent and mainstream publisher do not pick us up, we can always have the book published via print-on-demand services such as CreateSpace (through Amazon), Lulu, Xlibris, et cetera. If we're very lucky, a traditional mainstream publisher might pick us up and print it as nonfiction, which I would love to see happen. We would then let the publisher worry about the Son of Sam law. There are ways around this law. I understand your concerns and fears, knowing that you want the book published as fiction because of these elements. However, if the publishing house were to posit otherwise, that your concerns and fears are unjustified, I'd ask you to reconsider. Unfortunately, it is not likely that a traditional publisher will pick up the book as fiction, even though it is based on and inspired by your own true story. Whatever way it goes, i.e., Print-on-Demand (self-publishing), or the traditional publishing route (be it nonfiction or fiction), there are still no guarantees regarding sales. You, my dear lady, and I, will probably have to be out there promoting the book. Madeline and I just launched our own publishing company titled Clearwater Books. I edited and Madeline formatted Arthur Cooper's book titled *Underground*: Memoir of a World War II French/Italian Wartime Journey ~ 1942-1944. Everything went smoothly, and the book was published on June 28, 2012.

I continue poring over my notes, viewing those *20/20* and *Court TV* tapes, listening to William Baxter being reprimanded by the judge, but not nearly to the extent that the trial transcripts clearly set forth. Together, tapes and transcripts make it abundantly clear that the man was not a good lawyer. But for Baxter to have served in the capacity of a criminal defense attorney is criminal in itself. Although it wasn't for incompetency, it's certainly not surprising that he's been disbarred. Baxter should have thoroughly ripped into Sergeant. Dennis Phelps and Detective Lieutenant Walter Warford when he had the chance. His questioning of witnesses for the prosecution as well as the defense left a lot to be desired.

Madeline and I don't do much traveling out of the country. The last time was in 1984 when we went to the Dominican Republic with our lawyer friend and his wife. I won't get on a plane with all that's going on in the world today. Wherever we go, we drive, travel, or boat —and that's good enough.

I was very glad to hear that Wallace and Rose visited you.

Very best regards,
Charles

****

Aug. 5, 2012

Dear Charles,

I have read and re-read your letters about the Son of Sam law. I've had 3 different people send me all kinds of information they could find on that law. I also went to the inmate's law library and looked it up for myself. I even talked to the lady who runs the library. No one knows anything about the law being declared unconstitutional or changed in any way.

It's wonderful you and Madeline have your own publishing company and T.V. show. Congratulations again. You both have to be two very intelligent people. I knew you were from the first letter I received from you.

You are, oh, so right. William Baxter should have ripped Sgt. Phelps and Detective Lt. Warford apart for lying on the stand like they did. My poor excuse for an attorney did not even know how to lay the proper foundation or to ask the witness the right questions. Also, I truly believe Baxter was intimidated and afraid of Judge Hershfield because when you don't know what you're doing, you run scared.

I can understand why you and Madeline don't want to get on a plane anymore. A lot of people feel the same way.

In my grammar book, I'm studying simple, compound, complex, and complex sentences. I'm beginning to understand—I think. I believe you'll see a marked improvement.

My very best regards to you both,
Caitlin

****

August 14, 2012

Caitlin Fitzgerald
#00G1442
Bedford Hills Correctional Facility
247 Harris Road
Bedford, New York 10507-2400

Dear Caitlin,

I do understand your concerns and will write your story as fiction as you wish, so you need not worry about that.

The commentary from legal and medical experts as to battered woman syndrome is most interesting and will be relevant with what I have in mind in terms of organizing your story.

Our publishing company is moving along nicely. I just had a call from an author who wants me to read his manuscript and evaluate the work. And Madeline *thought* she retired in 2003. Silly girl. But we're only going to be handling one or two books a year, inclusive of my own. Arthur and Thelma Cooper are ecstatic as to the book that Madeline and I put together for him: *Underground.*

This Thursday we have a taping at the Cablevision TV studio with two consummate outdoorsmen. One is a marine biologist, hunter, fisherman, photographer and falconer. Madeline and I actually went on a hunt with him and his red tailed hawk one Sunday morning. It's amazing to watch the bird go after her prey. The other gentleman is a veteran fisherman here on Long Island. He'll be talking about fishing the wrecks in the Long Island Sound during the fall season. It should be a very interesting day of taping.

The weather here has let up a bit as far as humidity is concerned. It's been a very muggy season as you know. But fall is right around the corner with cooler days and nights.

Take care.

Very best regards,
Charles

Chapter Twenty-Four

Corrections Officers Clash and Crash

August 25, 2012

Dear Charles,

Thank you again for a very nice letter. Great news that you and Madeline's publishing company is moving along nicely. It's wonderful you two work so well together.

Going on a hunt with your friend and his hawk sounds so interesting. You just don't stop doing fun things.

I am happy summer is almost over. Before I came to prison, summer was my favorite season of the year. But in here it's awful with no air conditioning. Some days I take 3 showers.

Today we were in lockdown until 10:20 A.M. We don't know the whole story yet, but two c/o's got in a fight in the parking lot at about 5:45 A.M—right before the shift changes at 6:00 A.M. On the weekends we all like to sleep in, but that didn't happen today. There was a very loud commotion. After the fight, one of the c/o's drove his car into a building that's called the Center. That's where all the guns are kept. If an inmate is going to be driven to court or a hospital, two c/o's are with you. One c/o gets out of the van to get guns for the trip. We don't know exactly what happened after the c/o drove into the building, but it's rumored that he took some guns to go after the other c/o. You can rest assured that no c/o will be bringing us any newspapers for the next week. We are not allowed to read any newspapers if it has any negative news about the Department of Corrections. The same holds true for the T.V. news.

I'm going to make this a very short letter because the heat is getting to me.

Best regards,
Caitlin

BATTERED

****

September 4, 2012

Caitlin Fitzgerald
#00G1442
Bedford Hills Correctional Facility
247 Harris Road
Bedford, New York 10507-2400

Dear Caitlin,

That's some story referencing those two c/o's you mentioned in your last letter. I'm sure censorship is the name of the game after an incident like that. Let me know if you hear anything more as I'm sure I won't.

Last weekend we enjoyed having a colleague of mine come for a visit. We taught English at a community college. He's getting up there in age, and his eyes are not good. Madeline and I were on pins and needles hoping that he wouldn't fall down the stairs. At one point, he did, but I was there to steady him. We took him out to eat at a local Italian restaurant on Saturday, followed by a drive out to Greenport and Orient Point, both beautiful towns here on the North Fork of Long Island.

I am working diligently on my next novel. Madeline is formatting it to be uploaded and printed by CreateSpace. The book will be published before the end of this year. We will, however, take advantage of the striped bass and bluefish fall run and go clamming one more time before the boating season ends.

Very best regards,
Charles

****

Oct 7, 2012

Dear Charles,

Sorry I haven't written in a while. I should have known by your letters that you taught college English. I know I told you that English was my worst subject in school. I'm sure over the years you have seen All in the Family with Archie and Edith Bunker. My Mother and Father sounded just like them. Even in grade school, my Mom would call out spelling words to me, never pronouncing them correctly. I should have studied more in school. Glad you enjoyed seeing your colleague.

Charles, is it possible you could send me one of your earlier books, a chapter or two at a time or maybe a complete copy? Or I could ask Wallace to order it for me. I'll have to tell him that the receipt has to come with the book or the prison won't give it to me. Or should I wait until it is in the bookstore?

Best regards,
Caitlin

****

November 5, 2012

Caitlin Fitzgerald
#00G1442
Bedford Hills Correctional Facility
247 Harris Road
Bedford, New York 10507-2400

Dear Caitlin,

By now you should have received one of my novels, a two-book set. I had e-mailed Wallace regarding your interest in reading one of my works. He sent a check, and I sent the books off to you on October 22nd along with a receipt as you said was needed, which indicated that they were paid for in full. Did you receive those autographed and personalized copies ~ Part One and Part Two?

We've weathered Hurricane Sandy. Our center console was on the trailer in the backyard, but the boat floated off with the rise in tide. I had to tie the boat to the fence and pier to stop it from floating away.

When the water finally receded two days later, Madeline and I were able to reposition the vessel properly. Also, we had seven inches of water in the basement from the ground being so saturated. The basement is finally dry. I'm going to get smart and have a sump pump installed.

We certainly can't complain as many people lost their homes and their lives due to the storm. A friend's home may be condemned because of home heating oil contamination. Staten Island is destroyed; lower Manhattan had no electricity for days. The schools were closed for three days. Subway and bus service was suspended. It's a mess. There was no gasoline being sold on Long Island. The stations are just beginning to open, but the lines are extremely long.

Very best regards,
Charles

****

Nov. 27, 2012

Dear Charles,

Sorry again I haven't written in a while. I'm glad that Hurricane Sandy did not do too much damage to your home and boat and that you and Madeline are safe. I've been working overtime in Commissary because we were weeks behind because of Hurricane Sandy. The trucks could not get here with food or beverages. The ground here could only take so much water. It was like a river. We never get paid for overtime at the commissary. But that's o.k. because the more hours I work and read, the faster the time goes by.

Yes, I received the two book set. Thank you for autographing and personalizing the copies. Since it was a Friday evening, I stayed up a little late and read half of Part One in one evening. Wow! I cannot tell you enough how much I am enjoying it.

I have to get back to my continued reading rather than writing. Call me selfish, but you have a fan. I can't put it down.

I hope you and Madeline had a great Thanksgiving.

Best regards,
Caitlin

P.S. I almost forgot to tell you. The story is that one c/o went after the other c/o over a woman here. Not a female c/o but an inmate. She's now housed in another Unit. The older officer was high on drugs and alcohol and threatened to kill the younger c/o. That's why he crashed into the building to get a gun to go after him. The younger officer had taken away his superior's motorcycle keys so he couldn't ride and hurt himself. But the older c/o somehow got ahold of the other man's car keys and drove that car into the building. Believe it or not, the younger c/o got the shaft, meaning he was fired, and the high ranking officer got transferred out of here. Go figure. But that's not the end of it. Later, in town, the younger man who got fired crashed a rented vehicle into the others man's brand new motorcycle. Hope you get this letter.

****

December 6, 2012

Caitlin Fitzgerald
#00G1442
Bedford Hills Correctional Facility
247 Harris Road
Bedford, New York 10507-2400

Dear Caitlin,

Wow! Some story. I won't comment on it here.

I'm delighted to hear that you received the two books and that you are enjoying the story. You certainly are a fast reader . . . half of Part One read in an evening. Wow!

All of my novels will now be sold through Amazon. I have a big monetary layout for new computer equipment, printers, monitors, packaging, promotion, et cetera. I have to show income in order to claim deductions of equipment purchases to the IRS. This will also help with our new Cablevision show (*Long Island Living with Co-hosts Charles & Madeline*). I have a tentative title for our book project —*Battered*, which won't cost you a dime and will *hopefully* make you a few bucks. I was totally honest with you from the onset; it's a tough business, Caitlin. However, you have a good story and a good writer behind you. Me. ☺

Very best regards,
Charles

****

December 2, 2012

Dear Charles,

    Can you believe it's almost Christmas?
    I want you to know that I finished reading both your books, and I have to say they are two of the best books I've ever read. They grip you and hold your interest; you can't stop reading because you want to know what happens next. You are a great writer! Also that's a good picture of you on the inside back cover of Book Two.
    Thank you. Thank you.

Very best regards,
Caitlin

****

December 8, 2012

Caitlin Fitzgerald
#00G1442
Bedford Hills Correctional Facility
247 Harris Road
Bedford, New York 10507-2400

Dear Caitlin,

    Thank you for the continued kind words regarding my novel. I'm very glad that you enjoyed the story. I hope that you tell everyone about the book(s) because anything positive that is said about my writing will help when your story is written and published. Please tell your friends and relatives to visit my Web site at www.CharlesWinfield.com, where they can read a synopsis referencing all of my novels and other writings. I'll autograph and personalize the books for anyone interested.

On another note: Many people are still coping with the aftermath of Sandy. Some homes are completely destroyed, and those folks have to start all over. Very sad.

Our Thanksgiving was wonderful as usual. Every year we go to a couple's home, which is about a half hour away. I went to college with the fellow, so we go back a long way. This year, the group was smaller, consisting of nine people, including our hosts. Their son, his wife, and their infant daughter didn't join us this year because the baby was sick. It would have been nice to see them.

My friend and his wife go all out for Thanksgiving. She roasted two turkeys, had all the trimmings, and about five desserts from which to choose. Needless to say, we were all very full. Madeline always has fun at their home because they have two cute little dogs that she loves to play with.

Very best regards,
Charles

****

Dec. 20, 2012

Dear Charles and Madeline,

Thank you for the beautiful Christmas card.

I'm spreading the word about your novels as best I can. Many of my friends on the outside are on fixed incomes, so I can't promise anything. Many of them had damage from Hurricane Sandy. One day I will read <u>all</u> your novels; I truly look forward to them. A friend of mine who is two cells down is reading your two volume set right now.

Lately, we've had lots of shakedowns. Something odd is going on, but I don't know what. Rumor has it that it has something to do with the inmate who was involved with those two c/o's. Rumor also has it that she's now involved with another officer here.

I just can't get over what happened in Newtown, Connecticut. It's a good thing the gunman killed himself. I'm sure thousands of people would have liked to kill him.

Have a blessed Christmas,
Caitlin

****

December 26, 2013

Caitlin Fitzgerald
#00G1442
Bedford Hills Correctional Facility
247 Harris Road
Bedford, New York 10507-2400

Dear Caitlin,

Madeline and I are sorry to hear that your friends were hit by Hurricane Sandy and incurred damage. A lot of people are still suffering from the "Perfect Storm." Don't concern yourself with asking friends to purchase my novels. I have to go through the motions in order to secure sales and keep my name out there. I do what I have to do. I'm glad that you gave the book to your friend to read.

My new novel, inspired by a serial killer trial in Suffolk County, is making its rounds via law enforcement folks, judges, lawyers, friends, et cetera. I believe I had mentioned that it was the first death penalty case on Long Island in almost a quarter of a century, which was shortly thereafter found unconstitutional because of the way one judge (presiding over another death penalty case during the same period) had *improperly* instructed the jury. The fact of the matter is that the state of New York cannot afford a death penalty because it costs more to execute a person than it does to feed him or her, appeals and other issues notwithstanding.

Madeline and I just returned from spending a week in Manhattan, staying at my son's apartment while he was in Europe. We rested, read a lot, and went to see a show at the Comic Strip Live, which is about five blocks from the apartment. The dozen acts were wonderful; very funny. We had a really good time. The audience was, for the most part, a young crowd. People were from England, Spain, Wales, Scotland, and Bosnia. The comedians certainly played off the young lady from Bosnia. First question asked by one comedian was, "Aren't they looking for you?" meaning the authorities here in this country. It was good that she had a sense of humor, for these comedians can be merciless.

When you get the chance, I want you to write down, in detail, more about what a typical Thanksgiving, Christmas, and New Year's is like for you at the correctional facility. Tell me about the Good, the Bad and the Ugly. Please refer to your letter of December 18th, 2011 to me so that you don't have to repeat yourself unnecessarily. Mary tells me that you keep all correspondence.

That's about it for now. Take care.

Very best regards,
Charles

P.S. I have the whole story involving that female inmate and those two c/o's you talked about in your recent letters. For obvious reasons, I won't go into that now, except to say that I am a pretty good investigative reporter. ☺ ☺ Tell you all about it when Madeline and I meet you personally. You won't believe your ears.

Chapter Twenty-Five

Holidays and Halfway Houses ~ Sex and Suicide

February 20, 2013

Dear Charles,

Well, you certainly have my curiosity. Can't wait to hear, but I guess I have to.

It sure sounds like spending a week in Manhattan was very enjoyable for you and Madeline.

I'm very sorry it has taken me so long to answer your letter, but ever since Commissary stopped selling cigarettes, I just don't get caught up anymore. Withdrawal makes you very tired and irritable. I'm so tired by the weekend all I want to do is sleep. Also, the holidays make us all very depressed: Thanksgiving, Christmas and New Years. Holidays here are always a bitch. I'm behind on my laundry and cleaning up my cell (which Administration always refers to as our rooms) because the c/o's keep messing it up with one shakedown after another. I told you something strange is going on here ever since those two c/o's got into a fight and one drove his car into Central. Also, I'm busy cutting other inmates hair with toe nail clippers for 4 postage stamps. Hint, hint.

Christmas is the saddest day of the year in prison for most of us. Of course we do have about 50 Muslims here who don't care about Christmas. I thank God I've only got 2 more Christmases to go. We are all thankful when New Years comes and goes because it marks another beginning to an end. In other words, you know there is light at the end of a very long and dark tunnel. That pretty much sums up what I told you before about the holidays Thanksgiving, Christmas and New Years. I told you the food sucks—if you can even call it that. Thin slices of processed turkey luncheon meat. The cheapest the state can find. Most of us <u>do not</u> eat it. The best part of Thanksgiving or Christmas lunch is 2 dinner roles with 2 pats of butter. On a personal *level, birthdays are very depressing too. And when someone dies here in prison or takes their own life, well, I don't even want to talk about that.*

Any day now I will be called to go to the Administration Building to sign up for a Halfway House. The Administration and the Governor want all inmates to spend their last 2 years there. But I'm not going to sign up. And for that I might be put in Administrative Segregation. But I would rather be there than a Halfway House. If you look up these places on your computer, you will understand why. The New York Times investigated them for 3 years. Rapes, gang violence and drugs run rampant. It is so bad that employees quit and inmates escape on a regular basis. If you think this is an exaggeration, check it out. You will learn that Halfway Houses throughout the State are politically corrupt money making systems. Millions of dollars are made. The governor's friends and relatives own and operate some of these Halfway Houses. Because we do not have access to a computer, folks on the outside have tried to get us all of The New York Times 15 page report about these Halfway Houses. But the mailroom took most of them along with the letters. I have 4 of those 15 pages. Here are a couple of sentences from one page.

"He took his pants down and grabbed my hair and pushed me down. That started the first four weeks of hell."

The maintenance man who assaulted the woman was put on temporary leave, and the woman was transferred to another facility.

I hope to have most of those 15 pages by the time I get to the Administration Building. I will show and tell the Board of Directors there that this is the reason why I would rather be sent to Administrative Segregation then be sent to a Halfway house. I'm also going to tell them that my judge didn't sentence me to any Halfway House.

Whenever anyone here writes to a radio or T.V. station, the letter never leaves the mailroom.

Best regards,
Caitlin

****

February 27, 2013

Caitlin Fitzgerald
#00G1442
Bedford Hills Correctional Facility
247 Harris Road
Bedford, New York 10507-2400

Dear Caitlin,

Thank you for the information regarding those holidays, et cetera. Very important.

Madeline and I checked out halfway houses on the Internet. Wow! *The New York Times* really gave these places a scathing report, so we understand your concerns.

Enclosed is a postal money order for $20 with our compliments.

Very best regards,
Charles

P.S. No need to apologize for not getting back immediately. Madeline and I have been extremely busy with promoting my latest novel, as well as editing my fishing book, which should be coming out this year. Too, I was just accepted as a member of the New York State Outdoor Writer's Association, so now I'm going to barrage other members, letting them know that I weave my outdoor experiences through my novels. Madeline calls it networking; I call it whoring. ☺ One must do what one must do.

Enclosure: Postal Money Order $20

****

March 5, 2013

Dear Charles,

Thank you so much for another $20 dollars. It's greatly appreciated. I'm sure I mentioned that twice a year we get to order a *food package if we haven't received any kind of a charge in the last year. All meats, poultry and seafood are fully cooked. Your $20 will go toward stamps and 1 pound of shrimp.*

Thank you again.

Charles, congratulations on being accepted as a member of the New York State Outdoor Writer's Association. And good luck with your books.

Take care. Keep networking and whoring. ☺

Wishing you all the best,
Caitlin

****

March 12, 2013

Caitlin Fitzgerald
#00G1442
Bedford Hills Correctional Facility
247 Harris Road
Bedford, New York 10507-2400

Dear Caitlin,

You're very welcome. I hope that you enjoy the shrimp.

Thank you for sharing the information regarding Enzo and *the Long Island Fishing Journal*. I had no idea that he gave the magazine to his employees and is only doing temperature charts. I won't, of course, say anything about you giving me that piece of news.

We just returned from a weekend in Connecticut at our friends' parents' farm. We went up to see how maple syrup is made and worked in the sugar house for three eight-hour days; we learned a lot. It's an amazing process. Madeline and I certainly got in a lot of exercise. The fire has to be constantly fed and stoked to keep the syrup in the evaporator at 219 degrees, which is when the sap becomes syrup. That was basically my job. I have a nice tan. ☺ ☺ It takes 50 gallons of sap to make 1 gallon of maple syrup.

Very best regards,
Charles

****

March 24, 2013

Dear Charles,

Yes, I did enjoy my shrimp. I'm glad you both enjoyed your friend's farm. I would never have thought it takes 50 gallons of sap to make 1 gallon of maple syrup. Now I understand why it's so expensive.

I have disturbing news. We have a new Administrator. Her name is Ms. Atkins. She is a real bitch! Ms. Atkins said we are all going to Halfway Houses sooner or later. There is no way out. I am expecting my name to be on the list any day now.

Before Ms. Atkins took over, if you refused to go to a Halfway House you were sent to Lock for about 10 days. Then you were housed in one of the Units in Max for a couple of weeks. Then you come back here to Grounds, where I am now, and you got your job back. You do not have a job at a Halfway House. Everyone is first put in a house prison. They tell you you will only be there a few weeks before being sent to a Halfway House. This is not true! I have had many letters from women inmates who have been in these house prisons for many months before they are sent to Halfway Houses. It is most of the young drug addicts who want to go to these prison houses and Halfway Houses because they know they can get drugs easily. These Halfway Houses get paid $40,000 for each inmate. And when you do something wrong, you come back here with <u>nothing</u> and start all over again. No T.V., hair dryer, curling iron, etc. Then this place gets another 40 grand. They keep you here a month, send you back, and the Halfway House gets still another 40 grand. It's all just one big money making operation coming out of taxpayer's pockets. And it seems there is nothing anyone can do about it.

I know I'm venting. Sorry.

Well, it's supposed to rain and snow here tomorrow. When is Spring really coming?

Best regards,
Caitlin

****

April 6, 2013

Caitlin Fitzgerald
#00G1442
Bedford Hills Correctional Facility
247 Harris Road
Bedford, New York 10507-2400

Dear Caitlin,

I hope this letter gets to you. From your last correspondence, things seemed up in the air for you as far as your being transferred to a halfway house.

I have written another letter to Governor Drew on your behalf regarding clemency in the hopes that my writing keeps your name in the forefront.

Very best regards,
Charles

Enclosure

****

Charles Winfield
72-61 113 St.
Forest Hills, N.Y. 11375

copy

April 6, 2013

The Honorable Christopher Drew
Governor of the State of New York
New York State Capitol Building
Albany, New York 12224

Dear Governor Drew:

I had written to you on March 5 and May 30, 2011, and again on March 3, 2012 regarding clemency proceedings (applications already submitted) for Caitlin Fitzgerald (#00G1442), incarcerated at the Bedford Hills Correctional Facility in Bedford, New York. Too, other folks, friends and family, have written you in the same regard.

I trust that you have given serious consideration to this matter in favor of Ms. Fitzgerald. She is, as I'm sure you know, a model prisoner. Certainly, your clemency statement and her release would show compassion and receive public favor.

Most sincerely,
Charles Winfield

****

May 25, 2013

Dear Charles,

I got your letter. I'm still here, thank God. Thank you again for writing to the Governor. Even to get a year off would be great. I keep praying this place doesn't put me on the list. The new Administrator, Ms. Atkins, told us she doesn't care if you are 100 years old and on a walker. It's mandatory that we go to the prison house and then the Halfway House.

Each day before 5 P.M., we get a movement list. If your name is on the list, you have to make arrangements with someone on the outside to get your T.V., hair blower and curling iron sent to them. Months later, after you are in the Halfway House, that person can mail those items to you there. I'm told your clothes get washed and dried inside a laundry bag.

Yes, I'm venting again. There is nothing I can do about any of this.

It's 11:30 P.M. I just finished reading a grammar book and starting another. My goal is to be a much better writer <u>than</u> [not <u>then</u>] I am. See, I'm learning. I know I make a million mistakes, but I'm learning a little bit each day. I went through some copies of my old *letters. We do not have access to a copy machine, so I must rewrite everything over in order to make a copy. I do this so I don't forget things . . . just in case I lose my mind or something worse happens to me. On my copies I write page 1 of 4, for example, along with the month, day and year. This way when we have a shakedown and the c/o's start throwing things around, I can put my papers back in order much easier.*

In going through some old letters to a friend I wrote when I first came here, I realized I didn't tell you about all the sex that goes on here. I was in Max North Hall, and at that time we had a knitting program. Whatever you made, except for a blanket for your bed, it went to a nursing home. This very pretty young black girl on my tier made a bikini. A black male c/o took pictures of her inside her cell and gave the girl 2 pictures of herself. She showed the pictures to some of the other inmates. During a shakedown, other c/o's found the pictures. The girl had to tell the c/o's name who took and gave her the pictures; and that c/o was fired. There were many sexual advances made toward that girl both by c/o's and other inmates. Believe it or not, that girl got out early because of those sexual advances. The rules have changed since then. You can sue the prison, but it doesn't mean you are going to win. Some win a few thousand dollars. Most do not win anything.

The second year I was here in the same building, a white girl, who is still here, liked having black women come to her room. This girl lived right across the hall from me. She left her door open wide. Another girl would stand near the doorway, warning them if a c/o was coming down the hallway to open the gate and walk the wing. The white girl and the black woman would have oral sex. I would close my door; I do not need to watch that. This went on for 6½ years.

Another woman on that wing would make herself dildos. When we had a shakedown, a c/o found them and started kicking them down the hallway in front of our doors, from one end of the wing to the other, announcing the woman's name and promising to introduce and fix her up with Jack Hammer, a pneumatic drill housed in one of the shop buildings. She was finally escorted out of the building and brought to the shop where tools are kept. The c/o actually started up an electric jackhammer and threatened to "pulverize her pelvis" if he ever found dildos in her room again. From that day forward, many of the inmates teased her mercilessly, wanting to know how she and Jack were making out.

The next story I'm about to tell you didn't happen on our wing, but news travels fast in this prison. A very pretty white girl had been giving a c/o blow jobs for gum. We are not allowed to have any kind of gum in prison. This young girl got mad because the c/o stopped giving her gum but still insisted on a blow job. One day he takes her into a closet and demands sex. She has a plastic bag in her pocket. The c/o unzips his pants, she gets on her knees and gives him a blow job. When he's finished, he laughs and tells her to go back to her wing. She quickly leaves, disappears down the hallway, pulls out the plastic bag from her pocket, spits his cum into the bag, then files a report for sodomy against the c/o. The outcome was that the c/o lost his job, his pension, and his wife and kids.

99 percent of all fights here are over another inmate; inmates that "turn gay for the stay." One inmate falls in love with another. After a while, one female gets tired of the other and goes after another one. Then the fight begins. Watching a fight in prison between two women is nothing like you would ever see on T.V. It's like being ringside with no holds barred. Watching a fight in prison with many women fighting at the same time is surreal and scary. Some of these women hit just as hard as a man. Some of them even look like they should have been a man anyways. They break jaws, arms, knock out teeth, and try to kill one another for real.

In Max Compound, the women get into fights 10 times more than they would in Grounds. But the sex goes on just as much. Across the 6 foot hallway is a 29 year old woman who has a much younger girlfriend who lives on another wing. They have sex almost every day. They do not have anyone watching at the older woman's doorway for a c/o to walk by because the c/o's in this building are very lazy and only walk the wings at count time, which is at 6 A.M., 11 A.M., 4 P.M., 8 P.M., and 10 P.M. Of course, everyone knows when count time is and that you better be in your room and alone. Other than that, it's easy for two girls to get together for sex.

In 2006, 2007, and 2008, a lot of women here hung themselves. During those 18 months I was in Fishkill State Prison, I would get a letter from an inmate in Bedford Hills telling me all about it. When I got back here, the scuttlebutt was that most of the women who supposedly hung themselves didn't really hang themselves. It was suspected that a c/o murdered several of them and made it look like a suicide. In other words, the women here believed that there was a serial killer in their midst. I knew two of the women very well and would stake my life on the fact that no way, no how, would these two women ever take their own lives. They were tough as nails and could deal with anything the c/o's could and would dish out. Eventually, this suspected c/o was transferred and the hanging spree suddenly stopped, with only an occasional young girl taking her own life.

I was here the first time a young girl hung herself in the hospital. She had a husband and 2 children waiting for her to come home in 6 months, but she had turned gay. As we all walked to the mess hall, we had to first pass the little hospital. From a hospital window, this girl had run a finger across her throat, signaling to her lover who didn't know what the young girl was trying to say until it was too late. We were told that she didn't leave a note. They always have at least 4 to 6 c/o's in that very small 6 room hospital. The very next day, maintenance painted all the hospital windows brown so no one could see in or out.

As widespread as sex or the occasional suicide is in here, it's far worse in a halfway house.

I told an inmate all about you. Her name is Brenda Smith, and she is hoping you will help her write her story. If you have time, she would like for you to write her. I'll give you her address if you're interested. She is a large black woman, about 58 years old. Her stories are a lot more interesting than mine. Brenda was a gangster who killed a few people. She is reading your two books now and sees that you're a very, very good writer. Her words.

Tell Madeline hello for me. I'm sure by now you have your boat in the water and are catching nice fish.

Best regards,
Caitlin

Chapter Twenty-Six

Chitchat: Books and TV Shows

June 6, 2013

Caitlin Fitzgerald
#00G1442
Bedford Hills Correctional Facility
247 Harris Road
Bedford, New York 10507-2400

Dear Caitlin,

Your last letter was outstanding in terms of fodder for our project. That kind of behind-the-scenes information is what folks want to read. With reference to Brenda Smith, I truly do not have the time to take on another writing project or start a correspondence. In fact, you are my swan song, meaning that your story is my last book. However, I have an idea. If Brenda wants to impart information of her life before and/or during prison, I might add her as a secondary character in the novel. For openers, she could either send me snippets from her story, or she could impart certain information through you directly, which you would then include in your correspondence. I would then juxtapose that info into a cohesive narrative. It might really work well and something for the two of you to think about.

If Brenda agreed to either of these suggestions, it would have to be with the understanding that the Caitlin Fitzgerald story is the Caitlin Fitzgerald story, not the Brenda Smith story. The agreement that you and I made if the book sells is the agreement between us; it does not include Brenda. Be up front with her on this point. To be quite candid —and you should tell her this—the book written as fiction will have about as much of a chance of becoming a best seller as you have of receiving early release. How's that for being blunt? But there is always that hope. We have no control over Governor Drew's decision regarding clemency. We do, however, have control over the book's success if *we're* willing to promote it. Success is not always or necessarily measured by a monetary barometer. If we sell a thousand copies, we'll have made a dent. If we sell ten thousand copies, I'd say the book is a success. If we get lucky and sell a million, from my mouth to God's ear, I'd say the book is a huge success. In order to accomplish this, there has to be an underlying theme, a motif, a message that appeals to many people. That's what I'm striving for.

In any event, keep writing, especially with the kind of prose you included in your last letter. From what you said, your story might not be as fascinating as Brenda's life as a gangster, but keep firmly in mind that your experiences certainly are. I'm more interested in imparting lessons in life that you learned the hard way than I am in purely entertaining an audience. The message of awareness is the message I wish to send. If I can do this in an entertaining way, so much the better.

Stay well. *You're* almost there. In terms of the book, *we're* almost there.

Very best regards,
Charles

****

June 15, 2013

Dear Charles,

Actually, I'm glad you're not taking on Brenda Smith's story. I did not mention your idea about her being a secondary character. I've lived with her for 4 years and can tell you firsthand that she wouldn't be second to anyone. I simply told her that you're too busy, which is true. She asked me to ask you for the names of other writers and their addresses. I told her I'd mention it.

The one point I would like you to bring out in the book is that battered women all believe that their husbands or boyfriends are going to change. They are not. They are damaged and wish to hurt and damage others both mentally and physically. There were many years I worshiped the ground Jimmy walked on. When he said jump, I jumped.

I know you know that I left him several times but that he always found me and talked me into coming back. That's the trap. I went full circle with Jimmy, from loving him to fearing him to hating him. We have many women in here that killed their husbands, but they didn't shoot them 5 times. I know I hated him when I killed him. I guess that's why I pulled the trigger so many times. But I also know why he was getting out of his office chair. It was to beat me one last time. It's like I told the judge at my trial. Someone was going to die that night. I was truly defending myself. I did not plan on shooting him like the prosecutor said. I also know that if the police had escorted me that night, they would have calmed Jimmy down but only for the moment. It was only a matter of time that he would have beaten me to death if I let him. As I told everyone, I just couldn't take anymore beatings. When Jimmy got up out of his chair, he had murder in his eyes. His rage was something you could almost touch.

I have to change the subject. I get sick to my stomach when I relive that moment. I should have just disappeared like I did when I went to California after I left my first husband. Start all over again with nothing. For the years I spent here and the remaining years I still have, I could have built a new good life. Shoulda, woulda, coulda. I hope, no I pray, you can get that message across in the book. The smears you see on this page are my tears. Sorry.

I'm sure you're busy with your T.V. show. How's it going? Good I hope. I wish I could watch it.

Wishing you and Madeline the very best always,
Caitlin

****

June 26, 2013

Caitlin Fitzgerald
#00G1442
Bedford Hills Correctional Facility
247 Harris Road
Bedford, New York 10507-2400

Dear Caitlin,

Our TV show is going very well. Every month we have a new guest, and we cover quite a range of topics and personalities: authors, baymen, artists, sport fishermen, consumer advocacy, park rangers, marine biologists, boat captains, fashion designers, librarians, master gardeners, criminal justice, outdoor photographers, horticulturists, and on and on.

Referencing Brenda Smith, I'll mention her to a local author's group. As I am not at liberty to give out their addresses, *if* one or two members are interested, they'll contact her directly. However, tell Brenda not to hold her breath because I believe many of these writers would charge a pretty penny for the time involved to tell her story. But you never know.

Sorry to be so brief, but I have a lot on my plate at the moment. You take care.

Very best regards,
Charles

****

July 5, 2013

Dear Charles,

Wow! You really do cover a lot of people and topics on your T.V. show. That's got to be a lot of work for you and Madeline.

Charles, you sure do have a way with words. I'm glad you're handling Brenda Smith the way you suggested. I think it's better that way.

Hope you and Madeline had a nice 4ᵗʰ of July. We had 1 hot dog and 1 very small hamburger, French fries, and a small cup of ice cream. Ironically (how do you like <u>that</u> fancy word?) the food was better than our Thanksgiving and Christmas meals. We were all very happy.

Wishing you and Madeline the very best,
Caitlin

July 26, 2013

Caitlin Fitzgerald
#00G1442
Bedford Hills Correctional Facility
247 Harris Road
Bedford, New York 10507-2400

Dear Caitlin,

Yes, the television show is a lot of work in preparing for the guest interviews, but it is very interesting for Madeline and me. We meet a lot of interesting people that are into all sorts of endeavors. Our latest guest was the owner of a farm here on the east end of Long Island. He and his family (a wife and 8 children) own 200 acres. Some of their children work the farm; others have their own pursuits. The farm is known for their super sweet corn. In 2003, they ventured into the wine-making business. Their wines have won awards throughout the country. He was a very good guest.

We are experiencing extreme heat as I'm sure you are, too. It feels like we're living in Florida during its hottest summer days. Our Fourth of July was pretty quiet. We asked a few friends to stop by for hamburgers and hot dogs and to watch the fireworks from our dock. The town sponsors the show, and we can see it clearly since we're so close to town. The fireworks were good, but we've seen better displays. It was nice to get together with friends.

I'm giving a book talk tomorrow and next month, hoping to sell some of my novels and my new fishing handbook. Tomorrow's talk is at a boating store, West Marine, promoting my fishing book, so that should be fun.

Take care.

Very best regards,
Charles

****

Aug. 11, 2013

Dear Charles,

I received your nice letter; they are always so interesting.

Our new administrator, Ms. Atkins, keeps changing all the rules. There is no one here that likes her. 15 years ago, she was a c/o here. Before that, she worked in a men's prison. I'm so thankful I only have 18 months and 25 days to go. So far, I haven't been picked and sent to a Halfway House. Thank God!

I'm not letting anymore inmates read your books because Book Two is falling apart, and I want to take both books with me when I leave here.

A friend of mine for over 30 years, Nancy Summers, came to see me Aug. 3. She told me she ordered and read one of your books, saying it was graphic. I had to laugh because that's one of the reasons why I couldn't put it down, wanting to see how the serial killer would be brought down by the protagonist. How's that for a 10 dollar word? See? I'm reading about writers. I just love that gritty character. Anyhow, to each his own. I wonder if my friend read the court transcripts or heard the prosecutor's portrayal of me she'd still be my friend. She has led a sheltered life and could not handle <u>anything</u> graphic. I think graphic is what's needed in a novel or nonfiction book for people to <u>see</u>, not <u>envision</u>, what serial killers actually do to their victims. "Don't tell me; show me," is a quote from a book on writing that I'm reading. Not that I'm planning on writing my own story, God forbid, Charles! I certainly know my limitations. But I am getting a very good sense of what writers like you do in order to paint pictures with words. I'm learning all about similes, metaphors and analogies.

Changing the subject: You are so right. The last heatwave lasted 7 straight days. Yes, you would think you were living in Florida in July and Aug.

Take care. It always sounds like you and Madeline have a great life.

Best regards,
Caitlin

****

August 17, 2013

Caitlin Fitzgerald
#00G1442
Bedford Hills Correctional Facility
247 Harris Road
Bedford, New York 10507-2400

Dear Caitlin,

We're happy that you haven't been picked to be sent to a halfway house. Does 18 months and 25 days translate to March 8th, 2015 as the day you leave Bedford Hills? I'm doing the math from your dated letter of August 11, 2013.

As a point of information, three of my five novels to date are being republished with new covers as Madeline and I now have complete control over their publication. Eventually, all my novels with the exception of my fishing book will be published as e-books, making them considerably more affordable because readers will be able to download them onto their computers. Those who want print books as opposed to digital books will, of course, pay the cover prices.

I've given a couple of talks on the fishing book's content: spin, bait, fly-fishing, canoeing, kayaking, clamming, crabbing, and smoking fish. That book might be more to Nancy Summers' liking than my serial killer thrillers. ☺ ☺

Recently, I've given several talks referencing my mystery and serial killer thrillers, explaining how one follows the other and discussing the storyline. Each novel can stand by itself, but they're more enjoyable if the reader follows the series. One day you'll have all of my books, including the one that *you'll* relate to; that is, your story, Caitlin.

My audiences find it very interesting in how I build verisimilitude (believability) into my work. I actually lectured at Kirby Forensic Psychiatric Center for the Criminally Insane on Ward's Island in Manhattan. Then I sat down with the head of Suffolk County Homicide in order to build credibility into my fiction. It's amazing how one thing leads to another.

I'll send you a copy of my next novel in the series shortly.

Meanwhile, take care.

Very best regards,
Charles

****

Sept. 7, 2013

Dear Charles,

Thank you for still another very informative letter. It's good to know what order all your books are written in. As I've said before, I really enjoyed reading the first in your series. Your writing is incredible. Like myself, some of my friends here can't wait to read the next page to see what is going to happen next. They can't put the book down. It is very interesting to see how you build believability into your work. Oh yes, I would truly appreciate it if you would send me your next novel. Please don't forget that it would have to have the source of sale (invoice) inside the package.

My release date is March 8, 2015, but I just found out that this new Administrator is not letting anyone leave here on a Sunday, so I won't be getting out until Monday, March 9, 2015. There is nothing I can do about that. Wallace and his wife Rose will be picking me up. I'm sure I'll be at the gate at 7 A.M., jumping up and down like a 5 year old.

Charles, the things you do like lecturing at Kirby Forensic Psychiatric Center for the Criminally Insane on Ward's Island in Manhattan, then sitting down with the head of Suffolk County Homicide in order to build credibility into your fiction is so great. You are so intelligent; my grammar must really make you laugh.

Best regards,
Caitlin

****

Sept 14, 2013

Dear Charles,

I just received the book and couldn't wait to tell you. Thank you so much. On the very first night, I read until Chapter 21. I just couldn't stop reading. I'm going to slow down because I don't want to finish this book in one weekend. This novel is fantastic! Just as great as the first. You're really something! I can't wait to read the novel you're writing about me.

Hope you and Madeline are enjoying the beautiful weather we are having.

Best regards,
Caitlin

****

September 24, 2013

Caitlin Fitzgerald
#00G1442
Bedford Hills Correctional Facility
247 Harris Road
Bedford, New York 10507-2400

Dear Caitlin,

I have both your letters of September 7th and 14th. I'm thrilled that you're enjoying the read and very much appreciate all your kind words. Truly. At the rate you're going, I'm sure you've already finished the story. And while on the topic of writing, don't knock yourself as you do. You communicate just fine. As a matter of fact, your writing has improved dramatically since we started writing one another, beginning with my first letter to you dated October 8th, 2010. That's almost three years ago. To put it another way, "Everything's easy once you know how." ☺ I could hardly begin to upholster a chair, let alone a couch—or cut someone's hair—God forbid!

Thanks for informing me of your release date (March 9, 2015). I *know* you'll be jumping up and down like a little kid. It's very nice of Wallace and Rose to offer to pick you up. Where will you be in New York once you're released? Any decision yet?

Very best regards,
Charles

****

Oct. 1, 2013

Dear Charles,

 I slowed down on reading your book because I wanted to have something good to read for the weekend. But I couldn't put it down and finished it Saturday night. What a book! How in the world you think of all these things is unreal. I loved the ending.
 I wrote my friend Mary Jennimgs and told her how great it is. I just received a phone call back from her tonight. Mary is begging me to live with her. But I might go back to Macon, Georgia and live with Aunt Katherine who will be 85 years old this December. God only knows if she'll be alive if and when I do wind up there. I think I should go back to where I was born and raised. I still have a plot just outside of Macon to be buried. I sure don't want to be buried next to Jimmy in Flushing Cemetery. These are the things you think about at our age. Actually, I wish Mary had asked me a little earlier. Then again, I have to see if I can even parole out to Georgia. You never know what they may say.

Best regards,
Caitlin

****

October 21, 2013

Caitlin Fitzgerald
#00G1442
Bedford Hills Correctional Facility
247 Harris Road
Bedford, New York 10507-2400

Dear Caitlin,

Madeline and I just returned from our first-ever cruise a couple days of ago, visiting New England and Canada. We visited Boston, Mass; Bar Harbor, Maine; Halifax, Nova Scotia; Sydney, Nova Scotia; Saguenay and the Saguenay Fjord, Quebec; and Quebec City. We were supposed to visit Prince Edward Island after Sydney, but Mother Nature prevented that from happening. The winds were blowing at 50 miles an hour, so our captain thought it best not to dock lest we all end up in life boats! From Quebec City, we took a train to Montreal, where Madeline and I met up with our son and his girlfriend. Montreal is a mini city compared to New York, and has a very European flavor. Churches are everywhere! The voyage was a wonderful experience. The crew and the entertainment staff aboard ship were superb. You wouldn't believe the amount and variety of food they offer. I'm enclosing a picture of the dessert extravaganza that the pastry chefs held one evening.

I'm very happy you enjoyed the novel. You are a fast reader. I strive very hard to write good endings as I'm usually disappointed in those I see in movies and read in books.

Madeline and I are glad to hear that you're narrowing your decision on where to live once you leave Bedford Hills. I'm sure that your choice will be the right one. Your friend Mary is a very nice person. Not too many people would make an offer to have a friend, even a good one, live with them. I hope that the parole board grants your request to reside in Georgia with your Aunt Katherine— if that's what you really want.

Well, after a two-week vacation, it's back to the grindstone. I'm editing one of my manuscripts for future publication.

Very best regards,
Charles

Enclosure

****

Oct. 30, 2013

Dear Charles,

Sure sounds like you and Madeline had a wonderful trip. I love the picture of all the desserts. I've only been on one cruise and gained 10 pounds. Did you and Madeline gain weight?

I hope I'm making the right decision wanting to live back down in Georgia. This will mean I really have to say goodbye to my friends in New York. Also, I have no idea how or when I'll be able to visit you and Madeline. Anyone who's been in prison over 5 years has to first get a learner's permit and cannot take the driver's test for 3 months after that. Even to leave the state, I will have to get permission from my parole officer.

I didn't know you were writing another book. You had said my book would be your last one, but I think you will still be writing 20 years from now. You are so good at it.

Very best regards,
Caitlin

****

November 12, 2013

Caitlin Fitzgerald
#00G1442
Bedford Hills Correctional Facility
247 Harris Road
Bedford, New York 10507-2400

Dear Caitlin,

We woke up this morning to snow. I hope this isn't going to be a nasty winter.

Surprisingly, Madeline only gained two pounds on our cruise, and I didn't gain an ounce. When they had that dessert extravaganza, we didn't partake because we had just finished a huge dinner. We only went down to the Lido deck to take pictures.

As you've given considerable thought about where you're going to live, again, I'm sure you'll make the right decision. Any decision is going to be a good one because it means that 'You Are Out of There.' In any event, think positively. Everything will fall into place for you over time. However, if you're still weighing your options, maybe you should rethink Mary Jennings' offer to live with her. Your aunt may be upset, but it's still your life. Just a thought. As you said, parole officials may not even let you leave New York.

The novel I'm presently editing is one that had been written a while ago. I have two others as well and will be working on them, too. Your book, as I've mentioned to you along with several other friends and acquaintances, will be my swan song. Then I promised Madeline that I'll kick back. I'll probably still continue to write articles since that doesn't take an inordinately long period of time.

Back to work now. Take care.

Very best regards,
Charles

****

Nov. 23, 2013

Dear Charles,

I received your nice letter on the 15th, but we keep having shakedowns, and I didn't want to start a letter to you and then have the c/o's come in and read what I write to you.

It's great that you and Madeline have such willpower to turn down all those lovely desserts on your cruise.

If parole doesn't allow me to live in Georgia, I surely will move in with Mary. It would also be a lot easier for me to come and visit you and Madeline for a day.

You might know that Court T.V. and ABC's 20/20 showed my case in the middle of the night over the last 13 years. Different T.V. channels bought parts of those tapes and put together segments to broadcast at least 10 times over these last 13 years. I've had mail from people all over the country as far away as Texas write to me. I've even

*had women c/o's from different prisons write to me and say they saw
me on T.V. and are praying I get out soon.*

*This past Monday, my c/o called me up to her desk and said, "Ms.
Fitzgerald, I was at a party last night and guests there were talking
about you. Most of the people were law enforcement officers who saw
you on T.V. At first I didn't know they were talking about you. When
they said you were from Georgia, and killed your husband in Flushing,
New York, I realized they were talking about you. I told them I've
known you for over 4 years and that you are a model prisoner."*

*Later she called a female Sergeant from another area who came
to see me and said, "Ms. Fitzgerald, I've seen you all these years, but
I didn't know who you were. I'm so sorry you are still in here."*

*Can you see how I've learned to handle quotation marks,
Charles?*

*Anyhow, I asked her if she and/or others could write a letter to
anyone who could help me. "No Way," was the long and short of it.
Both women were very nice but could do nothing for me.*

Charles, you and Madeline have a nice Thanksgiving.

Best regards,
Caitlin

****

December 8, 2013

Caitlin Fitzgerald
#00G1442
Bedford Hills Correctional Facility
247 Harris Road
New York 10507-2400

Dear Caitlin,

It wasn't that Madeline and I exhibited any sort of willpower in
passing up on all those wonderful looking desserts, it was because they
feed you like there's no tomorrow, and we had just come from having
dinner in the main dining room on the ship. However, other people

piled up their plates—high. Madeline and I used to be able to eat a lot at one sitting, but now that we're getting older, we eat far less. One day, perhaps in a few years, we are hoping to go on another cruise. Madeline and I are presently devoting 2014 to finishing up editing and publishing my manuscripts. So it will be a busy year for us. Your book is scheduled for 2015 publication. By then, we will *need* a serious vacation. ☺☺

It would be very nice to have you for a visit if you are in the area and living with Mary. I guess you'll just have to wait and see what the parole board says.

We are not hooked up to cable or Direct TV in our home, so we don't watch TV. We rent movies from Netflix and enjoy them before we go to bed. If we were hooked up to television, I'd be watching outdoors hunting and fishing shows all day and wouldn't get any work done. No, I didn't realize that segments of your story were being rerun. Maybe, just maybe, someone in power will see the injustice and incompetence that exists in our legal system.

I hope that you enjoy my new novel. It's a shorter thriller, so don't read it all in one night. Streeeeetch it out. ☺ ☺ It will be coming to you shortly.

Best wishes to you this Christmas from both Madeline and me.

Very best regards,
Charles

****

Dec. 19, 2013

Dear Charles,

I haven't answered your letter right away because Commissary is so busy that we are working overtime. Yes, you did tell me you are not hooked up to cable T.V. Do you get all your news off the computer?

I think you'll find it interesting that I was called out 2 nights ago to the package house. I just knew it had to be your book. I was very excited. The c/o takes the wrapper off and says, "Ms. Fitzgerald, you can't have this book." And I'm like, "Why not?" He says, "Because of the blood and rope on the cover." Well, I had a little fit. He wanted to

255

know who would send me a book like that. I said, "The famous author Charles Winfield; that's who!" Now he's interested and reads what you wrote to me inside. I got the book. And I'll just bet he buys your novel!

Thank you so much. I'm not going to start reading it until Christmas day, when I'm off work, of course.

You and Madeline have a wonderful day.

Best regards,
Caitlin

P.S. Because you have sent me money in the past, I feel I have to give you this new information. The Administration is changing the way we receive money as of last week, Dec 15. Money received through money orders must include the form provided; please photo copy. You can also send money via the Internet or a 1-800 number. But your credit card information must be provided. That option is up to you, of course.

I turned 71 on Dec. 7. I hate telling my age but thank God I don't feel a day over 30. I'm telling you this because you told me we are both the same age.

Chapter Twenty-Seven

Weathering Winter on Both Fronts ~ 2014

January 9, 2014

Caitlin Fitzgerald
#00G1442
Bedford Hills Correctional Facility
247 Harris Road
Bedford, New York 10507-2400

Dear Caitlin,

A belated Happy Birthday to you. I'm sorry to be getting back to you so late, but I've been down with a very nasty cold/flu that has knocked me out for a month. The holidays were no fun because I was pretty sick. However, I'm beginning to recover, and Madeline is taking good care of me.

I received the form regarding the new procedure for sending you money. I'll follow up shortly.

When I hadn't heard back in a while after sending you my latest novel, I said to Madeline, "I'll bet that the people who handle the mail didn't give her the book because of the cover." I was glad to hear that you finally received it, albeit with some "insistence" on your part. I laughed when you said that the c/o might buy a book.

To answer your question regarding how I get the news, I listen to the radio. Madeline gets her news from the Internet. We focus on both liberal and conservative slants then compare notes. Being as objective as we possibly can, we both agree that the liberals are destroying this country.

We had 8½ inches of snow here along with subzero temperatures when considering the wind chill factor. But it's getting warmer as this polar vortex is heading back up north. The birds are standing on the river as it's completely frozen over. Two ice eaters that stir up the warmer geothermal waters from the subsurface around our dock are keeping the pilings and floating dock from seizing in the ice. The joys of winter!! ☺ ☺ Madeline is more than ready for some warmer weather. I hope that you are warm.

Take care.

Very best regards,
Charles

****

January 19, 2014

Dear Charles,

I'm very sorry to hear you've been sick. I have it too. I feel awful.

On Jan 19, I woke up and put my feet on the floor then fell back on the bed. I've put in 2 sick slips; each one costs $5.00. I don't mind that, but now you wait 7 working days to see a so-called doctor. That really sucks, and it's just not fair.

We now have another new procedure here for inmates receiving any mail, be it letters, books, packages, money orders, etc. In addition to my I.D. number, an SBI (State Bureau Identification) number now has to be put on the mailings. My SBI number is 000488273B. The same applies to outgoing mail we send. On letters I mail you, you'll now see my name and I.D. number followed by my SBI number: Caitlin Fitzgerald #00G1442/000488273B. Please put this on the envelope like so. Otherwise, I won't get my mail.

The reason for this, the way I understand it, is because many released inmates keep coming back here on new drug charges. So they get a new State number. The SBI number stays with you until you die. I just learned that 90 percent of the women in this prison are in here because of drugs. They robbed banks, stores, houses and people. I really thought it was around 30 percent. When you stop to think about this, 90 percent is a staggering figure. I heard this from a nurse who has worked here for many years. I know one inmate who has been back here 7 times for stealing.

Now, about your latest novel. How in the world do you do all the research you do? It's truly amazing! I started the book Christmas day and was trying to make it last a while. I finished the book on New Year's Day. It's very hard for me to put down any of your books. They are so interesting that you can't wait to read another chapter. Your books are unbelievably great. And thank you for signing and personalizing all of them.

I hope you are totally well from this cold/flu that's going around. I'm looking forward to Spring.

Take care,
Caitlin

P.S. I just saw on T.V. that 37 states in this country have this cold/flu that's going around.

****

January 26, 2014

Caitlin Fitzgerald
#00G1442/000488273B
Bedford Hills Correctional Facility
247 Harris Road
Bedford, New York 10507-2400

Dear Caitlin,

You'll note that your SBI number, following your I.D. number, is on the letterhead as well as the envelope. This should ensure that you get your mail without a snag.

Yes, I'm on the mend but still have a persistent cough. Sorry to hear that you're under the weather, too.

I'm not surprised that a majority of the women in your facility as well as throughout the United States return to prison on drug-related charges. The recidivism rate, in terms of percentages, is indeed high. Information on the Internet is filled with rhetoric. Depending on one's agenda, the percentages presented increase or decrease dramatically. But what one really can't argue is that drug abuse puts people behind bars. It's a given that if you return to drugs when released from jail or prison, you are going to be incarcerated anew. Most of the crimes on the East End of Long Island are drug related. There was a holdup on a street in town where the perps pulled an air pistol on a victim and demanded money. They beat the guy when he wouldn't move fast enough. I just read that they caught one of the guys—a homeless fellow on drugs—a pretty common occurrence in Riverhead.

In your next letter, please describe your cell in detail: colors, size of the space (pace it off if you have to), approximate height of the ceiling, the position of your bed, chair, table, lighting, et cetera; anything that you have inside. I want readers to have a very clear picture of that space. Perhaps you can also take an area at a time as we correspond through the months [no longer years]. It's what writers refer to as 'spatial description.' Very important visually to your story.

I'm happy that you liked the novel; thanks very much for the kind words.

I'm mailing out a money order to JPay for you. It takes a while for the money to get to you, but I wanted you to know so that you can expect it.

Very best regards,
Charles

****

Feb. 5, 2014

Dear Charles,

I received a receipt tonight saying you sent me a $20 money order. Thank you so very much. I was surprised to get this receipt this soon. Everyone else's is taking 3 to 4 weeks.

You asked for the dimensions of my cell: ceiling, 8 ft.; window, 2 ft. wide - 4 ft. high. Only half the window opens, and the bottom half is painted, so you have to stand on the bed to see out. As you enter the cell door, to the left is a 2 ft. square sink area. Straight ahead, the longest part of the room is 9 ft. 5 inches. The widest part is 6 ft. 5 inches. Next to the sink is the toilet, taking up 4 square feet. Moving through the cell in a counterclockwise fashion is a 6 ft. locker. Ahead of the locker is a 35 watt bulb. In that corner of the cell is my 13 inch

T.V. that sits on a large cardboard box. Crossing the cell, in the far right corner is that single window with bars. Beneath the window, against the far right wall, is my 6 ft. 3 inch long bed. A trunk sits at the foot of the bed. I also have 6 storage boxes. No table or chair.

There is only one other building here made this way on what I've mentioned is called Grounds. The other half of this compound is called Max.

I hope this answers your questions and hope you're feeling better. I'm feeling a lot better now.

Take care,
Caitlin

****

February 11, 2014

Caitlin Fitzgerald
#00G1442/000488273B
Bedford Hills Correctional Facility
247 Harris Road
Bedford, New York 10507-2400

Dear Caitlin,

Thanks for your thorough letter explaining your cell.

I'm feeling much better, but this hacking cough is persistent. Perhaps when the weather gets warmer it will disappear. I'm glad that you're feeling better, too. The weatherman says we're in for another snowstorm and very cold temperatures. It was 17 degrees when I got up this morning.

I'm going to write Governor Drew another letter. I'll make a more persuasive argument. Don't get your hopes up though. I'm just going through the motions, but you never know. I don't always tell you and copy you with my letters to him and other bureaucrats, lawyers, et cetera. I actually wrote Drew six times over the last four years.

Hopefully this weekend, Madeline and I will be heading upstate to our son's first home. The weather is always a factor. It takes us about six and half hours to drive up there, and we'll probably stay several days. I don't like to travel that distance for just a weekend. We're anxious to see his new digs.

Too, I'm glad you got the money order receipt quickly.

Take care.

Very best regards,
Charles

****

Feb. 18, 2014

Dear Charles,

We're all behind with our work because of all the snow. Today was my first day back to work. No inmates got to go to work except for those who work in the kitchen. Even today we couldn't go to work until 12:30. With all the snow and ice, the mailroom was closed. Not even enough c/o's came to work. Everyone is so sick of the snow. I volunteered to shovel 3 times. At least it gets me out of the building, plus I love fresh air.

We are having more shakedowns than ever before, but I have to say the c/o's don't mess up my stuff like they used to. I think it's because they know me and know I don't have anything I'm not supposed to have.

Thank you for taking time out to write Governor Drew those six times. I know it's a lot of trouble.

I hope you and Madeline had a nice trip visiting with your son.
Take care.

Best regards,
Caitlin

****

February 24, 2014

Caitlin Fitzgerald

#00G1442/000488273B
Bedford Hills Correctional Facility
247 Harris Road
Bedford, New York 10507-2400

Dear Caitlin,

It seems like everything stops when the snow and ice hit. It's a very good idea that you volunteered to shovel. As you had said, you get some fresh air and exercise.

I'm glad the correction officers realize that you're a model inmate and do not mess with your things like the used to.

Some further questions regarding an earlier letter from you:

Does your cell door slide or pull open?

Is the light bulb in the ceiling?

Do you sleep with your head toward the window or the trunk?

Also, write whatever comes to mind that you feel might be of interest to readers.

I'm going to be very busy writing your story, so you won't hear from me for a while.

That's your homework, Caitlin. ☺

Very best regards,
Charles

****

March 3, 2014

Dear Charles,

Received your letter. Oh, you are so right. Everything stops here when we get snow and ice. We got an inch of snow, but there's ice under the snow. But the mayor says the children here will still be going to school. I think it's an accident waiting to happen. Vehicles here are

263

sliding all over the place. But who am I to voice an opinion.

My cell door here in Bedford Hills opens like a door you push in. But in Fishkill State Prison, they slide open and closed. Also, in Ad Seg (Administrative Segregation) here they slide open and closed. This 35 watt bulb is on a wall about 6 ft. high. I sleep with my head toward the trunk and door. I was told that this is not a good way to sleep in prison because an inmate could hit me on the head with a lock in a sock. But I will tell you why I sleep this way.

My first little cell was in North Hall Max Compound. They gave us one large granny gown to sleep in. I was sleeping with my head toward the window until one morning after a headcount was cleared at 6:30 A.M. I was called to come to the gate on my wing. I put on a robe over my gown, of course. This first shift officer who was a female said, "Ms. Fitzgerald, you have to sleep with your underpants and bra on. I could see all your body parts last night." I said to her, "Sorry, I cannot sleep with underpants and bra on." So I simply got myself a longer gown and still sleep the same way, head toward the doorway, feet toward the window, which she said was okay but still dangerous for the reason I just explained. To me, sleeping with bra and panties would be like sleeping with all my clothes on.

I think I answered all your questions.

Best regards,
Caitlin

****

April 23, 2014

Caitlin Fitzgerald
#00G1442/000488273B
Bedford Hills Correctional Facility
247 Harris Road
Bedford, New York 10507-2400

Dear Caitlin,

I've been very busy writing your story; hence the delay in getting back to you as I had mentioned earlier. The book is coming along nicely.

The weather this winter has not been great as you well know. We have yet to put the boat in the water. Most the work is done except for a few little items. Hopefully, we'll have it in sometime next week. Madeline and I did a little playing in the past couple of weeks. We took our canoe down to Laurel Lake, a very pretty lake not far from our home. We tried to catch some fish but had no luck. It was a sunny day, so that kept us somewhat warm. Last Sunday we drove into Smithtown, which is about an hour west of us, and we went fly-fishing for trout in the Nissequogue River. You get assigned a section of the river to fish for four hours. You make your way slowly through the stream and cast for fish in deep pockets of the water. Madeline caught two rainbow trout, and I caught one brook trout. She always does that to me. That woman almost always catches the first, the biggest, and the most. It's a beautiful stream that reminds us of being in England—not that we've ever been there, just what we've seen in pictures. Very peaceful.

We'll be going back up to our son's home in the very near future to spend some time helping him and his girlfriend with things that need to be done.

Stay well. We're counting the months till your release as I know you certainly are.

Very best regards,
Charles

Chapter Twenty-Eight

Serious Health Concerns

May 7, 2014

Dear Charles,

Your letters are always so interesting. I enjoy hearing all the things you and Madeline do together. It really sounds like the two of you have a great time with all the different things you do. You two are definitely soul mates.

I haven't written to you in a couple of weeks because I've been depressed. On April 8 I was called into our clinic and told the mammography I had on March 7 showed a lump and that it could be 2 months before I could get a sonogram. Two months! "No way," I said. I have a few women friends on the outside that I know—Mary being one of them—call our medical director here and complain on my behalf. On April 23, I was called out of work and taken to the Max hospital for an ultrasound. The woman doing this asks me to show her where the lump is. I show her and find another lump one inch apart. I had to have my same friends call the hospital because I insisted on getting a biopsy.

Last night I was called back to the clinic to sign papers for a biopsy. But they won't tell you when it's scheduled for. I don't know if you and Madeline pray, but if you do, please pray I don't have cancer.

I have some other bad news. The southern states don't want any more parolees from other states. I haven't even told my Aunt Katherine and other relatives yet.

You and Madeline be good to each other. No one is promised tomorrow.

Fondly,
Caitlin

****

May 14, 2014

Caitlin Fitzgerald
#00G1442/000488273B
Bedford Hills Correctional Facility
247 Harris Road
Bedford, New York 10507-2400

Dear Caitlin,

Madeline and I are very sorry to hear of your health problems. Considering the circumstances, it is amazing how fast you were able to get those initial tests done. Way to go! We hope that future tests give you some good news. We realize the shock and anxiety you must be feeling, but a positive attitude helps. I truly believe that the mind has a powerful influence over the body.

Madeline here, Caitlin: I had a similar experience about ten years ago. I felt a lump and the doctor told me that I had two choices: He could monitor the lump with a mammogram every three months or take it out. I hate having mammograms, so I chose to take it out, and the biopsy showed that it was benign. I was lucky. I truly hope that you have the same luck.

Charles here: Once again, I recently received notification from the New York State Parole Board that my letter to Governor Drew referencing your Executive Clemency application was placed in your file. Yeah, so what else is new? We were hoping for, at the very least, a year off your sentence. At this juncture, it remains a countdown to March 9th of 2015.

For an innate reason that I won't elaborate on at this time, I feel you'd be better off living up here with your friend Mary Jennings rather than living with your Aunt Katherine in Georgia. Of course, it's not my business, but it's such a strong and strange feeling I have.

Anyhow, I'm glad you find my letters interesting. In the beginning of our correspondence, I felt uneasy telling you things about the *outside* because I felt it might cause you some degree of depression, seeing as how you are incarcerated. But you were and are so close to release that I thought a few photographs and news of Madeline's and my activities (fishing, boating, traveling, et cetera) would be uplifting and help take your mind off, if only for a moment, the horrible world in which you exist. I remember what you said what you would do upon hitting the ocean after all these years . . . clothes and all. But of course the month of March is not going to be the moment to take the plunge, Caitlin. ☺ ☺

So, let's see. Further news from the *outside*:

As you know, our son and his girlfriend purchased their home upstate. A lovely, peaceful place. Well, now that he's in the country, he desperately needed a pick-up truck for that neck of the woods. We decided to give the kids our old but well-maintained 22 year old Toyota 4 x4. Madeline drove our Camry sedan, which is 23 years old, and I followed behind Madeline as she had the GPS and it was our first trip up there. It wasn't a nice day because it was drizzling on and off the whole trip. We're on Route 17 when we see a New York State trooper's vehicle on the side of the road, lights flashing, giving a motorist a ticket. The next thing I know, the state trooper is coming after *me*, siren wailing and lights flashing. I pulled over to the side of the road, and Madeline pulled up ahead of me.

The state trooper (female and cute) says to me, "License and registration." I made sure she saw my pistol license and other pertinent cards as I'm *fumbling* through my wallet. "Do you know why I pulled you over?" she asks. "Well, let's see now," I answer, telling her the story about when I first purchased the pick-up truck and had a cap put on the back so that we could transport our dog comfortably and securely. I told her that a highway patrolman pulls me over on the Long Island Expressway and says, "When you have a pick-up with a cap and no commercial plates, you have to have a portable toilet, a fire extinguisher, and a small refrigerator in the vehicle." What???? It was a supposed law hanging somewhere in a "gray area" at that time (20 years ago). "Bullshit," I told the officer. "I'm on an expressway, not a @%$*&%# stretch of sandy beach on an off-road fishing trip. (See, you really don't know me yet, Caitlin). I was also pissed because he took my 'Get Out Of Jail Free' card that my buddy had given me whose son is a state trooper. The patrolman also told me he better not see me on the L.I.E. again, or he'd write me a ticket. When I got home, I called the Forest Hills Police Department. They told me the guy was just being a prick and that the vehicle cap law was in that proverbial "gray area." I called and wrote my congresswoman and complained.

Subsequently, that stupid so-called law was, indeed, shot down.

I then proceed to tell this female state trooper that another reason why I thought she might have pulled me over was that I didn't have my headlights or windshield wipers on even though it was raining, but that I had Rain-Exed the windshield and the water just beads off. "By law, officer, I don't have to have my headlights on if I'm *not* using my windshield wipers. Those are the only two reasons why I'm thinking you might have pulled me over." By this time, the state trooper is rolling her eyes, probably wishing she had never pulled me over in the first place. She says, "Don't you know about changing lanes?" I said, "I was in the far right lane." The trooper then explained to me that when there are lights flashing on emergency vehicles, you have to immediately move over a lane to the left. It's a relatively new NY State law. I truly didn't know that; obviously, neither did Madeline. After checking Madeline out and going through the same litany, noticing that she also has her handgun license and similar cards, in addition to official hats positioned at the back window of the Camry (FBI and Riverhead Courts), the officer lightened up. The officer came back to me smiling, saying that she was not going to write us up. I thanked her for the break, and Madeline and I continued on our trip.

In retrospect, I'm wondering what the officer was thinking when she pulled me over and Madeline immediately pulls over, too. Two civilians with handgun carry permits—maybe carrying. *That's Bonnie; I'm Clyde*, I'm envisioning. Gotta smile ☺, no? Anyhow, we caught a break.

Let me know immediately (if not sooner ☺) what the results of your tests are. Madeline and I are surely concerned. You are certainly in our prayers.

Very best regards,
Charles

****

May 24, 2014

Dear Charles and Madeline,

Thank you both for your nice letter. The only reason I got an ultrasound is because I had people on the outside call our Medical Director in Albany. This place is supposed to give anyone over 50 years of age a mammography every 2 years. Mine was 3 months overdue. I made the trip to the hospital on May 13 and thought I was getting a biopsy. But this place never sent the test results to the Doctor, so I wound up getting nothing. After riding to and from the hospital in what we call a dog cage (4' by 4'), I couldn't get out by myself without help. A female c/o had to drag me out because you go in handcuffs hooked onto a large belt, plus your legs are together with shackles. I have two bad knees that I messed up doing exercises that 30 year olds do here. So the trips to the hospital and back were the trips from hell. I was told by a c/o who wanted to bust chops that "The cages were never made or meant for dogs because that would be inhumane." Keep in mind that these vans are all new, so they were purposely designed to cage you like an animal.

Next, I was taken to the clinic here and was told that the Doctor studied the results and that he doesn't think either lump is cancerous. The lumps are very different because one is soft and feels like jello. The other one is round and very hard. He doesn't think I need a biopsy. Well, I'm asking—no, actually begging—to please go to the hospital for a second opinion and if necessary a biopsy. But I'm almost sure by the time I get an appointment I'll be out of here.

I have mentioned that I cannot be paroled to Georgia because of a new law that they are not taking anyone from out of state. But I'm curious. Why do you think I will be better off not living with my Aunt Katherine in Macon, Georgia? I'm sure her children and all the family want me there because they know as Aunt Katherine gets older I would look after her. She is 85 but still does everything for herself except drive. If I stayed with Mary Jennings in Flushing, which she insists I do, I'd move out as soon as I could afford it because I don't want to be a burden to anyone. But she said I could live there for as long as I wish. Her children are married and have homes of their own, so there's no problem there. She says she has all the room in world for the two of us.

That was a funny story you and Madeline experienced with the State Trooper on your way upstate. I'll bet she couldn't wait to get away from you.

Keep looking out for each other and enjoy each day.

Oh, and thanks for letting me know you got notification from the New York State Parole Board about the Executive Clemency application being placed in my file.

Very best regards,
Caitlin

* * * * * * *

June 3, 2014

Caitlin Fitzgerald
#00G1442/000488273B
Bedford Hills Correctional Facility
247 Harris Road
Bedford, New York 10507-2400

Dear Caitlin,

Your trip to the hospital for naught does sound like a trip from hell. You're right in that you should get a second opinion. Will you be going back there for other tests and perhaps a biopsy? Hopefully, you'll get that second opinion sooner than later. Too, I'd push for a biopsy to be on the safe side. Remember, the squeaky wheel gets the oil.

Mary is a truly good friend. Does your aunt know at this point that you won't be able to stay with her? I just think that staying with relatives will cause more problems, only because it's family . . . that's been our experience. You know the adage: You don't pick your family; however, you do pick your friends. Less of a headache, me thinks. ☺ ☺

Madeline and I were nailing weakfish after weakfish when fishing recently. However, yesterday morning, we were skunked. Not a bite. It's like the fish disappeared overnight. Hopefully, we'll have better luck next time; we'll be trying again soon. Meanwhile, I'm back to your book then finishing up a fishing article re a monthly publication for which I write.

Stay well, and keep me posted on your progress re the tests, et cetera.

Very best regards,
Charles

Chapter Twenty-Nine

Cancer Makes its Call
Radiation Treatments are in the Works

July 20, 2014

Dear Charles,

Sorry I haven't written sooner, but I've been on a roller coaster ride.

Your fishing trips always sound so great. I hope this letter finds you both enjoying the summer.

I'll tell you the latest like you asked me to. As you suggested, I pushed for a biopsy. Two Doctors tried to talk me out of it. They said they didn't think either lump looked like cancer. They wanted me to wait until next year when I got out. Believe it or not, I got the biopsy. Actually, I had to go back to the hospital for a second biopsy on the smaller lump. I asked the one Doctor why the other Doctor didn't do a biopsy on the smaller lump when he did the bigger lump, especially when he made a big incision right next to the smaller lump. She didn't know why. On July 9, I was called out of work and told by my Doctor that I have Ductal Carcinoma (breast cancer). The good news is that I don't need chemotherapy, only radiation treatments at the hospital. I was hoping this was all over. I know I can beat this because I'm healthy and as strong as a horse. But please, Charles and Madeline, keep me in your prayers.

Love,
Caitlin

****

July, 30 2014

Caitlin Fitzgerald
#00G1442/000488273B
Bedford Hills Correctional Facility
247 Harris Road
Bedford, New York 10507-2400

Dear Caitlin,

Madeline and I are so sorry to learn that you have breast cancer. Neither Madeline nor I can understand why they just didn't do a biopsy on the second smaller lump when they did the first. When Madeline had her breast lump, she insisted on having it taken out. The doctor had wanted to monitor it and have her go for mammograms every three months. Madeline just thought that the radiation from the mammograms would only worsen the situation. Being persistent in your treatment requests got you to see the doctors. I'm certainly glad that you don't have to go through chemo.

As I'm writing this book as fiction, all names and locations are, of course, being changed. I have you at another correctional facility for women in New York. The transition is smooth and believable. Even your ID number is changed to correspond with a closely related number of an inmate there during her 2001 incarceration. For obvious reasons, I'm not going to detail certain information. Mary Jennings will fill you in when she sees you shortly.

Enclosed, you'll see how I updated the Author's Note. I probably rewrote it twenty times. What I learned a long time ago is that writing is rewriting. To quote a famous writer and poet, Dorothy Parker, "I hate writing; I love having written."

Very best regards,
Charles

Enclosure: Author's Note

****

Aug. 5, 2014

Dear Charles,

Yes, Mary came to visit me recently. You are a Frigging Genius! The Authors Note is just wonderful. I even like my new name.

Many things have changed since I last wrote to you. On July 22, I was taken back to the hospital for a third time. On July 23, the Doctor took the lump out along with the main lymph node and some other lymph nodes. I didn't get back from the hospital until Friday the 25th of July. On July 28, a large red bubble popped up, right where the Doctor took out the lymph nodes. I sent in medical slips to see a Doctor here. Last Friday I was taken to the Max hospital here. All three so-called Doctors we have here looked at this bubble and said it doesn't <u>look</u> infected. One Doctor here tried and tried to get in touch with my surgeon at the other hospital, Northern Westchester, about 15 minutes away. One of the Doctors here saw on the computer that the surgeon over there would be doing Teller Meds on Aug. 5, so she put me in for an 8:20 A.M. appointment this morning.

Me and 4 other inmates never made it to the hospital until 9:00 A.M., too late for the 4 of us. I'm now back in my Unit.

Charles, if any of them so-called Doctors is a real Doctor, well, I'm the Virgin Mary.

I'm told that whenever this bubble goes down, I will be back at Northern Westchester Hospital in Mount Kisco, 5 days a week for 6 weeks for radiation treatments. The good news is that no cancer was found in any lymph nodes.

Thank God!

So hopefully I still won't have to do chemo.

I can't stand not working, but I'm not allowed to use my left arm for any lifting. My job is on hold. What I really think is funny is that 2 girls are doing my job in Commissary, taking on half day turns each.

You and Madeline take care of each other.

Best regards,
Caitlin

****

August 13, 2014

Caitlin Fitzgerald

#00G1442/000488273B
Bedford Hills Correctional Facility
247 Harris Road
Bedford, New York 10507-2400

Dear Caitlin,

I'm glad that you like the Author's Note and your new name. I'm certainly no genius, but I'm going to write your story as accurately as I can.

You certainly have been on a medical go-round. But your attention to your health is, of course, most important. Remember, even as an inmate, the squeaky wheel gets some things done at both Bedford and Northern Westchester facilities. In the meantime, try to adjust to not having to do all the work you normally do. They'll appreciate the fact that you do the work of two, which probably keeps you physically fit.

As I had mentioned in a previous letter, Madeline and I are not hooked up to cable TV, but we order movies through Netflix. We've been watching *Orange is the New Black*. We just finished season one. It's about an upper middle class woman who gets involved in drug smuggling and is imprisoned for a year. The show is quite interesting. Since the series is not on mainstream TV, the producers can be, and are, very graphic. I see similarities in the show from what you have been telling me through the years. Is the show available to you? If so, what do you think of it?

I'll soon be sending you out a copy of the fourth and final book in the series. Keep an eye open for it.

Other questions: Where are the six storage boxes located in your room? What do you have in them? Also, what's in your 6-foot locker on the left side of the cell? How wide, how deep? I want readers to have a good picture of your possessions.

Again, Madeline and I are indeed sorry for what you're going through medically and otherwise. It's good that you appreciate the positive side of the coin; that is, radiation versus chemo. Keep your spirits up; you're almost *home free*.

Very best regards,
Charles

****

Aug. 22, 2014

Dear Charles,

Again and again, thank you for another nice letter. I'm looking forward to receiving your next novel.

I actually measured all the 6 storage boxes with a 12 inch ruler. Interestingly, I learned that some other inmate's boxes are new ones, and the measurements are printed right on the box. 4 of them are 23" x 16.7" x 9" high and are made by Rubbermaid. The other 2 boxes are made by Sterilite and are 24.5" x 17.75" x 7.13" high. 4 boxes are under the bed. The other 2 sit on top of the trunk at the foot of the bed.

One box is half full of picture albums and hundreds of loose pictures in large envelopes. Also I have 13 yearly reports on me because we get one each year. Copies of these were sent to the Governor along with the clemency forms. All your letters and letters from friends fill another box. In another are 3 kinds of writing paper, envelopes, all 13 calendars, an address book I made, pens and a composition book that I write in each time I see a Doctor.

By the way, I was taken again to the Northern Westchester Hospital last Thursday, Aug. 14 to meet an oncologist. He told me everything my surgeon had already told me. And I still don't know when I'll be starting radiation treatments, 5 days a week. Friday was my first day back to work.

Back to the other storage boxes. Another contains 4 laundry bags, radio, and a large bowl for cooking spaghetti in a microwave. Another large storage box contains food items from the commissary: coffee, creamers, sugar, cheddar cheese sticks, hot pepper cheese sticks, peanut butter, chili with beans and pork, beef stew, chicken breast in a pouch, cookies, V-8 juice, candy and mayonnaise. In another box is clothing: large terrycloth bathrobe, coat, work gloves and scarf. In the last box are plastic bowls, cups, plastic spoons and forks.

In the 6' x 1' x 1' wall locker with 8" shelves are sodas, a box of oatmeal, box of Raisin Bran, saltines, snack crackers, tortilla chips, potato chips, string beans in a can, macaroni and cheese, hair blower, curling iron, lotion, powder, deodorants, soap, vitamins and aspirins.

Oh, and the 13 inch T.V. that sits on top of the cardboard box *which is full of books. Yours included.*

The movie series Orange is the New Black, I only saw one hour of. We were told that we would see these shows at another time. I have no idea when this will happen or why they took this off. I really didn't see enough to know whether I like it or not.

One of our 3-shift c/o's is out of here and under investigation. An inmate in a dorm with 15 women said he came into the area at night, unzipped his pants, pulled his penis out in front of her, and made some lewd comments. Most of us don't believe this because none of the other 14 inmates said they saw nothing. Either no one was awake to see him or the woman is flat out lying. Also because he is not the type to do that. If it was some other c/o's here, I myself along with many others might believe it. But not this guy. We have a lot more male c/o's than we do female c/o's. I'm told that years ago this prison only had female c/o's.

Hope I answered all your questions.

Today I went to church, walked a total of 3 hours, then GI'd my cell. I'm so glad I have my own space rather than be in a dorm with 15 women. I'm so very happy to be back at work, but can only lift 10 pounds for now. I'm sure when I start radiation treatments I'll be put back on medical because going to Westchester Hospital in Mount Kisco is an all day ordeal. You are never back before 3:00 P.M.

I'm a little tired, so I'll close for now.

Best regards,
Caitlin

****

Aug. 24, 2014

Dear Charles,

I forgot to tell you a few things I also have in this little room: a typewriter I don't use because I let people use it before, and a letter is broken off the Daisy wheel, boots, shower shoes, slippers, and 2 pairs of sneakers. Except for the boots, the state does not give you any of these shoes. You have to buy them. I also have 2 fans, a trash can, 6 20oz. sodas, 4 large towels and 16 wash clothes. I guess that's about it.

Charles, thank you so much for the book. I'm saving it until I start my 6 weeks of radiation. I'm so tired from those 4' by 4' dog cage rides back and forth from Doctors at the hospital. All I do now is come back, take showers, shampoo my hair, and lay down. I never get back here in time to go to work at Commissary. Even if I did get back say at 12:00 P.M., I don't think I'd be up to it. It's really inhuman what the prison puts you through. But that's what prison's supposed to be like I'm forever reminded.

Thank you for writing what you wrote when you personalized and autographed the book. I consider you my friend also.

I made the trip a couple more times to Westchester Hospital. At least this past week, I got to work 4 days. And still it takes two girls to do my job. Until the Doctors say I can lift 100 pounds, I can't go back to the job I was doing the last 5 years in Commissary. But that's o.k. with me because I'm very tired. This year is the very first time in my life I feel old. I pray I can feel like 40 again when this is all over.

Wishing you both the very best always,
Caitlin

****

September 3, 2014

Caitlin Fitzgerald
#00G1442/000488273B
Bedford Hills Correctional Facility
247 Harris Road
Bedford, New York 10507-2400

Dear Caitlin,

I received your two letters dated August 22nd and 24th, 2014. Thank you for answering my questions re your storage boxes and items in such detail. It will certainly give readers a clearer picture of your area and belongings. I'm glad to know that you have a few snacks on hand. ☺

I'm happy that you're back to work if only part time. Good luck with the radiation treatments. Madeline and I feel that you will come out of this okay. You're strong both physically and emotionally, which is certainly important. We all get old in body, but it's the mind that helps keep us young. You've been bogged down of late with serious concerns coupled with full days of having to travel to clinics and hospitals to see doctors, which is certainly stressful on both the mind and body. You have to continue to keep strong both physically and emotionally, working through those obstacles that life puts in our path. I know, easier said than done. Think good thoughts and your body will follow. That's my mantra.

I can truly understand why prison officials only allowed you to watch an hour of *Orange Is the New Black*. Some of the things that you've been sharing through the years are addressed quite graphically on the show. As I had mentioned in a previous letter, the series is a Netflix production, so they are free to include scenes that would otherwise be banned on conventional TV.

To bring you up to speed on this powerful *Netflix* production, it is adapted from Piper Kerman's [that's her real name] best-selling memoir, *Orange Is the New Black: My Year in a Women's Prison*, which was made into a series. The title is abridged to *Orange Is the New Black*. Lead character Piper Chapman is a Waspy, bi-sexual blonde, University of Missouri graduate who winds up in a minimum-security prison in Litchfield, New York, serving thirteen months of a fifteen-month sentence for dealing heroine and laundering drug money. Piper Kerman, template for the Piper Chapman character, was a Smith College graduate. Although not an ivy-league college, Smith is a prestigious, private liberal arts institution for women, located in Northampton, Massachusetts.

Now, let's compare Piper Kerman's education, crime, and time served to your story.

Caitlin: high school ~ murder ~ initially 30 year sentence cut to 15 years

Piper: college ~ drugs and money laundering ~ 15 months cut to 13 months

Piper's story pales in comparison to yours, Caitlin.

Piper got around the Son of Sam law referencing her published memoirs.

Caitlin is in fear of that law.

I think you know where I'm going with this, Caitlin.

Piper is benefiting monetarily from her prison experiences.

So can you, Caitlin.

Piper Kerman serves on the board of the Women's Prison Association, addressing students of law, criminology, sociology, and creative writing to name but a few groups. Also, she speaks to groups such as the American Correctional Association's Disproportionate Minority Confinement Task Force, lecturing and educating federal probation officers, public defenders, book clubs, current and former inmates, justice reform advocates, et cetera.

As you insisted, your story is being written as fiction. Still, somehow, after your release, we should find a way to get you financially compensated via *legal* circuit tours; for example, TV talk shows, guest lecturer assignments, et cetera . . . if you so desire. I picture the three of us—you, me and Madeline—presenting before said groups and other audiences. Then again, you may want to put this whole business behind you and get on with your life. Give these options some serious thought.

Glad you received the novel. Enjoy.

Take care.

Very best regards,
Charles

****

Sept. 20, 2014

Dear Charles,

I am sorry I have not answered your letter sooner. I haven't worked in weeks. Yesterday was only my 13th radiation treatment. I have 20 more to go. It was moved from 30 to 33 treatments. I don't really know why. If my blood cell count does not drop, I will finish radiation a month from now on Oct. 20, but I still won't be able to go back to work because the left side of my chest will be burnt too bad. So far it's not the radiation that hurts, it's the trips in those cages that they wouldn't even put dogs in. Only us inmates.

Thanks for telling me more about Orange is the New Black. I understand what you are saying about the Piper Kerman story, but she didn't kill anyone. But I will give some serious thought to what you said.

Right now I am so tired from those trips to the hospital that takes 9 to 12 hours before I ever get back to the Unit and have something to eat. I can't eat breakfast or lunch because I would only throw it up in the cage. I have just enough energy to shower and go to bed. Last night, after 5 days of doing this, I slept 10 hours and 15 minutes without waking up. The first thing I did was drink 20 ounces of water before I ate. I don't drink anything all day because it would come up too. I just hope I can make the next 20 trips. Columbus Day I get a 3 day break.

Please keep me in your prayers.

Always wishing you and Madeline the very best,
Caitlin

****

September 26, 2014

Caitlin Fitzgerald
#00G1442/000488273B
Bedford Hills Correctional Facility
247 Harris Road
Bedford, New York 10507-2400

Dear Caitlin,

We're sorry to hear you're going through a very tough time. Hopefully, the time will pass quickly and that you'll be rid of the radiation treatments along with those long, inhumane journeys to the hospital. Keep your eyes and mind focused on March 9th 2015.

We're presently packing for a trip up to Peter's upstate home. Hunting season starts October 1st, so I'll try for a buck and a gobbler. Peter has put the pressure on me to provide the turkey for Thanksgiving dinner. ☺

In your descriptions of the cell/room, you never mentioned a table and chair. Do you write your letters sitting on the bed? By the way, our project is coming along nicely. You'll be very pleased.

Take care.

Very best regards,
Charles

******

Oct. 5, 2014

Dear Charles,

No, I do not have a table or chair in the cell; I write and read sitting on the bed. I finally got into reading your latest novel. Every Friday evening I sleep 10 hours. Can't tell you how much I look forward to Friday evenings. I've read to Chapter Eighteen. It's very good as are all your novels. I'm glad our project is going well. Can't wait to read that one.

I have 10 more treatments to go. Each one gets harder and harder. Half of my chest is burnt. Northern Westchester Hospital gave me a cream, but it does not really help.

Enjoy the trip upstate with your son. I'm sure you'll get a buck and a gobbler and that you'll have a great time. Does Madeline go hunting with you?

Best regards,
Caitlin

****

October 20, 2014

Caitlin Fitzgerald
#00G1442/000488273B
Bedford Hills Correctional Facility
247 Harris Road
Bedford, New York 10507-2400

Dear Caitlin,

Madeline and I returned yesterday from our three-week trip upstate to Peter's home. We're very sorry to hear that you are going through so much pain from the radiation treatments. By now, you must be finished with them or close to it. You are always in our thoughts and prayers.

Well, I spent a good deal of time learning the lay of the land upstate. Peter has 39 acres of property, so it will take some time. Initially, we saw many deer, but they are smart and quickly became elusive. A couple of days ago, we saw seven turkeys crossing the field out back. I quickly retrieved my shotgun, but they snuck into the brush out of sight. We'll be going upstate again soon, and I hope to get a deer for the freezer that Peter bought. He has a lot of confidence in my hunting skills, so the pressure is on! Madeline doesn't hunt, but she will help me track and retrieve a deer. We did that together a few years ago.

I'm glad that you're enjoying the novel.

Take care of yourself.

Very best regards,
Charles

******

Oct. 26, 2014

Dear Charles,

Thank you and Madeline for your prayers. My last treatment was Oct. 15. I went back to work Oct. 16. Radiation makes you very tired, weak and worn out. It can take months to get your strength back, but I plan on having mine all back in a few weeks. I can't stand not being able to anything I've been doing for years. I go back to the radiation Dr. on November 10. Under my arm is burnt very bad. The skin is black and peeling off. It's much worse than the boob.

Wow! Peter has 39 acres. I'm still sure you will get that deer and turkey before Thanksgiving.

Wishing you two the best always,
Caitlin

******

November 5, 2014

Caitlin Fitzgerald
#00G1442/000488273B
Bedford Hills Correctional Facility
247 Harris Road
Bedford, New York 10507-2400

Dear Caitlin,

We're very glad to hear that you have finished your treatments. We're also happy to see that your spirits are not dampened and that you expect to have your strength back sooner than later. Atta girl!

I'm working hot and heavy on your novel while Madeline is close to finishing up with formatting my next thriller, which will be published shortly. Then we will be entering the editing/formatting phase of your novel, *Battered*. Actually, I will have proofread the novel at least twenty times (quite seriously) before handing it over to Madeline. If she can find a couple of dozen points to discuss or argue in a 300-page book, that would be a lot. Needless to say, my novels are pretty well-polished.

Keep this in mind: As my letters get shorter, your novel gets longer, ☺ ☺ and longer. ☺ ☺ ☺ ☺

Very best regards,
Charles

Chapter Thirty

Game Changer ~ Chemo Combativeness

Nov. 15, 2014

Dear Charles,

    Thank you for another nice letter, and funny. I would guess you and Madeline are both pit bulls. Yes? I had no idea you were writing another thriller.

    I was taken to Northern Westchester Hospital again yesterday for the 40th time in that dog cage, of course, believing that this will be my last time for that awful trip. Well, I really got a big surprise. I'm thinking that Dr. Manual is just going to tell me what kind of pill I'll be taking for the next five years. I couldn't have been more wrong. The Dr. now wants me to take <u>chemo</u>*! I tell him, "No. No. You told me I'm cancer free and that I'm doing great. I'm back to work. He said, "Ms. Fitzgerald, if you don't do this chemo, your cancer can come back in a couple of years." I told him I'll take care of that in March when I'm released. He told me that my surgery is almost four months old, reminding me that my last radiation treatment was on October 15th. "We need to do this now," he said.*

    I'm crying and even the female officer has tears in her eyes. She has taken me on many of these medical trips. She said, "Ms. Fitzgerald, I have two friends who are dying of breast cancer right now." So I agree to do the chemo and start this Wed. or Thurs, whenever the Department of Corrections wants Central Transportation to bring me.

    Please keep me in your prayers. I wish you, Madeline, and family a wonderful and blessed Thanksgiving.

Fondly,
Caitlin

******

November 25, 2014

Caitlin Fitzgerald
#00G1442/000488273B
Bedford Hills Correctional Facility
247 Harris Road
Bedford, New York 10507-2400

Dear Caitlin,

We've just returned, once again, from upstate and received your letter dated November 15th. We are very saddened to hear that the doctors want you to undergo chemo treatments. We all prayed that your cancer would be nipped in the bud with radiation. This is a very hard time for you, yet we hope your spirits remain positive.

Our trip was peaceful but very cold. I went hunting on a 19-degree day, not counting the wind chill factor, and my gloved hands almost fell off. Stupidly, I had left my Hand Warmers back in Forest Hills (small chemical bags that fit into gloves and create heat). The wind chill factor brought the temperature down to approximately 10 degrees Fahrenheit.

On the bright side, quite literally, it snowed a couple of inches, which makes everything look beautiful. After a few days, it warmed up considerably, and the snow disappeared. We saw a few deer, which were very big, but I didn't shoot them because I had forgotten my hunting license and tags, too! To compound matters, Peter hadn't registered the truck we gave him; therefore, I couldn't have transported four big deer that I could have easily harvested but didn't. I figured I'd take a small doe for the freezer, which I could butcher myself—but not the size of those big boys and girls. They would need to be butchered professionally. I saw nothing small out there. Again, that transportation and license and tag problem was an issue, so we came back home and will go back up for Thanksgiving, weather permitting. North of the city is expected to get some serious snow. We'll see how it goes.

Usually, I'm more squared away than I was on that hunting trip. Needless to say, I was very frustrated. I've learned to leave nothing to memory and to work from a checklist. Anyhow, besides those four <u>big</u> deer upstate, Madeline and I saw a red fox and a very fat raccoon that walked across Peter's frozen pond. The time we spend up there is very peaceful and beautiful. On the way back home on Sunday, we stopped at a shop in Roscoe, NY, in the Catskill Mountains. *Fur Fin Feathers* looked like a dump from the outside, but looks are deceiving. The shop had quality equipment for fishing and hunting. The proprietors have been there for 39 years, so I guess they're doing something right.

We'll keep you in our prayers.

Ah, the tentative title for the book is *Battered*. Easy for folks to remember and pretty much says it all.

Very best regards,
Charles

******

Dec. 10, 2014

Dear Charles and Madeline,

Am not feeling well on chemo and try to tell them that I don't want any more. But they said I'm getting a second dose on Dec.12 at Northern Westchester Hospital and I say, "I am not!"

Caitlin

******

December 18, 2014

Caitlin Fitzgerald
#00G1442/000488273B
Bedford Hills Correctional Facility
247 Harris Road
Bedford, New York 10507-2400

Dear Caitlin,

Thank you for your Christmas card. That was very thoughtful of you.

Madeline and I are hoping that you do not get very ill on the chemo treatments, preventing you from working in the commissary. We know how you like to stay busy. Did you have your chemo on December 12th, or were you able to get out of it?

We'll be having a very quiet Christmas season. Peter and Karen are going to Ireland to see her mom and sister as they do each year. I came down with the flu, so I'm trying to take it easy. I guess not easy enough because Madeline keeps after me to take care of myself.

Be on the lookout for monies through JPay.

Very best regards,
Charles

******

Dec. 29, 2014

Dear Charles and Madeline,

Thank you so much for the $25.00. It is greatly appreciated. This month I was put down as a 'house person' for 14 days at a $1.40 a day. I received $19.60 for doing nothing. I have what is called <u>chemo brain</u>. Couldn't even do paperwork in Commissary. Made too many mistakes. I went for chemo Dec. 12, but was still so sick that the doctor waited another week. I wasn't going to take any more chemo. But here is what happened. I had two female relatives look up Invasive Ductal Carcinoma (grade 3) on the Internet. Both told me they would take the 6 doses of chemo if it was them. I still had not made up my mind. But going through last year's Christmas cards, Elizabeth Saunders, Jim's oldest sister, said on her card that she had breast cancer and had done the radiation treatments but didn't do the chemo! In April of 2014, I get a letter from Elizabeth's husband Christopher telling me Elizabeth died on April 11, so I made up my mind that I'm going to do this chemo. I want to live at least 10 more years. Elizabeth only lasted 4 months. As I'm sure you recall, both of these people testified for me at trial.

Regarding chemo dosage, my oncologist said that they always go by weight and height but that he would make the dose smaller next time. I went back yesterday on Dec. 19 and got two small bags. That was 1/3 of what I got before.

I can't remember if I told you or not, but I went bald and lost my eyebrows too; no hair anywhere. I look like a cadaver. I was so pissed off at the oncologist I could have hit him. The S.O.B. told me he would leave out the chemo that takes your hair out. We have a girl in Bravo who has breast cancer. She still has a full head of hair. I know because I cut it with toe nail clippers. And while I was getting radiation, she was getting chemo once a week.

I never answered your letter of Nov. 25, and am very sorry. Just haven't felt like writing.

Battered is a great title for the book. And you are right in that people won't forget the name.

Oh, am sorry to hear you have the flu. Hope you are feeling much better by the time you receive this letter.

Am sure there are many mistakes in this letter. The doctor told me that chemo brain does not go away. No matter what I am doing, I have to slow down.

Anyone who has been in prison for more than five years has to first get a learner's permit in order to drive a vehicle again. Then 2 to 3 months later they have to take the driver's test all over again. I pray I can pass. If I couldn't drive anymore, I don't know what I would do. I love to drive anywhere.

Thank you for all you do for me. I hope you and Madeline have a blessed Christmas. Thank God this is my last one in here. I've had 14 birthdays and 14 Christmases in prison, but still can't say I'm sorry I killed Jim. By law, I'm glad I won't be penalized for holding onto my conviction.

Take care of each other.

Best regards,
Caitlin

******

December 22, 2014

Caitlin Fitzgerald

#00G1442/000488273B
Bedford Hills Correctional Facility
247 Harris Road
Bedford, New York 10507-2400

Dear Caitlin,

Enclosed is a copy of the letter that I sent to Governor Drew on December 19th on your behalf. We must keep plugging away. You never know.

I also found an article that I thought might be of interest to you referencing cancer survivors.

Very best regards,
Charles

enclosures

copy

Charles Winfield
72-61 113 St.
Forest Hills, N.Y. 11375

December 19, 2014

The Honorable Christopher Drew
Governor of the State of New York
New York State Capitol Building
Albany, New York 12224

Dear Governor Drew:

I had contacted you on March 5 and May 30 of 2011, again on May 3, 2012, then once again on April 6, 2013 regarding clemency proceedings re (applications already submitted) Caitlin Fitzgerald, #00G1442/000488273B, incarcerated at the Bedford Hills Correctional Facility, New York. Of late, at age 72, Ms. Fitzgerald has been diagnosed with breast cancer and has undergone radiation and now chemotherapy treatment that is making her quite ill. Ms. Fitzgerald has been transported and continues to be transported inhumanely to medical facilities for well over 40 times in a bantam-sized, cage-like compartment that is "not fit for dogs let alone people," correction officers are quoted as saying. I implore you to show compassion and grant Ms. Fitzgerald her immediate release; we're talking a few months. If you act immediately, you'd be giving the woman three months of her life. Would that be too much to ask? Her scheduled release is March 9, 2015.

I firmly believe that a compassionate clemency statement and her early release would receive public favor. Please give this request your utmost consideration.

As an aside, going back to 1991, my working with renowned criminal attorney Barry Slotnick, his colleague Mark Baker, and Mike Taibbi, resulted in the release of an innocent young man from prison who had contracted cancer while incarcerated. The young man, Richard Tchilinguirian, died shortly after his release. The only good thing that resulted from law enforcement's debacle was that Richard Tchilinguirian did not die in prison.

Thanking you in advance for any consideration.

Most sincerely,
Charles Winfield

******

January 31, 2015

Caitlin Fitzgerald
#00G1442/000488273B
Bedford Hills Correctional Facility
247 Harris Road
Bedford, New York 10507-2400

Dear Caitlin,

As we haven't heard from you in a while, Madeline and I were concerned, so we called Wallace. He told us that you're okay but very tired from the chemotherapy, which Madeline and I figured was the case. We hope that you bounce back soon.

Of course, I have not heard from Governor Drew's office referencing my latest correspondence, stating that I had sent him <u>two letters</u> regarding your early release. Actually, I had sent him <u>four letters</u> re clemency, <u>seven letters</u> in all. I just didn't want to remind him of the fact that I'm relentless. It truly doesn't matter because he probably doesn't read any of them anyway. His staff responded to half of them, while I'm sure the other half goes into file 13 (that is, the garbage).

This is important for the cover of the book, Caitlin. Is there any way you can secure the make and model of that 4-foot x 4-foot dog-type cage in which they transport you to the hospital? When I told Wallace what I had in mind, he told me, in so many words, that they're not necessarily fabricated on site (which I didn't even entertain), but rather manufactured elsewhere. If you can secure that information, I'll contact the company for further details. If they're located in the area, I'll make it my business to travel there.

And talking about traveling, I learned from Wallace that it's not yet written in stone you'll be heading to Macon upon release until you secure permission from the powers that be: the state, probation, whomever. Let me know when you know things are finalized. I asked Wallace if he had any objections to Madeline and I being there on the day of your release. He said it was fine with him, just so long as it was all right with you.

I didn't want to get ahead of myself with Wallace because things have not yet been finalized, but if you have to remain in New York, or temporarily stay with friends in the area, Madeline and I would be more than happy to take you there. This would save Wallace the trip until such time as you are able to travel to Macon. If he's still going to make the trip, we wouldn't hold you up other than to give you big hugs and be on our way . . . only insisting we buy you, Wallace, and Rose (if she's coming), the best meal at a restaurant that *you've* had in fifteen years—then we'll head on out. Of course, we'll abide by your wishes and handle this moment any way you decide.

Very best regards,
Charles

cc: Wallace

******

Feb. 1, 2015

Dear Charles,

I am so sorry I haven't written to you in a while. Can't even remember the last time I wrote. Chemo is killing me. And I've only had 3 doses. I was taken to Northern Westchester Hospital for the 45th time yesterday. My left breast is swollen so big I refused to get any more chemo until it gets back to normal size. And the oncologist agreed with me. Am now anemic. Low red blood cells and also low white cells. I am exhausted all the time. Am told by 2 doctors it wouldn't do any good to give me iron pills because chemo eats them right up.

Don't know if I told you this. I was approved to live in Macon, Georgia with my Aunt Katherine, who is 87 years old. She was my Dad's youngest sister. Katherine also had the same kind of breast cancer 12 years ago, but hers was stage 1. Mine is stage 3. At Aunt Katherine's age, am not sure who will be taking care of who. ☺

Wallace and his wife Rose are picking me up at 7 A.M. on March 9, 2015. We will take 3 days to get to Macon. They will be staying in Macon for a few days to take me everywhere I need to go: parole officer, social security office, D.O.M.V. for a learner's permit. Anyone who hasn't driven in the last 5 years has to get a learner's permit first. Then I go to the cancer doctor. I have to buy clothes to wear to all these places. I leave here in a gray sweat suit that we all have to buy and wear when we're not in uniform. God, are those sweats ugly. Wallace's wife is buying me a red wig. I've been a redhead most of my entire life, and I think maybe I'm due for a change. I hope we can stop somewhere so that I can buy a salt and pepper colored wig. After I get settled in and get a cell phone, I would like to call you. Please send me your phone number. As of March, 9, my new address will be Macon, Georgia—not the Graybar Prison Hotel! ☺

Hope the book, Battered, is going well. Also hope you and Madeline are doing well and feeling well.

Always,
Caitlin

BATTERED

******

Feb. 2, 2014

Dear Charles,

I just spoke with Wallace on the phone, not having gotten your letter of Jan. 31 until after I sent you mine yesterday, Feb. 1. He said you and Madeline wanted to come here on March 9. <u>That is fine with me</u>. I am thrilled. I would love to meet you and Madeline in person. Wallace said you wanted to take a picture of the van with what I call a dog cage. No one here would ever allow you to do that. When a van brings me to the parking lot to meet Wallace and Rose, I won't be in a cage; I'll be in a Department of Correction car or van that doesn't have the "dog cage" because I'm not going to court, or the hospital. But Central Transportation has a hub somewhere near the Downstate Correctional Facility in Fishkill. You might have luck finding it there.

If you come here on March 9, it's no use for you to get here at 6:30 or 7 A.M. because court doesn't clear until sometime later. Wallace has to be here at 6:30 A.M. to tell them he is picking me up. Later a correction officer comes and drives me to the hospital where we go over all the cancer medications that will last me 2 weeks. This can take a while before I'm driven to the gate parking lot. You and Madeline would be better off meeting us at the shopping center at Kohl's, 777 Bedford Road, Bedford Hills, sometime after 7:30 A.M. It's only 5 minutes from here.

Wishing both of you the very best.

Always,
Caitlin

******

February 7, 2015

Caitlin Fitzgerald
#00G1442/000488273B
Bedford Hills Correctional Facility
247 Harris Road
Bedford, New York 10507-2400

Dear Caitlin,

Madeline and I are looking forward to meeting you as well. We'll be waiting at Kohl's on Monday, March 9th around 7:30 a.m.

Thanks for the tip about the Central Transportation hub near the Downstate Correctional Facility in Fishkill. Madeline has been researching these transport vehicles on the Internet. She hasn't found anything yet but is continuing her research. I might have to come up with a different cover design. No big deal; I have other ideas.

Very best regards,
Charles

******

Feb. 14, 2015

Dear Charles & Madeline,

Yes, our letters crossed in the mail. My fault for waiting so long. I now have your much earlier letter of Jan. 31, 2015. I am very excited about March 9, but am also afraid about my condition. The doctors here need to go back to medical school. Also, my oncologist needs to learn more about cancer. My left breast has swelled to twice its size, and no one seems to know why or what to do. The 5th floor at the hospital is always dirty. Thank God I'll be out of here in 17 days and a wakeup call.

Charles, I have received a card and a letter from a very dear friend, Tanya. She was in prison with me here for several years. She went home to Ridgewood, Queens on May 13, 2013. We became close. Tanya and her husband Larry want to meet us at Kohl's. Wallace told me you and Madeline invited him, Rose and me out to breakfast. Would you mind if Tanya and Larry join us? Tanya knows that we may never get to see one another again. I hope you and Madeline understand. I'm sure they will pay for their own breakfast.

Can't wait to get to this Kohl's. ☺

Very best regards,
Caitlin

February 21, 2015

Caitlin Fitzgerald
#00G1442/000488273B
Bedford Hills Correctional Facility
247 Harris Road
Bedford, New York 10507-2400

Dear Caitlin,

Well, kiddo, we're coming down to the wire when you'll be a free woman.

We're going to scratch that van transport business for a couple of reasons. I consulted with my Photoshop guy about superimposing an image within the van. It would lose the impact I initially had in mind. Madeline and I are working on other ideas that will be just as powerful. As important as the words are upon a page, so too is the book's cover and design: front, back, spine, colors, contrast, size trim, graphics/photo, and title. Madeline and I will come up with an appropriate cover for *Battered*. Apart from the covers (front and back) and the last chapter, the book is done. I will write the last chapter shortly after we meet, homing in on the moments and feelings of freedom after leaving Bedford Hills' maximum security Correctional Facility State Prison.

Madeline and I hope you're feeling better and pray that this cancer will go into remission. We're both looking forward to meeting you, Wallace, and Rose. No problem hooking up with Tanya and Larry, too, on Monday, March 9th, at around 7:30 a.m. at Kohl's in Bedford. From there, we'll all go to the Bedford Diner & Restaurant, 710 Bedford Road (¼ mile away) for a nice breakfast.

Wallace and I have each other's cell phone numbers, so he'll let us know what time we'll hook up at Kohl's, followed by breakfast.

Very best regards,
Charles
cc: Wallace

Chapter Thirty-One

The Feelings of Freedom

A week before leaving to meet Caitlin, Wallace, and Rose in Bedford, New York, Charles contacted Enzo Margola and his wife Janine, informing them of Caitlin Fitzgerald's upcoming release date of March 9th, 2015. Enzo (former police officer, owner and publisher of *The Long Island Fishing Journal* from Bayside, Queens) was the man whose boat, vehicles and home Jimmy Fitzgerald had threatened to blow up. Additionally, Jimmy had promised to murder Enzo, his wife Janine, and their two daughters (one of whom was Caitlin Fitzgerald's goddaughter, Anna) for taking sides and supporting Caitlin after having been both psychologically and physically abused by her vicious husband. Anyone who knew the Fitzgeralds knew of Caitlin's emotional abuse. Few knew of the physical abuse she suffered at the hands of Jimmy. The Margola family certainly knew. Caitlin, not wanting to wear out her welcome, had stayed with the family for a short period time while she was out on bail.

Charles and Madeline arrived at Kohl's at 7:30 a.m. sharp. Charles called Wallace McKenna on his cell phone. Wallace explained that he and Rose had been waiting at the prison since 6:30 a.m. for Caitlin's release. When Caitlin finally arrived at the prison gate with boxes of her possessions, she unselfishly suggested that rather than hold folks up any further by her first going off to shop at Kohl's for necessary items—namely, to purchase then change into a more suitable outfit in lieu of the presentable, nondescript gray prison sweat suit she wore—that everyone meet at the restaurant for breakfast. Wallace coordinated the change in plans. Rose had bought and brought along a red wig for Caitlin to wear as she had lost all her hair as the result of many chemo treatments.

Enzo and Janine, along with their daughter, Anna, arrived at the Bedford Diner & Restaurant and surely surprised Caitlin when she entered. Charles and Madeline arrived next, followed shortly by Tanya and Larry. The group shared hardy and heartfelt handshakes, many hugs, mighty embraces, kisses, and strong emotions that could neither be articulated in a sentence nor several paragraphs. All ten folks were finally seated for breakfast: Tanya and Larry; Charles and Madeline; Wallace and Rose; Enzo, Janine, and Anna; and the finally free woman of the hour, Caitlin. Tears of joy and sheer happiness fell freely from Caitlin's bright-green eyes, yet she felt compelled to tell all present that they were exactly that and not to be confused with anguish or anything of the sort just because her shoulders shook violently while the fingers and palms of her hands held back the blessedness of the moment . . . a freeborn baptismal with floodgates unable to control the flow of rebirth . . . far from the flings of any ephemeral feeling of freedom. The gathering lasted a good two-and-a-half hours before everyone said their good-byes.

Wallace, Rose, and Caitlin had a long ride ahead of them to Macon, Georgia. As the group broke up, Charles and Enzo discussed what a totally different outcome there would have been had James Fitzgerald come by the Margola residence to make good on his threats of murder, for Enzo, in a heartbeat, would have justifiably shot and killed the madman. Enzo, with his service revolver, had been waiting and ready for Big Jim to show. It would surely have been a showdown.

"That poor woman was locked away in a cage for fifteen years," Enzo lamented. "It's Jim who belonged in that cage. Either that or a box six feet below the ground."

"Amen, to that," Charles concluded, taking Enzo's hand in farewell.

Chapter Thirty-Two

Revenge is a Dish Best Served Cold

It was a dark and cool early April morning in 2015 as long-retired Sergeant Dennis Phelps and his nephew finished loading their gear into the 22-foot center console located at the end of a finger pier at the Bayside Marina in Queens. The pair looked up as a smiling woman approached, boat bag with long straps slung over her right shoulder.

"Hey," the older man said, smiling, too.

"Hey, yourself," the woman replied. "Plan on doin' a little fishing, are ya?"

"Lady, after the winter we just had, that's all me and my nephew here have been doin' since the end of March.

"Makin' up for lost time, are ya?"

"You betcha."

"Funny, because that's exactly what I've been doin', too. Makin' up for fifteen years, in fact."

The nephew put aside a few rods and reels and looked up queerly. "You know . . . you look familiar," he remarked, a look of sudden concern scrawled across his handsome wind-driven red face.

"I imagine that I would look somewhat familiar to you, Taylor. In fact, I was hopin' you *would* notice and remember. You were in the courtroom and whispered in my ear as I was being led away after sentencing: 'Hey, Caitlin', you said, 'you're finally bein' escorted *home*, just like you wanted to be. But your home will be three walls and a cell door for the next thirty years. Oh, by the way. My uncle Sergeant Dennis Phelps from your murdered husband's fishin'/huntin' club said to say bon voyage. You're just gonna love Bedford Hills's maximum security Correctional Facility State Prison for cunts, Caitlin. Rapes there are on the roster regularly. Trust me on that. I already made arrangements to make sure that happens to you soon after you arrive. You see, I know people. One c/o there in particular is just gonna love your old but lovely butt.' Remember, Taylor? Yes? I'll just bet I spit that out practically word for word—aside from my usin' contractions and colloquial grammar, whereas you spoke so clearly, slowly, and quietly in my ear. Recall those words, Taylor? You see, I know people, too, who are helping me improve myself in that regard."

Caitlin Ann Fitzgerald turned her attention to the retired police sergeant. "I understand you lasted another three years with the 107th Precinct, Dennis. Ever think about me? Ever think about the lies you and your superiors told about me there in the courtroom?"

Dennis saw Caitlin's hand reach into the boat bag. "It was them; it wasn't me," Dennis Phelps' voice trembled slightly. "I had no choice."

Caitlin watched as Dennis' shoulders shivered, wishing she could see them shudder there for a century, just as her whole body shook on and off for fifteen long, hard years. She wished she could see his tears, but there weren't any. "You didn't call Jimmy and then tell me it was safe to go home? No?"

Dennis Phelps said nothing, but his mind was racing at a hundred miles an hour. He had no weapon on his person or on the boat. He knew his nephew had a 9mm semiautomatic strapped to his ankle.

"Before you die Dennis, I just want you to know that every single word I said about what happened with Jimmy that evening was true. He got up and *out* of his chair to come after me. He would have killed me."

"It was your own goddamn fault, lady. You had a good lawyer, and you let him go. Then you hired that incompetent, William Baxter. You bought and used an illegal handgun. You were going to do time no matter how you cut it. Your own fault," Dennis Phelps repeated. "You made a big mistake, and now you're making another one."

"A big mistake, you say?"

"Do you really want to go back to prison for killing me? Do you? Do you think you're going to get away with this, in front of a witness? Huh?"

Caitlin smiled a sad smile. "I'm not going back to prison, Dennis. That's a given."

Taylor knew in that instant there was not going to be a witness . . . that his uncle and he were both marked for death . . . it was do or die. In what seemed like a single motion, the nephew crouched and leaned to his left as if to scratch his ankle, unsnapping the strap of the holster, grabbing the handgun's grip.

In a flash, Caitlin withdrew a pistol from her canvas boat bag.

The bullet that exited the mouth of the silencer reported no more than a whisper. Dennis Phelps' nephew flew back against the console, the body falling between it and an ice chest—a hole in the hollow of his ear less than the diameter of a dime. What exited the opposite side of the man's mandible was a fragmented, bloody, bony mass the size of a golf ball.

Dennis stood frozen in shock.

"What I really didn't get to say at my grand jury hearing, Dennis, or what my lawyer failed to bring up during trial is that, yes, I'm left handed, but I'm also ambidextrous. I can sew, sketch, scribe or shoot a gun with either hand. But I favor my left hand, not my right. Again, what I told you and all the others was the truth about what happened with Jimmy and me that fateful evening. I carried that handgun in my pocket book for protection, but it was not premeditated murder like the prosecutor wanted the jury to believe. When you told me it was safe to go home, I wanted to believe you, although in my heart of hearts I feared the worse. I had my handbag over my left shoulder, and when Jimmy got out of that chair and started to come after me again, cursing and screaming at me for calling the cops, I reached in the bag with my right hand, withdrew the weapon and fired. Had I *planned* on shooting Jimmy, I would have had the bag draped over my right shoulder, just like it is now, then reached across with my left hand and withdrawn the weapon. Or I would have simply had the weapon in hand and at the ready as it is now. At which point, had there been a gun in my hand, Jimmy never would have lifted himself *up* and *out* of that chair like he did. Jimmy was a bully when he had the upper hand. But if he knew he was about to be bested, he became a big, whining crybaby. Believe me. I lived with him for all those abusive years.

"Yes, Dennis, I can shoot a handgun or almost any gun for that matter with either hand—but really not that well with my right hand. Not like I can with my left as your nephew learned too late."

"Listen to me, lady—"

"Caitlin," Caitlin stated evenly.

"Caitlin, please." Dennis now wept bitterly, looking back and forth between the body of his bloody nephew and the woman who was about to murder him in cold blood. "Pl-please, I'll make a full confession as to everything that happened and the reasons why. I swear it." Dennis looked into Caitlin's cold, dead eyes with pleading eyes of his own.

Suddenly, Caitlin's eyes brightened, and she began to smile again. "Dennis, if you did do all that, don't you think that folks would say that your confession was made under duress, seeing as how I'm holding a gun to your head so to speak?"

"I really had no choice. There were others, Caitlin. It wasn't just me," he repeated.

"We both know that."

"So why do you want to kill me?"

"Because it all started with you, Dennis. You outright lied. That's why. You could have stopped the madness by telling the truth; not lying under oath like the others. Do you understand?"

"I understand that you'll be going back to prison for what you did here to my nephew, Taylor. Authorities will hunt you down and throw away the key."

"I'll let you in on a little secret that I never told anyone, Dennis. When I first got sent to Bedford Prison, I was raped repeatedly by a c/o for the first month. And do you know what he told me before he finally left me alone, Dennis? He said, 'Taylor Warford,' that's Detective Lieutenant Walter Warford's son, your nephew laying there before you, Dennis, 'sends his fondest regards.'"

Dennis Phelps slumped to his knees beside to his dead nephew and wept uncontrollably for a full minute. "I ha-had— no, no idea," he finally droned, his voice dropping to a mumbled murmur. "No idea at all."

"It doesn't matter, Denny."

"Why don't you go after Warford?" Phelps said pleadingly. "There are bigger fish to fry than me. He's now Chief Superintendent/Detective Walter Warford."

"Oh, but I have, Sarge. I started with the chief. Sad to say the c/o who raped me in prison later died of natural causes. Then there's Taylor, here. And now I'm finishin' up with you."

"You'll fry, Caitlin Ann Fitzgerald."

"Nah. First off, I took back my maiden name, Reeves. So there's no need to be quite so formal, Denny dear. Secondly, I have little time left. So if and when the authorities do suspect me, they'll first have to prove it. I may be long gone. Get it? The cancer has eaten away at most of my body, except for my brain. I'm thinking with a clear mind, but admittedly, a black heart. What more is there to say, Dennis?"

Phelps had stopped listening as he slowly stood, reversing the center console's swingback seat set atop the bloody white cooler. Dennis sat down, looking up and facing Caitlin standing on the dock. He contemplated his move, realizing that trying to grab for the gun still strapped at Taylor's ankle would be foolish and fatal. Although much younger than Caitlin, he would have to move lightning fast to overpower her.

Caitlin repositioned the boat bag to her left shoulder, placing her weapon within—as if it were a gigantic holster. She knew exactly what Dennis had in mind. Caitlin placed both hands firmly on her hips.

"You see, Dennis, as you lunge for me, you'll be completely *up* and *out* of your seat, just as Jimmy was. My shots won't nearly be as deadly as the one to Taylor's ear, which is where I aimed so that the bullet could whisper my goodbye. I'll probably even close my eyes after the first shot like I did with Jimmy, but I'll empty the gun this time and hope for the best. Givin' you more than an even —"

Before Caitlin finished her sentence, Phelps, like a vicious jungle cat, charged her with a vengeance. Five muffled shots were fired in an instant. Three of the bullets found their mark: two at the top of one shoulder; one bullet through the very top of Dennis' balding crown. The ex-cop toppled over the stern and into the cold current of Little Neck Bay, running along the Cross Island Parkway.

"Bon voyage, fellas," Caitlin said and sighed, untying the bow, mid, and stern lines, sending the craft adrift. *Be awhile before anyone discovers that one of you went for a final dip while the other lay lazily about the bottom of a boat on the bay,* Caitlin entertained satisfactorily.

The first sign of dawn was dimly lighting the east as Caitlin left the deserted docks. She headed toward a car waiting for her beyond the parking area, hopefully far enough away from any surveillance cameras.

"Everything all right?" the man behind the wheel calmly asked.

Caitlin nodded somberly and carefully climbed into the back seat, laying down and resting her head on a pillow in a corner. "I think you can now conclude the final chapter of your book, Charles."

"That's what you told me at breakfast in Bedford back in March."

"You'd call that an ending?" Caitlin teased.

"What would you have called it, Miss Smarty Pants?"

"I'd have called it a wimpy dénouement."

"Define the word for me, please."

"Well, in terms of the book, I'd define it as narrative in which the strands of a plot are pulled together, following its climax, and matters are finally explained or resolved."

"And we didn't do that over breakfast in celebrating your freedom at the Bedford Diner?"

"Nope. Not like we did here this mornin'. *This* is an ending!"

"I just hope it's not a beginning to a dreadful end, Caitlin."

"Don't be such a worry wart. I worried for fifteen years about my freedom, and now I have stage three ductal carcinoma breast cancer. And the great irony is that now I'm finally free. How about *them* apples, fella?"

"Caitlin, you know I can't put this in the book as a final chapter."

"Sure you can, and you will. You're writin' fiction, right? Just don't tell your readers who's drivin' the getaway car," she bantered playfully. "They just might jump to conclusions that it's Wallace, but he's back home with Rose and relatives, and I'm with Aunt Katherine back in Macon. Half a dozen family members will swear to that."

"And what about Tanya and Larry? Enzo and Janine? Everybody's going to be a suspect."

"The four of them are together on a cruise ship as we speak."

"Then that leaves Madeline and me swinging in the wind."

"There's no wind today, fella." Caitlin laughed lightly and smiled brightly, her grin hidden behind a hand as the glow from the sun rose to light a new day. "Current's pickin' up nicely, though, so I wish you'd stop worryin'. Your alibi is—and that's even if anybody asks—that you're visiting with Mary Jennings and her uncle, a publisher of a huntin' magazine. Madeline is already there as I know you know she is. So please just relax. Everything's been taken care of."

"And everybody's just going to lie for everybody if the going gets tough."

"It's what families do best, my good friend. Especially when they feel it's justified. Like those in Jimmy's family who believed the police and prosecution. Jimmy's sister knew better, but the truth carried very little weight in court when weighed against a stacked deck. I know it doesn't make it right because two wrongs don't make a right neither. But sometime you have to fight fire with fire. I know I'm soundin' like one cliché after another, but I can't put it any simpler. I haven't harnessed the right words to have ready at my command."

"No, Caitlin. You're making yourself quite clear. I sometimes wonder if you should have taken the stand like you wanted to initially."

"I wasn't ready. I wasn't smart. A sharp prosecutor like Philip Morrow would have ripped me to shreds. I think you know that. But I've come to learn a lot of things over the course of fifteen years in prison."

"Still can't spell worth a crap though," Charles needled good-humoredly. Caitlin took the pillow from beneath her head and gave him a playful tap upon a shoulder. "You said my spellin' and grammar improved dramatically over the years of our correspondin'."

"I lied."

"You did not."

Charles unsuccessfully looked for her in the rearview mirror. "Caitlin?"

Caitlin dozed for a good fifteen minutes before she stirred. She would be dropped off shortly then find herself safely back with her family in Macon before nightfall. Alibis were all set firmly in place.

Epilogue

In the days, weeks, and months that followed, authorities had not come looking for Caitlin or asking questions of any family member or friends in connection to the murders of Chief Superintendent/Detective Walter Warford, Dennis Phelps, or his nephew, Taylor Warford. Nor had Caitlin's probation officer in Macon, Georgia made any mention.

Charles Winfield abided by Caitlin's wishes, writing the last chapter as she had suggested, settling all accounts as they pertained to a most special recipe for revenge—"a dish to be best served cold." Charles, of course, did not offer any account to the characters involved, and no one asked. The three murders remain unsolved and are among many of law enforcement's cold case files.

How justifiably fitting, the author contemplated.

Caitlin had handed Charles a long list of names of those who had abused their power and therefore had no right being in the responsible positions they held. Too, she provided the author with sufficient evidence to support such allegations. The series of names was meant for publication. Charles had promised Caitlin that he would follow up by writing subsequent books much in the vein of *Battered*. However, this time around (and they both agreed) those stories would not be published as fiction but as pure fact.

PRAISE FOR THE NOVELS OF
ROBERT BANFELDER

THE TEACHER

"BRAVO! As a forensic psychologist specializing in psychopathy, I have been researching authors who write fiction in the field of forensic psychology. I am impressed with Banfelder's well-researched, credible, and unique plots regarding the criminal mind."
~ Dr. Jason Dunham, Forensic Psychologist

KNOTS

"THRILLERS THAT TAKE YOU AWAY TO A DIFFERENT PLACE, LIKE GOOD THRILLERS SHOULD. Just when you think you have figured out where the plot is going, Banfelder pulls out the rug from underneath you with heart-pounding effect."
~ Russell F. Moran, author, *The Time Magnet Series*

TRACE EVIDENCE

"A MASTER OF HIS CRAFT! . . . Banfelder captures the essence of the serial killer."
~ Linda L. Chase, Forensic Anthropologist Specialist

THE AUTHOR

"UNRELENTING IN HIS ABILITY TO MOVE YOU ALONG AND INTO HIS PAGES. You are running fast, and just when you think it might be safe, Banfelder hits you with another curve."
~ Patti Ann Bengen, author, *Sex*, *Danger in the Tulip Fields*, *The Devil's Dance*, *New Beginnings*

THE GOOD SAMARITANS

BANFELDER EXPERTLY WEAVES THE SUBPLOTS together at the end, and delivers a thrilling denouement. This book is one of the best crime thrillers I have read in a long while.

~ Russell F. Moran, author, *Justice in America: How It Works, How It Fails*, *The APT Principle*, *The Time Magnet Series*

DICKY, RICHARD, AND I

"I HIGHLY RECOMMEND this book to readers who enjoy the fast pace of a suspenseful and well-written psychological thriller with moments of humor and a surprising ending that is anything but expected." ~ Edward Fitch, North Carolina

Robert Banfelder is a mystery/thriller novelist whose Justin Barnes series won "Best Suspense Novels" from NewBookReviews.org.

Robert is also an avid outdoorsman, penning approximately two hundred articles for such magazines as *Fur-Fish-Game*, *Deer & Deer Hunting*, *The Fisherman*, *On The Water*, *New York Game & Fish*, *Hana Hou! The Magazine for Hawaiian Airlines*, to name but a few. Robert's book on fishing titled *The Fishing Smart <u>Anywhere</u> Handbook for Salt Water & Fresh Water* has been endorsed by Lefty Kreh, internationally renowned angler and author. He is currently working on *The North American Hunting Smart Handbook*, which will include, as a bonus feature, hunting Africa's five most dangerous game animals. Robert maintains an online monthly report at *Nor'east Saltwater*; he is a member of the Long Island Outdoor Communicators Network and the New York State Outdoor Writer's Association. Robert weaves his knowledge of the great outdoors into the fabric of his fiction.

Along with Donna Derasmo, Robert co-hosts Cablevision TV's *Special Interests with Bob & Donna*, which broadcasts throughout the East End of Long Island, New York. Visit Robert at www.robertbanfelder.com, follow on Facebook and Twitter @Bob_Banfelder.